The Garden Club

and the
Kumquat Campaign

A NOVEL

Des Kennedy

Whitecap Books
Vancouver/Toronto

This book is a work of fiction. Names, characters, places and incidents are either products of the author's imagination or are used fictitiously. Any resemblance to actual events or locales or persons is entirely coincidental. For additional information please contact Whitecap Books Ltd., 351 Lynn Avenue, North Vancouver, BC, V7J 2C4.

Edited by Bernice Eisenstein
Copy edited by Elizabeth McLean
Interior design by Margaret Ng
Cover illustration by Stanislaus Gadziola
Cover design by Steve Penner

Printed and bound in Canada.

Canadian Cataloguing in Publication Data

Kennedy, Des
    The garden club and the Kumquat campaign

    ISBN 1-55110-403-2

    I. Title.
PS8571.E6274G37 1996   C813'.54   C95-911135-2
PR9199.3.K4179G37 1996

The publisher acknowledges the assistance of the Canada Council and the Cultural Services Branch of the Government of British Columbia in making this publication possible.

For those who grow,
Those who defend the old growth
And all who engender magic in the world

Acknowledgements

A first novel does not always come as easily into the world as this one did.

When a first draft of the story went to editor Bernice Eisenstein, I was wracked with apprehension. But as a long-time resident of Pickles Road, I was delighted to learn that my new and unknown editor, although thousands of miles away, lived on Olive Avenue. Under her insightful and sensitive guidance, the drafts gradually improved, without any of the psychodramatic fireworks that can illuminate the writer/editor relationship. For whatever delight the reader may take in the pages that follow, a portion of credit should be addressed to Olive Avenue rather than Pickles Road.

Special thanks to Karen Connelly for her chiselling and Elizabeth McLean for her polishing.

Meanwhile, my dear companion Sandy did all that could be done with someone in the peculiar mental state of novel writing. Her loving presence in the process and in the garden made the exercise a pure delight.

1

Caitlin Slaney beams as she slides into the passenger seat beside me, closing the door. "How's tricks, J.J.?"

"Trickier than thou; got everything you need?" Caitlin's notorious for leaving things behind.

"Got my satchel," she slaps the old brown leather satchel on her lap. "Got a ride. Got you close beside me. What more could any red-blooded woman want? Floor it, big fella!"

That's Caitlin for you. She's wearing a long green cotton dress, no makeup or jewellery, and her wild red hair's tied back with a green silk ribbon. Lord, she's beautiful, I think to myself. Again.

"Your place looks fabulous," I tell her as I slip the stick shift into first and ease my pickup out of her yard. And so it does. It always does, and especially today, bronzed in a golden September evening light. Caitlin's a fanatical gardener, a born natural, bold and flamboyant in her plantings. In June, when they're in full bloom, her antique roses massed against one another in opulent explosions of fragrance could make you weep for love and ecstasy.

Caitlin and I are neighbours on this little west coast island, us and about five hundred other people, give or take. She and I are each on twenty acres, so it's hardly a chat-over-the-backyard-fence kind of neighbourliness. There's a steep gully dense with huge trees between us. A footpath runs through the woods connecting our two places, and that's usually how I go over. But we have a meeting tonight and I've driven around to give her a ride to the hall.

"Can you imagine a more gorgeous day?" she asks, exhaling with pleasure. It's one of those late summer days that rival the giddy mornings of May for the very best the year has to offer.

"And can you imagine," I say, "how hard it was pelting rain just two days ago?"

"Wasn't it lovely! I danced on the lawn in that rain," Caitlin says, with a sideways glance that telegraphs the next bit. "I was naked, J.J., stark naked to the world! The warm rain splashed against my flesh and soaked my hair and I danced for joy until I thought I'd drop. Did you too?"

"Drop?"

"No, dance."

"No, I didn't."

"Jenny was convinced I'd gone completely mad."

"I tend to agree with her," I say. Though it's true that out here on the coast that first late-summer rain, after months of parching drought, comes like a gift from the gods, misting our sunburnt souls with a cool and blessed freshness.

Squatting in the rainshadow cast by the mountains of the big island, Upshot Island, our home, has what they call a winter wet/summer dry regime. For about three hundred days of the year it can be godawfully wet—if it isn't outright pouring rain, it's at least dripping with fog and mist. But come July and August, the wind swings over into the northwest, and everything on the leeward side of the mountains dries up completely. Wells run dry. Reservoirs drop. Unwatered lawns shrivel into miserable miniature Serengetis. The woodlands snap and crackle like dry cedar kindling waiting for a spark. Some years it'll stay dry right through October; there won't even be enough moisture to bring the wild chanterelles up. But not this year.

"I ran into old Waddy down at the store last week," I tell Caitlin, as we thread our way under the big trees that canopy her driveway. Waddy's an old bull-of-the-woods from way back when.

" 'Been listenin' to the frogs?' he asks me."

"Good question," Caitlin says.

" 'Tree frogs been singin' a rain song all week,' Waddy says to me. 'Rain comin', you watch.' "

One of the problems with Waddy Watts, and he's not the only one around here, is that he's about equal measure folk wisdom and b.s., and it's really hard to determine just which you're getting at any particular moment.

"Waddy knows his signs and portents," Caitlin says.

"He's solid on frogs, anyway," I say, "because once he'd drawn my attention to it, I noticed the tree frogs really were singing a rain song all last week. Did you notice them?"

"Yes," she says, "I did. Jenny's an honorary member of the Frog Clan, and brings me regular reports." Jenny's Caitlin's daughter, five years old and very wise. "Did you sing with the frogs?" Caitlin asks me.

"What do you mean?"

"I mean, go out in the dark without any clothes on, and squat near a frog pond in the rain and join in the frog chorus."

"No, I can't say as I did."

"Oh, it's great fun," Caitlin says, "and you learn a tremendous amount."

"Such as?"

"Oh, all sorts of things. Size counts. Big frogs in small ponds."

By last Friday evening even we humans could smell rain drifting towards us across the Pacific. I awoke in the middle of the night to a new sound: raindrops popping against the cedar shakes on my roof. After drought that's a sound as sweet as a winter wren's singing, and I lay in bed wafting in and out of sleep bathed in lush contentment.

It rained steadily for most of the night and all day Saturday. On Sunday morning when I stepped out into the garden the sky had cleared and all creation was throbbing with beauty. The air was rich and heavy, redolent with scents of humus and decay. Crickets were chirping maniacally, and the tree frogs had changed their tune from last week's mournful dirge into an ecstatic aria. Everything in the garden was burnished, shining bright, the leaves all wet and trembling, the edges of things sharp and individual, vivid as dreams.

Today's been another splendid day and I had a hard time getting down to any kind of serious work. After supper, I drove my pickup around to fetch Caitlin for the meeting. Her old Volvo's over at Blackie the Mechanic's for repairs. Again.

We emerge from Caitlin's woods out onto the road. The sun is hanging over the smoky blue mountains of the big island off to the west. The long slanting rays light up the fields and trees, illuminating everything in a golden wash, like a long-vanished Constable landscape.

We take off down the narrow road, lined with gilded hedgerows full of birds. To the locals, it's simply "the road," because for years and years it was the one and only road on Upshot. It forms an irregular loop around the island, so that no matter where you start from, you'll end up back there again. An imperfect circle. All the old homesteads front onto the road, either on the water or upland side. The only deviation from this elongated loop is—or, rather, was—a short spur that runs down to Rumrunners Cove on the southwest side. That's where the ferry from the big island docks and where a few small boats are moored at a decrepit government wharf.

"So down to the ferry first?" I ask Caitlin.

"If you'd be so kind," she says, smiling half to herself. "Elvira's getting the key to the hall. We'll pick up Mistral first, if that's all right with you."

"Fine," I say. "I'm intrigued to meet your Mistral Wind. Let's hope she's made the ferry."

We're on our way to the regular monthly meeting of the Upshot Island Garden Club and Horticultural Society. I've been a member for going on six years, and have more or less faithfully attended the regular meetings on the second Monday of each month, 7:30 sharp, at the community hall. We can usually expect around thirty members at a meeting. Caitlin is club president this year. Although barely out of her twenties, she's arguably owner of the island's finest mind. Admittedly, this might not be saying much. But Caitlin really is quite remarkable. Not long ago we had one of these forest company show-and-tell sessions, where company flacks explain what splendid things they're going to do with their forestlands on the island. It's transparent windowdressing, of course, a public relations exercise designed to impress the rubes. Most people ignore them, but not Caitlin; she's an absolute fanatic on the topic of industrial deforestation. Two of the reps were foresters and the other one a lawyer, but Caitlin took them apart—gently and respectfully, but nevertheless took them apart—piece by piece, as though they were a freshman debating team. It was both awful and wonderful to watch.

I guess Caitlin comes as close as anyone to being a love interest in my life. Not that I've told her this exactly. I'm a dozen years older than her, and painfully conscious of thinning hair, fattening waistline, and evolving wattles. I have long since crossed the borderline into lonesome middle age. The last thing I need is to make myself ridiculous in pursuit of a winsome younger woman.

Plus Caitlin's not easy. She's what you might call enigmatic. When she's on her game, the woman has a mind like a steel trap. It's why she was elected president of our garden club, and why she often gets called on to chair public meetings on the island, which can be a handful, believe me. She can organize a rose show and subdue bellicose drunks with equal dexterity. She's a silversmith by trade; her original designs, based in Celtic imagery, are in high demand in the city. Their intricate designs are like Caitlin herself, complex and lovely.

Brilliant and glittering one day, the next time you see her, she might be down in the dismals. Then she's completely hopeless. She calls them the dismals herself—mopish, brooding moods that might leave her pensive and abstracted for weeks at a time. Her tumultuous love life is usually to blame, and has become the stuff of legend on Upshot. She's taken up and bedded down with some of the most peculiar characters we've had around here, and that's saying something.

She threw her most recent lover out last spring. She'd caught him in a dalliance with a sweet young waif who'd come in by kayak and was camped down at the park. The guy had a history of waif-related incidents, though he fancied himself a poet, and therefore entitled. After each transgression he'd gradually weasel his way back into Caitlin's grace, and bed, with outpourings of explicit metaphors. Down at the Preening Peacock Cafe he was valued less for his poesy than as a source of particularly juicy gossip. He was our own Prince Charles, this poet. Poor Caitlin, each new episode concluded, how did she put up with him?

But Caitlin sailed above the talk, like Boadicea on the field of battle.

"I'm hardly the type to play whinging victim to some philandering little tomocock like him," she told me once. "But I'll tell you this: that versifier's got a tongue on him any woman would die for."

Did she mean his similes? I asked.

"He's a cunning linguist all right," she winked and tossed her red, red hair.

Caitlin takes perverse delight in saying things to shock me, though she's not alone in this. There's something about me, I don't know quite what, that people like to scandalize. It's as though I give off some pheromones or something that trigger in people a desire to say lewd things to me. Caitlin's the worst of all, partly because she and I share an Irish Catholic upbringing and she takes her revenge on its morbid graveyards and confessionals by skewering prudishness wherever she finds it. And she thinks she finds it in me.

I try not to think of myself as a prude. Prudent, yes; I'll accept prudent. In fact, I'm prudence personified. From very early in life, from the very dawning of consciousness, from perhaps as far back as the collision of prudent parental sperm with prudent parental egg at which I sprang into being, I have accepted as my life's work the keeping of my head down, the not rocking of any boats, the not making of waves.

"You watch your p's and q's, mister," my dad would growl at me, when I was all of six or seven, "or you'll get a good clip on the ear." A considerable chunk of my early life was devoted to the avoidance of getting a good clip on the ear, which seems in hindsight an awful squandering of great potential.

My father specialized in time. He owned a little shop where he repaired clocks and watches. Jones Clock and Watch the place was called. We lived—he and my mother and me and a succession of depressed canaries—in a walk-up apartment above the shop, on Jane Street in Toronto. My father spent most of his closely watched time in the shop, staring through a lens at intricate moving parts. He used his lens for so many years, always with the left eye, it had etched a permanent circle around the eye, so that when he glowered at me, it was like he was looking through a lens right into my secret self.

Hovering in the background, always cooking or cleaning something, my mother would never interfere when my dad was threatening me, but she'd take me aside afterwards and hug me close to her and say, "There, there, it'll be all right. You just behave yourself, and everything will be fine."

I took their point.

They named me Joseph. Joseph Jones. Never Joe. To this day I resist any attempt at being called Joe Jones. Caitlin has settled on J.J., and Waddy likes Joey-boy. Some of the others around here, Elvira Stone for one, call me Brother Joseph. Partly for a lark, but also because for many years—an interminable stretch between the clock shop and washing ashore here on Upshot Island—I was a member of a monastic order back in Ontario called the Brothers of Blessed Columkille the Lesser.

Columkille was a medieval mendicant friar renowned throughout the Gaelic-speaking world for his great sanctity. However, he ran afoul of the church in Rome by devoting himself to undoing the work of Saint Patrick and reintroducing snakes and toads to Ireland. It was this quirky streak in Columkille that attracted me into the monastic order he'd founded, that and my own desire for a sheltered and well-ordered life, away from the tumult and shouting of a world that I knew instinctively from an early age was quite mad. Columkille's quirkiness had prevented him from ever being canonized a saint. Something of the founder's eccentricity stayed with his order, however, and it's hard to imagine a grander aggregate of crackpots than the good brothers with whom I spent so many years. We wore thick leather sandals and a long brown habit of coarse wool, cinched at the waist with a thick cord from which a long rosary of black beads dangled. The beads clicked together as we walked in silence through the cloister. Monastic life extended my long tutelage in prudence well into mid-life.

The past seven years I've spent living here on Upshot. Caitlin Slaney, living next door, has taken it upon herself to try to purge at least some of the prudence out of me by saying, and sometimes doing, the most outrageous things. As I say, I'm not nearly the prude she takes me for.

Anyway, last spring she tossed her philandering poet out for good, like a threadbare carpet at spring cleaning. "A worn-out little squire," she called him. Retreating to a tarpaper shack on Krapukniuk Place, the spurned versifier poured out passionate lyrics about Caitlin's body parts. Every morning he'd cycle up on his mountain bike to Caitlin's and deposit the steamy products of the previous evening's poeticizing in her mailbox. But Caitlin, once turned, was intractable. "There's nothing more pathetic than a Lothario who's tongue's gone limp," she laughed.

The Desperately Pedalling Poet, observers took to calling him, as he made his daily pilgrimage up the road past the Preening Peacock, past the hall, the school, and the general store on his mournful way to Caitlin's mailbox.

After a few weeks of this, his muse abandoned him too, and he left the island to begin life anew in Sedona, Arizona, with yet another new-found waif not yet versed in the rigours of literary criticism. Secretly my heart rejoiced to see him gone forever. I had not fancied myself lining up for Caitlin's favours behind the likes of him. Still, the fellow's vaunted tongue work daunted me immensely, and I'm not at all certain that, if called upon, I should make a sufficiently mellifluous replacement.

It was Caitlin's melancholy streak that the Pedalling Poet had proved so adept at exploiting. His lugubrious breath lines, the sticky concupiscence of his internal rhymes, spoke to her sadness in a way nobody else could. I don't know where her sadness springs from. It mystifies me, and stirs in me an urge to assuage it, but I don't know how.

7

"No doubt about it," she told me after she'd banished him permanently, "that little stopcock could lift my sinking heart."

Brilliant and peculiar, that's Caitlin. "She's a great romantic spirit," Elvira Stone says in her friend's defence. "It's the world that falls short, not Caitlin."

"Tell me about this woman who's speaking tonight," I ask Caitlin as we drive down the very road the Pedalling Poet had so frequently, and fruitlessly, pedalled up.

As I say, we used to have just the one main road on the island. In conversation, you might refer to westside road or eastside road if you were being particular, but more likely you'd pinpoint your position relative to the nearest property, as in: I'm broke down in front of the Overstall place.

Things changed on the island with the creation of Cascara Heights, our first small-lot subdivision, thirty-five lots on the island's east side. It was created in the early eighties by a consortium of Calgary speculators most of whom, according to the gossip down at the Preening Peacock, have subsequently either fled to tax havens in the Grand Cayman Islands or become ministers in the Alberta government.

At Cascara Heights, at least on the waterfront lots, everyone's rolling in dough. Designer homes nestle tastefully among big smooth-barked arbutus trees—the developers mistook them for cascaras—with matching guest cottages set off discreetly to the side. There are several tennis courts, a lawn bowling green, and even a swimming pool—Jimmy Fitz couldn't get over it when he was blasting and digging the hole for it with his backhoe: "A swimming pool under all them arbutus?" he'd splutter. "I told 'em: when arbutus ain't rainin' down berries, they're rainin' down leaves, and when they ain't rainin' down leaves, they're rainin' down bark. I told 'em straight out: that won't be no swimming pool, it'll be a goddamn settling pond, but they didn't listen, that type never do."

We might have tilted eastwards slightly under the new weight of Cascara Heights, but a couple of years later things got balanced out with a westside subdivision, between the ferry and the park, just down from where we're driving now. Our friendly island realtor Fibber Miller ("the realtor who makes your dreams get real") was mixed up in that development. It lacks any pretence towards sophistication, and in fact is pretty much of a joke. It sits half-heartedly in what nature intended to be a swamp. Though there's seventy lots in it, hardly anybody lives there. Some of the lots have been developed, for summer cottages and rentals, but the buildings are mostly dark and pokey little A-frames or dilapidated trailers. They discourage habitation. The vegetation is post-clearcut alder trees, wild berry vines, and Scotch broom. The lots are so small and the water table so high, everyone's wells and septic fields more or less commingle in one great pooled resource.

Nevertheless, despite their several imperfections, the two subdivisions have greatly expanded our road grid. Each of them has a feeder road running out to the main road, and a little network of secondary roads to service the lots. Over at Cascara Heights they've continued the native vegetation theme in the naming of their roads. Thus you get Huckleberry Lane and Salmonberry Way winding down to Ocean Spray Drive.

The westside subdivision's road names are, like the place itself, something else again. The developers, Fibber Miller and his cronies—in what the regulars down at the Preening Peacock Cafe interpret as a rather desperate bid for immortality—named all the roads after themselves. This worked passably well for Miller Drive, but most of the other investors in the syndicate—that's what Fibber called it, the syndicate—were of Winnipeg Ukranian stock, so the roads now bear magnificently inaccessible monikers like Rudnyckyj Crescent and Stryzyboroda Place.

We pass the westside subdivision and go gliding down the hill to the ferry landing. I ask Caitlin how she first met tonight's guest speaker, a woman calling herself, rather unpromisingly, Mistral Wind.

"The first time I met her was up on Quasimodo," Caitlin says. Quasimodo's an island north of us which has, in Waddy Watts' words, "more religious nuts than a rotting log's got termites." Caitlin goes up there a lot.

"She was giving a workshop on permaculture," Caitlin says. "I remember I was put off by the name: Mistral Wind. How self-indulgent, I remember thinking, when I first saw it in the brochure. Capricious without being charming. Besides, I realized, the Mistral is a male wind, the Master Wind, cold and dry. People used to think of it as a plague, the way it could buffet and chill those soft warm Mediterranean places. It can blow for ninety days or more, you know."

I say I had no idea.

"Oh, yes, a violent wind," Caitlin goes on, "a wind at the backs of barbarians, Huns and Visigoths, sweeping down from the steppes. That's the Mistral. Not a woman's wind at all."

Conversations with Caitlin tend to go like this. I park the truck. We're a bit early. The ferry's still well out in the strait, just rounding the point off Barren Rocks. Caitlin and I sit on a wooden bench on the wharf and look out across the sparkling waters.

"So when I first saw the workshop brochure," she continues, "I thought to myself, Here's some impressionable soul who's just got through reading *The English Patient*—or, worse, *A Year in Provence*—and is full of winds. But what'll it be three weeks from now, I asked myself: mycorrhizal fungi? pre-dynastic Egyptians? No, I thought, it's not a good sign, this changing names every time the wind swings. I almost decided against taking the workshop. But I was interested in permaculture and signed up anyway. My expectations were anything but great."

"And?"

"Well, the first time I clapped eyes on this so-called Mistral Wind, she took my breath full away. She was astonishing to look at, but more than that: there was a radiance about her, an extraordinary immanence." Caitlin pauses a moment, glancing across the strait, her eyes a gleaming vivid green. "I'd taken Jenny up with me to the farm—they provide child care during the workshops. The first time Jenny saw Mistral, she walked straight up to her—you know how shy Jenny is of strangers—and opened her arms and Mistral opened hers and picked her up and they hugged one another and started laughing and crying together as though they were two old souls who'd been separated for a long, long time, but remembered each other at once. It was the most remarkable thing."

Caitlin traces a design with her finger on the wooden seat, musing. Caitlin teeters precariously on the edge of mystical experiences. It's one of the things I like best about her.

"What about the workshop? Did it live up—or down, I guess—to your expectations?"

"I hate to admit it," she laughs, "but I scarcely remember anything about the workshop, the actual content, I mean. I seemed to be transfixed by that woman. Only the woman. I suppose it's what's meant by besotted. Yes, I was besotted, I know I was."

"Not you," I say with what I think of as a telling tone of irony.

"And so," Caitlin ignores my wit, "when the garden club was planning our fall speakers' series, I insisted we include Mistral Wind if she could come. I calculated that either I'd actually learn something about permaculture this time, which I would like to do, or else be besotted all over again, which is always grand fun while it lasts."

"Should be an interesting meeting either way," I say drolly. "What is it about her?"

"You'll see for yourself in a few minutes," Caitlin says, "I hope." The ferry's drawing closer; I can pick out cars on the open deck and a few people standing at the prow. "I couldn't keep my eyes off her," Caitlin continues. "She has probably the most striking physical presence of anyone I've ever met. She's tall and dark and extraordinarily handsome. But not what you'd call pretty, not an anorexic fashion mannequin by any stretch. Far more animal and angel than that. I suspect she's an androgyne."

"That's convenient," I try a little sarcasm. "You said she was dark. What nationality?"

"She told me she was Persian. We were talking about musk roses, she and I, during a break in the workshop, and she broke into an ecstatic rapture about wild roses on the hills of Isfahan. 'You cannot walk these sacred places without weeping for the sweet felicity of life,' she said, or something along that line. You'll see how she is, how her whole body dances her words. All her talk's poetry. I mentioned something to her about Iran once, something about the Ayatollahs, and she flashed like lightning. 'I am not Iranian,' she said to me, 'I am Persian, like the rosa mundi rose!' "

I'm intrigued by Caitlin's description, and by her infatuation with this woman. We sit silent for a few moments. I feel a curious sense of anticipation, of arousal, at the approach of this charismatic character. I'm forty-three years old and single. In another time I'd have been called a confirmed bachelor. I've never experienced what people call a "long-term relationship." I don't believe I've ever been truly in love. No more than a few vapid infatuations. I wonder sometimes if things will just go on like this, if I'm destined to be always alone, like some solitary bivalve on a beach, self-contained and dutifully loyal to the preoccupations of my prudent forebears.

But sitting there on the bench with Caitlin, watching the ferry, now turning in its slow arc towards the wharf, for just a moment I experience an extraordinary sensation. I feel as though there's something peculiar stirring inside me, some other, secret self, a rogue, a bold adventurer, perhaps a poet, lurking within, a genie in a bottle, alert for something, a magical touch of some sort, that will release that part of me from confinement, and transform my life completely.

2

I'm no great believer in premonitions and portents. In fact, I'm no great believer in much of anything at all any more, not since leaving the Brothers of Blessed Columkille the Lesser. Prior to that I'd believed altogether too much. Believed without any shred of doubt some of the most outrageous rubbish imaginable. For instance, that, after death, baptised Catholics in good standing would enter the Kingdom of Heaven, while everyone else would be consigned to some level of Purgatory or Hell, where they'd roast forever like weiners on a campfire. Believed utterly in the infallibility of the Holy Father. I knew beyond question that anyone practising birth control by any means other than coitus interruptus was committing a mortal sin that, if left unconfessed and unrepented, would damn the blackened soul to Hell for all eternity. I accepted whole leather-bound volumes of these incomprehensibilities as gospel truth, divine revelation. The faith of our fathers bore me up to accept it, however much it might defy human understanding or fly in the face of common sense.

My mother set me on the path of faith as surely as my father on the way of fear, and half my life was already lived before I began to break free of either. For fifteen years I lived a life of contemplative retreat with the Brothers in the Caledon Hills northwest of Toronto. We lived, as religious recluses through the centuries have lived, by the sacred vows of Poverty, Chastity, and Obedience. None of these seemed to me as oppressive as the stifling little apartment above Jones Clock and Watch on Jane Street. The golden monstrance on the altar never gleamed as monstrously as my father's enraged eye, framed, like the eye of a demented Cyclops, by the imprint of its habitual eye lens.

But when my mother died some years ago, the faith that she had nurtured in me seemed to die with her. I could not accept her loss, my faith could not encompass it, and I came to see that my monastic calling was not rooted in a faith of my own, but in hers. Denied the binding surety of her deep religious convictions, I began to see my life of spiritual seclusion, my mortifications of the flesh, the bendings of my spirit to the will of the abbot, as preposterous. With the linchpin of faith released, the contradictions and absurdities in the grab bag of dogma I'd accepted as truth came tumbling out like potatoes from a sack.

I vividly remember that morning when I realized my vocation had vanished. The abbot was reading from Philippians: "I have come to rate all as loss in the light of the surpassing knowledge of my Lord Jesus Christ. For His sake I have forfeited everything. I have counted all else rubbish so that Christ may be my wealth. I wish to know Christ and the power flowing from His resurrection; likewise, to know the fellowship of His sufferings by being formed into the pattern of His death. And thus do I hope that I may attain resurrection from the dead." Everything stopped for me in the middle of that passage, and I realized in a sudden flash of understanding that I did not count all else rubbish and loss, oh no. Every corpuscle of my being knew that life is full of splendid mysteries and beauties I was no longer willing to mortgage for another life after death. It wracked me dreadfully to pull myself away from that hallowed, hollow place, from the only way of life I'd known as an adult. But I could not remain there without going mad. Within a year I had set aside my monk's habit and applied to Rome for release from my sacred vows.

I came down out of the Caledon Hills like a defrocked prophet into the grasping frenzy of Toronto in the late 1980s. I saw little to my liking.

Executing perhaps the only truly elegant act of his career, my father had died not long after my mother, leaving me sole inheritor of the little shop on Jane Street which just happened to be smack in the middle of a planned massive redevelopment project. I leapt from holy poverty to relative wealth as lithely as a stag leaping a low hedge.

Eventually, I fled west, and one spring morning found myself, I'm not sure why or how, aboard that same slow ferry approaching Upshot Island. I've been here ever since, living quietly and contentedly among the trees and creatures and characters of this funny little place. My needs are few and simple. I pick up a bit of money here and there doing freelance editing work, arranged through an old contact in Toronto.

I'd gradually come to consider most of the Brothers of Blessed Columkille the Lesser certifiable loonies, but they couldn't hold a candle to some of the characters on these little islands, Upshot included. No Pope holds infallible sway in these parts, nor is much taken on faith, at least not for long. All is up for revision and discussion and reinterpretation, depending upon who you talked to last. You can't even get consensus on a simple historical fact, like how the place got to be named, for example.

The official explanation, in *Coastal Place Names*, is that the island was named after John Upshot, a petty officer on Captain George Vancouver's ship, H.M.S. *Discovery*, when it made an exploratory expedition into these parts in 1792. Intrepid seamen though they may have been, these fellows were apparently not blessed with great imagination when it came to devising place names. To begin with, they'd exhaust the names of the British royal family of the day. Next they'd resort to the names of their ship's officers, hence the otherwise forgotten Upshot. Thereafter, with the exception of an occasional burst of polysyllabic melancholy as in the naming of nearby Desolation Sound, they seem to have been reduced to monosyllabic descriptions of physical characteristics, leaving the coast unimaginatively cluttered with numerous Deep Coves, Long Points, and Mud Bays.

As my friend Elvira Stone says, the explorers could have saved themselves considerable effort by simply enquiring of the native people living along the coast what particular places were called. Elvira's grandmother was a Salish lady, the last full native person to be born on the island. In those days it was often still called by its native name, a word of such deliciously protracted sibilance that, if they enquired at all, must have confounded the monosyllabic stalwarts from Europe.

When Elvira says it, the name sounds to me like small waves slapping on a shingle beach. Translated it means something like "the island where things grow in great abundance." Instead, our lads called it Upshot Island, after the third mate.

That's the official version anyway. But, as I say, there's usually more than one. Some locals refuse to accept this British Admiralty version, preferring an alternative explanation offered in *Upshot Island: A History* by our own Elsie Pitfield. Here's how it reads, on page three:

How Upshot Island came to be named is yet another part of its colourful history. Once upon a time it was called Pitfield Island, after its first pioneer family. However, the story is told that Isadora Pitfield, an exceptional beauty, was courted by two different beaux. When she pledged her hand to one, the other, in a fit of jealous passion, up and shot the first, for which crime he was later hanged. But ever after, the island came to be known by the name Upshot.

When Waddy Watts first heard this version he demolished it with a contemptuous snort. "Heifer dust!" he said. But there are others in the community besides Waddy who'll mutter that Elsie's slender paperback, now in its third printing, is little more than a thinly veiled glorification of the Pitfield family. Even an unbiased reading suggests that Pitfields do pop up throughout the narrative with a regularity disproportionate to their numbers or their modest accomplishments.

For myself, I like the old native name, and not just because I love Elvira Stone. Mostly because it's bang-on accurate about this place. The Salish name relates to the physicality and spirit of the place in a way that Upshot never will.

For some reason that no one can adequately explain, gardeners are drawn to this little island like yellowjackets to a salmon barbecue. You see a gravel driveway disappearing into the fir trees and you'd maybe assume there's a cabin at the end and perhaps a derelict vehicle half strangled in salmonberry canes. Instead you're apt to find a couple of fanatics labouring to recreate the white garden at Sissinghurst.

I've become one of these people myself. After I'd settled in here, the idea of growing my own fruit and vegetables seemed appealing enough, but at the time I'd had no inkling that I was taking a radical turn in my life, stepping into a world of gardening that would eventually consume most of my existence. I came like a lamb to the slaughterhouse of horticulture, and though I've never regretted that definitive turn in my life, I do believe there should be warnings to the unwary printed on seed catalogues, the same as on tobacco products.

Just look at the old Moffatts, Ernie and Gertrude, up at the north end, for example. They've been going at it since 1946, building a pleasure garden that one enthusiastic freelancer working for *Gorgeous Gardens* magazine compared favourably to the landscape of Hidcote Manor. The

Moffatts do almost nothing besides garden, eat, and sleep. They never go anywhere, never take a holiday. "Why should we go anyplace else?" old Ernie Moffatt will grin at you slyly, "when we got all this right here, eh?" Then he'll twist his funny little face sideways, click his dentures, and wink simultaneously. Some days I fear I'm turning into another old Ernie myself.

Ernie and Gertrude were part of the great English immigration wave that washed onto the island after Hitler's war. Being English, of course, that generation was all mad for gardening. But island growing was already well underway long before they got here. The Hamigami family used to run fabulous market gardens down at Big Marsh, until the war with Japan broke out and they were rounded up and sent to detention camps in the Interior, ostensibly because their bok choy represented a perceived threat to national security.

And, of course, all the back-to-the-landers came piling in around the late sixties and early seventies. Self-sufficiency. Grow your own. Back to basics. There was a whole commune of them down at Cogg's Crossing who used to all work together in one big vegetable garden. When the weather turned hot, they'd peel their clothes off and work stark naked, men and women and kids. You couldn't see them from the road, but if you went up onto Ricketts Hill, along the old skid road, there was a gap in the trees you could look through with binoculars and see them plain as day.

Eventually there was a petition circulated to try to force the hippies to put their clothes back on, but it never really went anywhere. Partly because no one knew who to send it to, but also because some of the good old boys said they enjoyed themselves immensely sitting up on Ricketts Hill in their pickups. They said they got a real bang out of seeing those hippie buttocks bulge with the effort of pulling out burdock roots by hand. Said they hadn't had so much fun since the glory days of biffy-tipping when as kids they'd overturned occupied outhouses on long-ago Saturday nights.

So the hippies stayed, some of them, joining the pioneering Scots and expatriate Brits. Then a wave of straight shooters from points east. Then cyberpunks and grunge rockers and God knows who else. So here we all are: Islanders. Gardeners. Dreamers. Fools.

3

"There she is!" Caitlin exclaims as the ferry nudges into its berth and begins disgorging a small band of foot passengers and vehicles. Caitlin runs ahead, bursting like a schoolgirl, and embraces the woman on the wharf. The two of them hug away, overlong in my opinion, like human growth group graduates. Finally unclinched, they walk back along the wharf towards me, laughing and holding hands.

From what I can see without staring, Caitlin's right about Mistral Wind. At least her appearance, which is magnificent. Well over six feet tall, and no older than Caitlin, I should think, she moves with a lissome, muscular grace, the way cougars do. Her skin's dusky and her long hair a lustrous black, deep as the sheen on raven feathers. She's wearing a simple brown tunic of coarse fabric that reaches almost to her feet, and leather sandals. I think straight away of someone on pilgrimage. Striding beside her, Caitlin seems fair and smooth, her pale skin like alabaster.

As Caitlin introduces us, Mistral takes my hand in hers and looks straight into my eyes, so that I want to look away in embarrassment, but can't. Her gaze holds me, and there are things in her dark eyes I do not want to see.

"You have spent long hours in meditation," she says to me. Her voice is husky and seductive, inflected only slightly by foreign accent.

"Yes, I have," I reply, startled that someone would say such a thing upon first meeting. "Long ago."

"I see," Mistral says, smiling. She releases my hand and turns to Caitlin. "Shall we go?"

"Yes!" Caitlin claps her hands like a mesmerist. "There's business to be done this night." We squeeze into my truck and drive back up the hill to the hall.

The Upshot Island Community Hall sits just off the main road behind a row of enormous big-leaf maple trees. Its gravel parking lot doubles as parking for the Preening Peacock Cafe next door. As we pull into the near-empty lot, Caitlin lets me know that she and Mistral are meeting Elvira in the café to plan the meeting. She doesn't say I'm not welcome to join them, but that's the sense I get. Which suits me just fine, because I've been feeling uncomfortable around Mistral Wind, and Caitlin too for that matter. There's something vaguely provocative about the two of them together that makes me uneasy.

"There's Waddy coming down the road," I say. "Why don't you two go ahead and I'll chat up the old fart for a bit."

Caitlin and Mistral stride off towards the Preening Peacock, again holding hands and giggling like teenagers. I walk up the road a stretch and hail Waddy.

"Hi, Waddy!" I call. "So you were right about the frogs!"

"Tree frogs don't lie," Waddy says, coming up. He lets a squirt of tobacco juice go and it splatters in the gravel on the roadside. "Unlike some of them two-legged hyenas they pass off for homo sappy-what-ever-it-is."

We fall into step together. Waddy Watts is an old bull-bucker from way back when. He came from down south on the big island, retiring to Upshot long before I got here. Waddy's a card from the bottom of the deck. No matter when you see him, he's always got the same outfit on: flannel shirt, coveralls and slip-on boots, the kind loggers call Romeos. He used to run a bush locomotive back in the old days. Damn good at it too, at least to hear him tell it. "A Pacific Coast Shay she was," Waddy'd say with a faraway look in his eye. "Lord, she was a lovely piece a machinery. Nothin' could touch the Shay for haulin' in the bush. Ninety ton she ran, not too heavy for the trestles, smooth as a sewin' machine."

"Always called him Waddy," Albert Peatfield told me once, when I asked about the name. Albert knew Waddy back in camp. "Everybody did. On account of his chaw. Never seen him without a wad of tobacco on the go. Hit a spittoon from fifteen feet easy. Never heard him called anything else but Waddy neither, don't even know if he's got another name."

Once retired to Upshot, Waddy took to growing vegetables with the same rough-hewn passion he maintained for his old steam locies. He must be pushing eighty now, but he's one of those tough little nuts that has hardly lost a step. He'll think nothing of hiking down to the hall from his place, well over a mile up the road.

"Been watchin' the wasps?" Waddy cocks his head sideways like a banty rooster hearing voices.

"I've got a whopping big nest in one of my apple trees," I say, "big as a basketball; one of those where the whole nest looks like it's made from a single sheet of paper wrapped around and around."

"Forest wasps," Waddy nods.

"I think they're going to get more of the apples than I will," I say.

"Indian summer comin'," Waddy's definitive. "Wasps are still feedin' their grubs. That's a good sign. Indian summer for sure."

Dealing with Waddy, I've learned over the years, it's safe to let him warm to his topic with a bit of folklore, but fatal if he's allowed to build a full head of steam. Once he's got a clear track for folkloric dissertation, he's all but unstoppable, and he'll fabricate the most outlandish rubbish if he thinks he can get away with it. When the Overstalls first showed up, Peewee and Julia, Waddy convinced them they could forecast the size of next year's kiwi crop by the length of ground squirrel whiskers. You wouldn't think even English professors like them could be that gullible, but Waddy's a master, just like the Pope. You catch him before he gets rolling, or you're done for.

"So, decided to enjoy an evening stroll tonight, eh?"

"That's it," he says. "Figured I'd stroll down to the meeting and hitch a ride back with you or old Moffatt or somebody. Get it while you can is my philosophy; no sense lettin' the worms have all the fun."

Waddy spits again and scratches his groin. "So I barely set foot on the road," here he goes now, "when there's a whole gang of cyclists come whizzin' past, visitors I guess, all of them wearin' that black stretchy stuff and them big helmets. Like they're gonna fall over and bang their pointy heads on the pavement any minute."

"It's the law now, Waddy," I interrupt him. "You gotta wear one."

"Oh, sure you do!" Waddy's dripping with contempt. "Government knows best, eh? Just like with hard hats. Remember the time they first introduced 'em up at the old man's camp. New government safety regulations, they said, you had to have one of these hard hats on if you were doin' anythin' a'tall."

I await the inevitable arrival of Waddy's protagonist.

"Well, there's one old feller in camp, tough old Swede name of Jonson, damn good faller too, didn't matter which way she was a'leanin', he could put her down right where he said he would. Always wore a toque, old Yonny. He wore it workin' and he wore it eatin' and he wore it sleepin' too. Said it kept the bunkhouse cooties outta his hair. Said it was lucky for him. Hot weather or cold, pissin' rain or not, it didn't matter to old Yonny, he'd have that bloody toque on."

We sit down at one of the picnic tables outside the hall, and Waddy continues his tale. "So when them fellers from the city says everyone has to wear one of them tin hats when they're workin', old Yonny just about has a shit. For one thing, the hard hat won't stay on his head, keeps fallin' down over his eyes so he can't see what the hell he's doin'. Guess his head was shaped kinda funny. 'Yeesus Christ!' old Yonny finally says to the old man, 'Dis fockin' tin hat's gonna kill me for sure!'

"It took the old man quite a while to calm him down, but finally they work it out that Yonny can wear his toque like usual and they'll get extra long straps and strap the hard hat over top of the toque, to satisfy safety regulations.

"Well, sure enough, couple of weeks later, a widow-maker comes whistlin' down off a big old spruce Yonny is wedgin' over. Down she comes, and a branch just nicks him on the hard hat, so it goes flyin' off like a cracked egg, but Yonny's got his toque on underneath and doesn't feel a thing.

" 'Yust like I told you,' Yonny says to the old man back at camp that night—Jesus, he was hoppin' mad— 'dat tin hat she's a piece a shit!'

"There was somethin' in it too," Waddy's reached his moral, " 'cause Yonny never washed that toque, no sir, soap nor water never touched her, and it was so thick with shit and corruption it probably was harder than a hard hat."

Waddy snuffles and snorts like a racehorse, which is his way of laughing, and bangs his hand on the picnic table. He has the old storyteller's habit of repeating his punchlines for renewed effect, and he does it now. "Yes sir, it probably was harder than a hard hat at that."

Small clots of garden club members drift in and we mingle for a while outdoors, reluctant to trade the evening loveliness for the gloomy interior of our ramshackle hall. Gertrude and Ernie Moffatt are there, as always, chatting away excitedly about a new water lily they've just acquired, though how they'll ever distinguish it from the scores they already have I'm not sure. Waddy drifts off to gossip with Albert Peatfield, who's old family around here. Those two old bushwhackers can talk all night about the glory days of big timber logging. They're oral tradition types, guys like Waddy and Albert, they'll talk your ear off if you let them, up and down a story like ants on a plum tree.

Peewee and Julia Overstall glide in on matching million-dollar mountain bikes. I see Waddy glower at their helmets and let a good squirt go. Jimmy Fitz comes rattling up in his rattletrap old pickup. Jimmy doesn't garden at all, but he hates to miss anything, so he comes to all the meetings anyway. Then Geoffrey and Rose Munz arrive, stepping out of their big sedan like the Queen and Prince Philip. Geoffrey and Rose are invariably immaculate, just like their place.

By now we're up to about two dozen. Suddenly a thrumming buzz runs through the group when we catch sight of Caitlin and Elvira escorting our peculiar guest speaker across the lot towards us.

"Jesus Christ!" whispers Jimmy Fitz close beside me.

We shuffle into the hall and find our seats. I end up beside Waddy. Caitlin and Elvira sit at the table up front, facing us. Mistral is sitting in the front row, so that I can only see the back of her head with its mane of gleaming black hair.

Caitlin starts things off by having Elvira read the minutes from the last meeting. These are about as interesting as picking raspberries. Then we do additions and corrections to the minutes followed by business arising from the minutes. Just in front of me, Jimmy Fitz is starting to nod off already. Gertrude Moffatt gives the treasurer's report, and here things liven up a bit because, try as she might, Gertrude just can't get the books to balance. Seven dollars and eighty-three cents have disappeared into some financial black hole, and Gertrude is mystified as to where they could be. She's searched through her receipts three times over, she tells us, but can't trace that darn seven dollars and eighty-three cents for love or money. Visibly upset, Gertrude offers her resignation. A disturbed murmuring greets this offer, and Caitlin, barely suppressing her amusement, replies that the club couldn't possibly entertain the prospect of Gertrude not having her hands tightly wrapped around our purse strings. Gertrude has been treasurer for so long, hardly anyone can remember when she wasn't. By this point in the meeting I'm seriously questioning what exactly I'm doing with my life.

Elvira reads the correspondence, which consists of a promotion package for a new weedeater with click-on attachments that can transform it into an edger, a super suction vacuum, a cultivator, and a hurricane-force leaf blower. "It works like magic!" declares the letter.

"Ain't got no click-on manure fork, does it?" Waddy asks out loud, and everybody laughs.

"Now," Caitlin announces solemnly, standing up, "it's my very great pleasure to introduce to you our special guest speaker for this evening, Mistral Wind. Mistral has a wide-ranging interest in gardening matters, being a trained herbalist and a specialist in permaculture. I have no doubt that by the time she's done with us, we'll be as magically transformed as our click-on weedeater. Please welcome Mistral Wind."

Caitlin sits down and Mistral stands up to polite applause. She bows slightly to Caitlin, and turns towards us. Suddenly, it's as though we've all held our breath at the sight of her. Even Jimmy Fitz stirs. I've never seen anyone electrify an audience so quickly. She seems to discharge charisma as naturally as some people do halitosis. She plunges like a diver into her talk with a voice as husky and luscious as some forbidden passion fruit.

"God Almighty first planted a garden," she begins, quoting Francis Bacon, then off she goes on an extravagant discourse on the meaning of gardens in history and religion, and on the gardener's eternal quest for Paradise, for the lost garden. She speaks easily and without pomposity about the great goddess and the nature religions that flourished for thousands of years, about Eden and the forbidden fruit, about banishment and exile in an arid land, and our attempts to make the desert bloom, to make the earth whole again. She paces before us as she speaks, a dark leopard in a cage that cannot hold her, and I see what Caitlin meant when she said that all this woman's talk is poetry, that she dances her words.

I'm impressed, but I have to say I'm not moved. There's something not quite right in the performance—and that's how I see it, as a performance, a clever masquerade, rather than the honest truth. She's an actor, this Mistral Wind, I think to myself, an actor who's a bit too good at what she does. She could be selling cars or laundry detergent. She could be running for Parliament, just one more clever schemer with a gifted tongue and dynamite stage presence.

Plus her body. My God. I can see almost none of her except her face and hands, but she gives off a raw sensuality that no amount of clothing can disguise. She speaks more to my lust than to my soul. While the fine words of her spiritual vision glide above us, smooth as frigate birds, there I sit inflamed with shameless thoughts, salacious imaginings, the vilest sort of concupiscence. To heck with paradise gardens! I'd rather bury my face in the muscular flesh of that bawdy Amazon and rut like a satyr.

This would-be angel is igniting impure thoughts in me, the very thoughts that were the bane of my religious life. Oh, the shame of kneeling in the confessional week after week and admitting to some titillated father confessor that I'd touched myself sinfully while imagining the naked bodies of seductresses! The terror of taking the sacred wafer on my tongue if I'd sinned again and not yet confessed! She might be extolling the return to paradise, but to me Mistral Wind smells like a return to sulphurous Purgatory, to an endless loop of desire and frustration and shame. Thanks, but no thanks, I say to myself, I'd just as soon tend my garden in peace.

Recomposed, I try to focus again on what Mistral's saying. She's worked her way around to trees, the oaks and ash, the Yggdrasil and bo tree, the sacred groves where people would gather to worship. Magic trees. Shamans climbing the tree of life from earth up to heaven, into the spirit world. Geoffrey Munz and all that crowd—they're just sitting there with their jaws hanging down while Mistral continues to pace back and forth, like she's dancing, and all the while talking, talking, talking.

Suddenly she stops speaking and pacing. She stands perfectly still and looks straight at us boldly. It's like when the wind drops all of a sudden, and everything's still and silent for just a second, and you wait for the wind again. Then she asks us, almost whispering: "Where are the sacred groves today? Gone, are they not? Gone forever! The cedars of Lebanon. Pine forests of Greece. Tropical gardens of New Guinea—all of them cut and burned long ago. And now there's bare hills baked by the sun where there used to be forests braided by streams and teeming with magic creatures. All of them gone, and is that not half the trouble with the world?"

God she's good at it; she makes the preaching priests of my boyhood seem like soapbox bumblers. Then she pauses again, only this time she looks straight into my eyes, and I can feel my sack go tight under her stare, but I can't look away from her. She's got me, like a halibut on a hook. And she says, "So why are we all sitting here like docile lambs?" She's looking straight at me, as though she's speaking to me specifically. "Not putting up any resistance at all, just meek and obedient, while the last great trees are falling all around us, falling for toilet paper and junk mail."

Then I see what she's up to: Kumquat Sound. You'd have to be living in a cave not to know what's going on over there. Kumquat Sound's on the big island, and it's been all over the papers and newscasts. For months now there've been logging road blockades by people trying to prevent clearcutting of the coastal rain forest. Hundreds of people have been arrested. Celebrities have been pouring in from all over, movie stars and rock musicians, decorated monkey wrenchers and Yankee politicians. People are sitting in trees, getting married on beaches, getting carried around in canoes by the local natives. The whole thing's like an Oliver Stone movie that has spun wildly out of control. Activists are sitting in jail, local rednecks are hopping mad, and tempers are running hot.

"And what are we doing about any of it?" Mistral asks, and pauses, and the room is silent as a sarcophagus. "And are we content to do nothing?" The silence holds, terribly.

Oh, cripes! I think to myself, I can see it all coming already. Caitlin's going to get into this issue and try to drag me in as well. It's the worst part about living here, and especially next door to Caitlin—someone's always trying to sign you up for some crack-brained campaign or other. Save the Salmon. Stop the Clearcuts. Nuclear-Free Ports. There's barely enough time to do all that you need just to stay alive around here, what with gardens and winter firewood and leaks in the roof and everything else, without having to go charging all over the place saving the planet. I don't like taking hardline positions, I don't like confrontation, and I don't like telling other people how to live their lives. Live and let live, that's my philosophy.

"How do we feel about ourselves," that confounded Mistral carries on, "while students and grannies and people in wheelchairs are being hauled off to jail for defending the trees and the sacred places? How do we feel about that?" I personally feel fine about it, if that's what people want to do, but still her question hangs over us, so that we can't ignore it. This is what I'd seen in her eyes down at the wharf, a depth into which you could plunge at your peril, if you weren't careful. This and other things.

"What's stopping us from going over there as well," Mistral asks, "from standing for the trees? Why are we afraid?"

Mistral sits down. The moment is like that split second after a great concert performance is finished, before the applause erupts, that moment of fullness that suddenly shatters.

Waddy Watts breaks the spell. I become aware of him sitting beside me as though in a trance; he's even forgotten his chaw. Suddenly, he leaps to his feet, and stands there.

"Caitlin," he says—Waddy's never one to stand on formalities—"I'd like us to thank our guest speaker here, and after that I'd like to move a motion."

"Yes, all right," Caitlin says, coming forward again, coming out of some trance of her own. She thanks Mistral for the talk which, I'm astonished to see by the ancient Canada Dry clock on the wall, has lasted an hour and a half. It seems like just a few minutes. We give Mistral a disconcerted-sounding round of applause.

"Now, Waddy," Caitlin says, "I believe you have a motion arising from the presentation?"

"That's right," says Waddy, who's remained standing, like a banty rooster at dawn. "I move that the club send a delegation over to Kumquat to get busted."

Waddy sits down, and you'd have thought lightning had just hit the hall. What the heck's Waddy up to anyway? I mean, he's such a snarly old bull-of-the-woods, he's the last person in the world you'd expect to go running off on some crackpot anti-logging protest. But I can see the old guy has a glint of fire in his eye. I half expect him to let a big squirt go right there on the floor.

Julia Overstall pops up to second the motion. I can smell trouble coming sure as manure tea.

Geoffrey Munz leaps to his feet. "Point of order, Madame Chair," Geoffrey begins in his best House of Lords accent. "With all due respect to our guest speaker and to the mover of the motion, I must point out that this particular issue is well beyond the purview of our club." There's a burst of spirited clapping from a few members in support of Geoffrey's position.

"However much we may as individuals be in sympathy with this particular issue," Geoffrey carries on, buoyed by the applause, "and notwithstanding any misgivings we may have with respect to the tactics being employed by groups and individuals involved in this particular issue"—Geoffrey always pronounces it "iss-yew" the way Brian Mulroney does—"nevertheless, I believe it to be incontrovertibly the case that the constitution of this society expressly limits the activities of the executive and the membership to horticultural matters on or near Upshot Island."

"What did he say?" Jimmy Fitz whispers in the silence following Geoffrey's sally.

Caitlin calmly extracts from her battered satchel a copy of the society's constitution and bylaws and reads aloud from the section headed "Purposes of the Society" Clause Six, Section B, Subsection Three, which states: "To do whatever else in the opinion of the membership shall be deemed appropriate for advancing the well-being of flora generally."

"Flora who?" This is Jimmy again.

"I do believe," pronounces Caitlin, with immense politeness, "that the motion is well within the parameters of the constitution." This ruling's greeted with another burst of applause, somewhat louder than the one Geoffrey elicited.

As luck would have it, there's a twenty-fifth wedding anniversary being celebrated elsewhere on the island this evening. The celebration has siphoned off several of the more strait-laced club members. Geoffrey, their champion, realizing that he stands tonight as spokesperson for a temporarily reduced rump, harrumps several times and sits down.

Someone calls "Question!" and the motion—that a delegation representing the Upshot Island Garden Club and Horticultural Society should proceed to Kumquat Sound and participate in the civil disobedience campaign underway there—is put to a vote by show of hands.

Damn! I'm seized by panic. What am I going to do? If I vote for the motion, I'll end up getting dragged along into who knows what insanity. And if I vote against, Waddy and Caitlin will be all over me like deerflies.

"All in favour?" calls Caitlin. A bunch of arms shoot into the air, but I can't put mine up, not in good conscience, I just can't. Caitlin, counting hands, catches it, of course. She would. Out of the corner of my eye I see Waddy give me a look that would curdle cream.

"Opposed?" calls Caitlin. Geoffrey and his few followers stick their hands up in a doomed attempt at opposition. I can't vote that way either.

"Abstentions?" Caitlin asks, as though these were a communicable disease. She looks straight at me with an infuriating blend of mockery and accusation. Damn it all anyway! I put my hand half up, feeling a perfect fool, and Caitlin makes a grand production of recording "One abstention!"

They pass another motion for the club to donate one hundred dollars to assist the protest group with expenses. At which point Geoffrey and Rose and several of their followers rise from their chairs with magisterial dignity and stalk from the room in protest.

The worst of it is having to drive Caitlin and Mistral back to Caitlin's place after the meeting. The two of them are high as kites, laughing and carrying on and going over the meeting. They don't mention my abstention, though I can see it plainly in Caitlin's smile when we're saying good night at her place.

"Thank you for the ride, Joseph," Mistral says to me, touching my hand on the steering wheel, "both ways. I'm sure we'll meet again."

"Good night," I say to her. "Your speech was wonderful."

"Oh, J.J.," Caitlin shakes her head and gives me a sisterly peck on the cheek, "you're such an unconvincing liar. Sweet dreams."

And then they're gone, arm-in-arm into Caitlin's house, and I drive home alone.

4

I decided to lie low for a couple of days until this Kumquat fad fades. Folks around here can work themselves up into a real lather at times, genuine tempests in teapots, but if you just ride it out for a bit, the furor eventually dies down and life pretty much goes on as it always has.

I know I'm on the outs just now. My phone hasn't rung for three days, not since that confounded meeting. I can feel Caitlin's displeasure next door, looming over me like an ice field. I suppose I should go over there and have a clearing with her, but I have a toxic reaction to melodrama. Life's weird enough as it is, without having it dissolve into soap opera. Working on the potato beds seemed to me a preferable alternative. As Waddy Watts says, if more people grew root vegetables, they wouldn't be running to therapists and counsellors every five minutes.

I start cleaning out a bed of early reds, Norlands. I've been eating them since June, but the crop's been a bit of a disaster. A lot of the largest tubers—tubby customers that give a little rush of pride when you first turn them up out of the soil—are, on closer inspection, diseased. They aren't heavy enough for their size, and when you tap one against your pail, it sounds punky. Somewhere on the skin, there'll be a small hole, and if you slice the tuber in half, the inside'll be hollow and mottled with sooty black.

"Hollow heart," Caitlin told me back in June, holding one of the big rotters in her hand. "Too much moisture in the spring brings it on. They set me thinking of my tribe, you know, the potato famine, the flight from blighted Ireland." Caitlin can say things like that. But why was I thinking of her again? Her sisterly kiss still lingers on my cheek, then she called me a liar, the brazen-face! And what monkey business were she and that prancing Mistral up to all night, going off entwined in sisterhood like that? I almost wish that crackbrained poet was still slobbering about, so I could dismiss Caitlin from my mind and be done with it.

I work my way along the bed, stuffing the shrivelled potato tops into a large pail, and separating sound tubers from the hollow hearts. I feel adrift. What about this Mistral Wind—is she just a charismatic charlatan, or is she something else, something wonderful, as Caitlin and Elvira believe? All my instincts tell me she's a fake. Ever since my own feckless plunge into the spiritual life, I've been extremely wary of people who parade around in religiosity as though it were a fashion statement. But Caitlin is nobody's dupe, and neither is Elvira. Could this be a woman thing going on, one of these Earth Mother rituals I don't understand, but which invariably seem to involve plump and naked females smeared with organic materials?

The work soothes me bit by bit, and gradually I forget these preoccupations and fall into the intoxicating rhythms of sweat and soil. After I've cleared off the potatoes, I dig the bed over by spade. I love the sweet flood of sensations released by a spade slicing deep and clean into garden loam and turning it over. The musty, rich pungency of fresh-turned earth. Pink earthworms curled up in tight knots, like bird nest noodles, centipedes like tiny Chinese dragons. Billions of microorganisms seething in the soil.

I level the bed with my rake and plant it with fall rye for a cover crop. I work the rye into the soil with quick little scratchings of the rake, to keep thieving birds from getting all the seed. Finished, looking at the smoothed bed, I feel an honest satisfaction, as though at least this one small portion of the planet is blessedly, for the moment, in comprehensible good order.

I pause for a bit, hands on the nub of my rake handle, chin on my hands. A pair of flickers dance along the swinging branches of an elderberry bush just beyond the fence, plucking the small blue fruits from flattened clusters. How beautifully the muted blue elderberries hang beside the orange-red berries of mountain ash. I'm charmed by the carefree perfection of the composition, and my spirit is calmed. This is what I seek, this tranquillity.

The telephone rings inside. I lean my rake against the fence and sprint towards the house, counting as I go: three rings I'm at the steps, four rings I'm through the door, five rings I'm grabbing the phone, hoping whoever it is hasn't gone. "Hello?"

"Well, if it isn't the great abstainer!" Elvira Stone.

"Hello, Elvira," I say, glad to hear her voice.

"Hello yourself. So what's the big idea?"

"Pardon?"

"Don't play me for the fool," Elvira counters. "I've just racked off some rhubarb wine that ought to be tested. Why don't you come over?"

"You mean you're looking for a guinea pig?" I had to get in a bit of a shot. Elvira's winemaking is notoriously erratic. One batch might be unbelievably good—"Julio Gallo, eat your heart out!" Elvira will proclaim triumphantly, glass in hand, during the solemnities of testing. The next batch might be so bad you could use it as spray to kill cockroaches. But you had to drink it through, no matter how foul it was—"You take the bad with the good in life," Elvira will say, "and no bellyaching either."

Elvira says into the phone, "I'm looking for a real man. You in or not?"

"I'll be right over," I tell her.

Elvira lives in one of the old farmhouses on the east side, just down from the Overstalls. She's third generation on that land. Her house is set back from the road, and the driveway up to it is lined with tall Lombardy poplars, so it feels a bit grand as you come up the drive, like a colonnaded avenue, with the big farmhouse at the end forming a classic focal point of interest. Glimpsed between the poplars, off to the right, the old barn is sagging badly now and cries for a new roof. Here and there, broad cedar boards have popped loose off the sides, leaving gap-toothed blanks in the walls, where barn swallows swoop and glide in and out.

As usual, it takes me a good ten minutes to get up the driveway, having to stop about every six feet to allow numerous ducks, chickens, guinea fowl, geese, and peacocks to first stand in front of, then slowly get out of the way of, my pickup. Elvira's place is overrun with barnyard birds. It's the land of the Pharaohs suffering a plague of fowls at the hands of a wrathful Jehovah.

The birds are running amok, at least indirectly, because of Elvira's husband, Freddie. He disappeared three years ago, and to this day it's still an unsolved mystery what happened to him. He'd been working at a copper mine up north on the big island and driving down on weekends. Elvira and her daughter Mona looked after the farm on their own, though by then it wasn't real farming any more, not something you could make a living at. Fred got in his pickup truck one Friday evening and drove out of the minesite on his way back down to Upshot, and he's never been seen or heard from since.

"That's not like Fred at all," Elvira said at the time, "you guys know that. He's as steady as stones, old Freddie."

Foul play was suspected. But Freddie's truck never showed up either, never a trace, and after a year or so the RCMP told Elvira there was nothing more they could do and closed the file.

"My heart just aches for anyone who's had a family member go missing," Elvira will say, but she somehow can't attach tragedy to Freddie—"He just ain't the tragic type," she'll say. She senses him alive, somewhere.

One time Elvira brought in a psychic who specialized in missing persons—Fibber Miller had met her down in the city at a convention and thought maybe she could come up with something. Fibber even paid her way up, which everyone thought was real decent of him.

Elvira and the psychic went up to the minesite together, and slowly worked their way back down the highway. Elvira drove her big old station wagon and the psychic sat alongside her with her eyes closed. Somewhere near Dark Creek the psychic picked up a strange disturbance. In fact, Elvira told us later, the psychic started cawing loudly, in a pretty lame imitation of a raven's cry. Elvira stopped the car and they walked down a dirt road for a bit. Night had fallen already, but the landscape was lit up in brilliant moonlight, and they could see snowberries and thorny wild roses in the hedgerows.

"It's very strong here," the psychic kept saying, in between caws. "It's very strong here." But that was all she could get.

People more or less concluded that the psychic was a fake. But, several months later, Gertrude Moffatt was lighting a fire in her woodstove when she happened to notice a small news item in a back issue of the Mid-Island Times about a reported UFO siting near Dark Creek around the time of Freddie's disappearance. Two high school students had seen a mysterious cigar-shaped craft with twinkling lights hovering above a corn field.

But when Elvira finally tracked down who the kids were, and called their homes, their parents wouldn't let her talk to them. "Uptight like you wouldn't believe," Elvira reported back to us. She figured the kids—a boy and girl "at the age when" as Elvira put it—had been eating magic mushrooms and maybe having a tumble under the snowberries. The parents must have discovered it somehow and then thought the kids had made up the UFO thing to cover their dalliance.

But, as Elvira reminded us, Fred was a real UFO buff, even subscribed to a UFO magazine from the States, and if there'd been anything strange hovering over Dark Creek that fateful night, he'd have been the first one to head right in and investigate.

Elvira became convinced that Freddie was taken off in a spacecraft, truck and all, and is still alive. She believes—in the same unshakeable way I once believed my own articles of faith—that she'll surely be meeting up with him again eventually and that he'll have what she calls "some hellacious tales to tell." Mona, who's now studying for a law degree at Dalhousie University, makes a point of sending Elvira any clippings about UFOs she comes across.

Shortly after Fred's disappearance, Elvira decided to become a vegetarian. This decision was partly due to a careless remark let slip by Jimmy Fitz at a New Year's party when we were hoisting a glass of wine to Freddie, wherever he might be, and Jimmy blurted out that he sure hoped the Martians or whoever it was didn't eat humans. After that, Elvira said she couldn't face flesh any more, not even a leg from one of her own chickens, without feeling pitchy.

She was even tempted to go vegan, she said, and do away with all animal products entirely, same as Caitlin has. But that was maybe going overboard because she still had all these birds at her place, laying eggs in every nook and cranny. Besides, it's widely conceded that Elvira makes the best eggs benedict on the island, which was something she didn't want to lose the knack for, because it was always Freddie's favourite. Spared execution by axe and chopping block, the ducks and geese and all the rest have the run of the place now, and Elvira's yard is aswarm with squawking birds and squishy with their droppings. You never wear your best shoes to Elvira's.

"C'mon in," Elvira hails me from her porch, shooing off a big barred rock rooster with her broom. A prim little white picket fence runs around Elvira's front yard, with a fancy lattice arbour over the front gate. She has a pair of beautiful camellias, one on either side of the path, and a huge forsythia in the middle of what was a lawn before the birds got at it.

But what really catches your eye, especially in May when it's in bloom, is her wisteria. Elvira thinks her grandmother planted it the same year they built the house, 1907, right at the corner of the porch. It's got a trunk like an apple tree now, twisting up to the porch roof. From there its arms spread out like the tentacles of a giant squid, grasping the whole front of the house, coiling out along the hydro lines and up the TV antenna.

Every so often, Elvira gets her pole pruner out and whacks the new runners back a bit. Sometimes you'll see her hanging out the front bedroom window upstairs, slashing at the runners with a machete as if she were cutting sugar cane. "That vine's a damn nuisance all right," Elvira says. "The house is so dark inside in summer I can't see my hand in front of my face. But let's face it," she laughs, "it's the only thing holding the old place up."

And when the huge pendulous blue racemes hang down in May, the wisteria is entirely splendid. A full-colour photograph of it had once appeared in a fancy gardening calendar for 1992, which Elvira keeps pinned to her kitchen wall. "I want Freddie to see that when he gets back," she says. "He always wanted to cut that wisteria down."

Elvira leads me over to her kitchen table, which is half covered with ripening tomatoes. She plunks down two thick glass tumblers and fetches a gallon wine jug from the pantry. She's wearing her standard issue blue jeans and T-shirt. Her thick black hair, now peppered with grey, looks freshly permed. Her broad face is lined and leathery as a desert rat's. Swarthy and thick-set, with muscular arms and calloused hands, Elvira's not just salt of the earth, as Caitlin says, she is the earth.

"Now for the moment of truth," she announces. The rhubarb wine gurgles and splashes out of the jug into the glasses. I stand solemnly, holding my glass, and she stands holding hers. "To absent friends," Elvira says.

"To absent friends," I echo. We clink our glasses together and take a swallow of wine.

We each pucker our lips judiciously and stare off across imaginary vineyards somewhere in the south of France.

"Well?" she asks.

"Hmm. Certainly a robust, fruity flavour," I venture.

"Piquant, wouldn't you say?" Elvira suggests.

"Piquant indeed," I agree, and we sip again. "Yes, piquant certainly, but there's just a touch of naughtiness too, don't you find?"

"I thought more pert," Elvira says, "Pert and piquant both."

"But still full-bodied," I add, needing to provide a final superlative. "Uncompromising. A marvellous spiritus frumenti."

Mercifully, this batch is not among Elvira's worst. She makes the stuff by the barrel-load in plastic garbage cans set behind her wood-stove. Rhubarb in spring, blackberry in fall.

Misadventures frequently attend Elvira's fermentations. On one occasion she inadvertently left the lid off a batch of blackberry wine overnight. She popped the lid back on the next morning and thought no more about it until, three weeks later, when it was time to decant the stuff into her secondary fermenter—another garbage can—she found a very bloated and very dead mouse floating on top of the wine.

"I guess I hadn't noticed the poor little beggar that first morning I put the lid back on," she said later. "I did think about throwing the whole batch away, but you know the work involved in picking enough blackberries to make twelve gallons of wine. And what harm's one little mouse going to do anyway?" Elvira made this disclosure at an intimate dinner party one evening, just as we'd finished drinking the final bottle of the vintage in question.

In the same vein, a cousin of Freddie's from up north came down for a visit one time. Lloyd his name was, and he'd come to offer Elvira con-solation over Freddie's disappearance. As she tells it, cousin Lloyd gets up to pee one night and mistakes her primary fermenter for an oversize potty. "I heard the splash," Elvira told several of us, again just as the final drops of that adulterated vintage had been consumed, "but I couldn't very well burst in there and tell him to hold his water, could I? The damage was already done. And, after all, Lloyd's a fisherman, so you have to make allowances."

Curiously, this tainted vintage had turned out to be one of her bet-ter-tasting batches, and all of us who assisted her in its consumption were in hindsight grateful that we'd known nothing, at the time of imbibing, about cousin Lloyd's nocturnal contribution to its success. Those of us who know her well have learned not to question Elvira too closely on the particularities of her winemaking.

"Marvellous!" I say as she refills our glasses and we sit at her kitchen table.

"Well, it'll get us through Christmas anyway," Elvira says, though you can tell she's really quite pleased. "Now, have you heard the latest?"

"Nothing," I say, "not since the meeting. What's going on?"

Elvira clicks her tongue and shakes her head. I can't tell if she's more dismayed by the meeting itself or by my pathetic lack of inside information.

Elvira Stone and I have a peculiar relationship. Although she's only a few years older than me, she seems in many ways far more experienced and wiser. Perhaps she's the older sister I never had. I feel easy when I'm with her, and I'm probably more open with her than anyone else, which admittedly isn't saying much. A friend for sure. Plus she's excellent at knowing whatever's afoot on Upshot.

"Tell me everything," I say.

"Well, you saw Elsie and Geoffrey and all that lot walk out of the meeting," Elvira sips her wine again and rolls her eyes in mock ecstasy. "And I'll tell you the phone lines were scorching that night. The sun wasn't up next morning before dark plots were already hatched."

"I'm all ears," I say drolly. I may not care for the blood and dust of battle, but, like most people, I do enjoy hearing about it.

"Next evening, Tuesday, they convene a secret meeting of their own. I only heard about it because I had my hair done this morning at Wilhelmina's, and she was at the meeting. Karl, of course, is one of the ringleaders—you know what he's like."

Indeed I do. Karl Muhlbacher and I have never seen eye-to-eye on much of anything. Karl and Wilhelmina, and three neurotic dachshunds, live over at Cascara Heights. Karl grows dahlias and nothing but dahlias. His idea of a garden is several hundred dahlias all lined up in straight rows, like the white crosses in Flanders fields. Wilhelmina is forbidden to even touch them. Blessed with great gifts as a hairdresser, she confines herself to houseplants and a few pots on the deck. Karl marches up and down his dahlia rows like the Iron Chancellor preparing for war. Anything untidy, anything disorderly or unruly, drives him into a cold fury. Dripping with anarchy as it was, the Kumquat expedition was guaranteed to enrage him, and if Karl had been at the garden club meeting, the strength of his presence might have forced a different outcome—or, at least, it would have been something to see him go up against Mistral Wind. Karl and Geoffrey taking on Mistral and Caitlin—

oh, it would have been delicious! But Karl and Wilhelmina had been at the anniversary dinner, and so missed the meeting.

"We all know there's no secret stays a secret very long with Wilhelmina," Elvira continues. "Especially when you're in the chair. The minute she gets her hands on your head, she starts talking and she can't seem to stop until she's done. It's as if she needs to work on what's inside your head at the same time as she's working on the outside. I was in for my regular perm and she's barely got me in the chair before she starts telling me about the secret meeting. Of course she tells me that the information cannot leave the room. That's what she always says when she's spilling secrets: 'This information absolutely cannot leave this room.'" Elvira refills our glasses from the jug.

"Who was at this secret meeting?"

"Rose and Geoffrey Munz, of course, the meeting was at their house. Wilhelmina and Karl. Elsie Pitfield—you know how she thinks the sun rises and sets on Geoffrey." Ever since publishing *Upshot Island: A History*, Elsie has considered her position in the community greatly enhanced. She is no longer just old family; she's now also a leading member of our intellectual elite.

"Who else?"

"The MacIvors, poor fools. I think that was the lot of them."

"Must have been interesting to have Geoffrey and Karl lining up on the same team," I say. "I thought they were still slugging it out on the beaches of Normandy."

"Amicable as all get out, apparently," Elvira says, "at least to hear Wilhelmina tell it. I can remember Geoffrey once referring to Karl as a stiff-necked Kraut, but that seems to be well behind us now."

"Strange bedfellows and all that."

"I guess. And, of course, Elsie was in there like last week's laundry, probably fluttering after both of them to keep them onside."

"What else did Wilhelmina have to say about it?"

"On and on about how smart Geoffrey is and how smart Karl is, but you could tell that their meeting had pretty soon become a good old-fashioned bitch session."

"How so?"

"Well, they started in about Caitlin, of course—Wilhelmina didn't say so in so many words, but I wheedled it out of her. How dare she do this, and how dare she do that, and all those shabby boyfriends, and that poor little girl of hers, so sweet, and isn't it all a shame, and what a disaster it was that she'd beaten Geoffrey out for president."

Geoffrey had been president of the club for two terms. He is, after all, highly regarded for his work with tea roses, and there's even a rose named after him, developed by an associate in England—'Geoffrey's Joy' it's called, although it's a rather pathetic yellow specimen that scarcely justifies the painstaking hybridizing required to create it. Sort of like Geoffrey himself.

Notwithstanding an impeccable pedigree, Geoffrey has a way of putting people's noses out of joint without even realizing that he's doing it. When Caitlin ran against him for the chair last spring, a few swing votes whom Geoffrey had offended in one way or another bolted to Caitlin's camp, thus sealing her victory. Geoffrey, it's generally conceded, has never altogether recovered from the sting of that rebuke.

"Then they got right down and dirty," Elvira continues. "I had a hell of a time prying this out of Wilhelmina, but it seems the talk got around to implying that Caitlin was having a lesbian affair with Mistral Wind."

"I'm shocked!" I say, although secretly I've been harbouring the same suspicion myself.

"Wouldn't you have loved to be a fly on the wall for that little parlez-vous?" Elvira winks. "According to Wilhelmina, Elsie dismissed Mistral as what she called a pretentious tramp. 'And you have to admit,' Wilhelmina says to me, 'there was something a bit off about that woman. Besides the silly name, I mean. I think she was quite promiscuous the way she presented herself.' 'But, Wilhelmina,' I said to her, 'you weren't even there.' She'd obviously just picked this up from one of the others, probably Elsie, or maybe Petty MacIvor."

Petula and Angus MacIvor also live in Cascara Heights. They've developed a wonderful alpine garden spilling down the rock bluff on that side. It really is a thing of beauty. But they're both such awful sourpusses—everyone calls them Petty and Angry—they ruin the whole effect of the garden. The one and only time I went over there to see it, I'd heard so much about it, the two of them nattered and bitched and whined the entire time I was there, so I couldn't enjoy the garden at all. Which is too bad, because they've done an incredible job with it. It doesn't surprise me to hear that they're in on anything nasty.

"Geoffrey especially seems to have a stick up his snoot about Mistral," Elvira continues. "Karl, of course, didn't see her; though if he had, he'd probably have spent most of his time staring at her breasts. Same as you," Elvira jabs me.

"That's cruel," I say, feeling myself blush stupidly. This is what I mean about people saying shocking things to me.

"Geoffrey was out and out mean," Elvira goes on, "at least from what Wilhelmina let slip. I guess he made a crack about Mistral's colour. 'Some gypsy wog,' he called her, and then Wilhelmina realized that maybe I'd take offence because of my native blood. So she tried to cover it up and got all flustered."

"What a bunch of klutzes they are!" I force a laugh.

"And then came the best part of all," Elvira grins. She must have one of the best grins of anyone in the world. Her broad face, lined and sun-tanned like saddle leather, seems perfectly constructed for grinning.

"Do tell."

"Wilhelmina goes on for over an hour—she obviously doesn't know that I'm in on any of this, or she hasn't stopped to put two and two together. Finally, my hair's done, and I stand up and I say to Wilhelmina, breezy as you please, 'Thank you so much, Wilhelmina, and don't you worry your head the least little bit. Not a word of any of this will pass my lips when we're on our way over to Kumquat.' Well, her jaw drops and she just gapes at me. It was absolutely priceless. Then I swing on my heel like the queen of England and waltz out of the beauty parlour cool as you please."

Elvira takes a swig of wine and beams at me broadly, pleased as peaches with herself.

"So, you're actually going along on this crazy expedition?" I wasn't exactly surprised to hear Elvira say so, because she's the type who'll do just about anything, no matter how crazy it is, but I've never known her to do this sort of thing. Being as she's recording secretary, she hadn't voted at the meeting, and I wasn't sure where she sat on the issue.

"Yes I am," she says firmly, "though I noticed you were less than enthusiastic yourself."

"Why would you possibly want to get involved in that circus?" I ask her, cleverly circling away from discussing my own participation. "You know it won't make any difference to anything."

Elvira smiles at me the way people smile at a puppy in the pound, as though I should be pitied for being out of the loop.

"Well, for one thing," she explains, a trifle more patiently than necessary, "I feel my few diluted drops of native blood beginning to beat. And you know as well as I do that what's going on at Kumquat, and all along the coast, is theft, plain and simple. It's outsiders—investors in New York or London or wherever, people who've maybe never even seen the place—making huge profits ripping off people who've lived there for thousands of years. That's not some political speech, it's the plain honest truth."

"Yes, of course," I say, "I agree." How can you not? "But isn't that sort of like saying how awful the civil war is in Rwanda or Burundi or wherever? I mean, what the hell can you realistically do about any of those huge intractable problems? Sitting on a logging road isn't going to change how transnational empires run the global economy."

"You're probably right," Elvira says, "but doing nothing will solve nothing for sure." Elvira's uncharacteristically solemn on this, and it disconcerts me. "And heading over to Kumquat for a day or two isn't going to kill anyone, is it?"

"I guess not," I admit. I'm getting uncomfortable with the track we were on; I'd rather be back in our familiar badinage, but Elvira's sombre tone forbids it.

"I'd go for Caitlin's sake, if no one else's," Elvira says. "You know how she feels about the issue."

"Yes."

"And about you."

"Me?"

"Don't play the innocent with me, Brother Joseph," Elvira raises her glass in mock salute. "Caitlin has a place in your life, same as in mine, and there's no sense your hiding from the truth."

One of Elvira's pet themes is that Caitlin represents what's missing in my life, just as Freddie does in hers.

As usual, I choose to humour her on this point. "I suppose not," I say, although hiding is precisely what I have in mind.

5

I needed to go down to the general store to buy a few supplies. It's been a couple of days since my chat with Elvira. I haven't spoken with Caitlin or anyone else in the interim. I've been quite content to harvest my tomatoes and get on with an editing job due in a couple of weeks.

The Upshot Island General Store and Emporium is a classic old island store. Its wooden shelves are crowded with a bizarre hodge-podge of groceries, hardware, tourist curios, video rentals, fishing tackle, local crafts, and eccentric oddments. Built in 1910, it retains its original edge-grain fir flooring and counters, though the oak barrel full of briny pickles and the great rounds of cheese have long since disappeared.

The second I step through the door, I sense that something is wrong, but I don't know what. The storekeeper, Margaret May, looks up at me from behind her counter with a disconsolate look I've never seen on her face before.

"Margaret May, what is it? What's wrong?"

"Look!" she cries, more a sob than a word, pointing to the wall behind me.

I turn to look, but for a moment fail to register what she means. Then I see: the bear head has disappeared.

For many years, long before I moved here, a large stuffed black bear head hung over the front door. The head reputedly once belonged to the last bear shot on the island, back in '53. Hanging beneath the head, an old framed photo showed the bear as a lifeless lump of fur on the ground and a half-dozen men standing proudly around the carcass, holding rifles and shotguns.

The bear head caused no end of trouble. The taxidermist responsible—it was an uncle of Gertrude Moffatt on the big island who'd done the stuffing—had tried his best to make the bear appear to be snarling in savage anger. But that wasn't the effect at all. Hanging on the wall like that, sundered from its once-magnificent body, the head seemed pathetic, disembodied, like the head of John the Baptist on Salome's platter. Its open mouth, though bristling with lethal teeth, seemed to be screaming in agony.

On several occasions, islanders attempted to have the bear head removed. Shortly after its installation, according to local legend, a delegation from the Ladies Auxiliary approached the storekeeper of the day—an irascible misfit named Mr. Konrad—saying that the bear head was causing certain children to have terrible nightmares.

"Just wait," Mr. Konrad told them ominously, picking his teeth with a red-cedar sliver, as he always did. "Just you wait. The day will come when they will dream of bears and be glad, because by then their world will have gone completely mad." Mr. Konrad had a talent for prophesying in apparently unconscious couplets.

The Ladies Auxiliary, so the story goes, despite boasting several quite formidable members among its ranks, faltered when faced with Mr. Konrad's gloomy predictions, and eventually withdrew in uncharacteristic disarray.

In turn, the new storekeeper, Margaret May, lifted her predecessor's gloomy sagacity into the realms of enlightenment. She took over the store some years ago, purchasing it with a handsome settlement from her late husband's life insurance policy. A big-bosomed woman of enormous warmth, Margaret May came to us like a fresh breeze in springtime after the morbid Mr. Konrad. Still, like most storekeepers, she has her own peculiarities.

"My late husband, Arthur," Margaret May would announce across her counter, "smoked himself into an early grave." She'd pause half a beat for effect. "But at least he had the good sense to buy solid life insurance. All in all, I'm not complaining."

From the very first, she absolutely refused to sell any tobacco products in her store. Nor would she permit smoking at the coffee counter. "Absolutely not!" she proclaimed. "It's a disgusting, filthy habit, and I won't be a party to anyone killing themselves!"

Announcement of this policy exploded like a car bomb among the small coterie of dedicated smokers who would customarily gather at the store's little counter for their morning coffee. Mr. Konrad's gloomy silences had suited the company perfectly. Perched on the five swivelling stools, they'd peruse their morning papers, drink bottomless cups of coffee, gossip a bit, and, mostly, smoke.

Jimmy Fitz's brother Johnny, who'd had his coffee at the store every morning for thirty years, turned several shades of magenta when told of Margaret May's new edict. He pounded the counter with a clenched fist so that the coffee cups jumped in their saucers. He bellowed at Margaret May face to face, flecks of his spittle splashing her awfully. He threatened lawsuits. He warned her he'd burn the bloody store down if she didn't relent.

But relent she would not. She lifted herself, enormous bosom and all, to a magisterial height and announced: "Johnny Fitz, you'll be dead within the decade if you don't mend your foolish ways."

That was it for Johnny. Within six months he'd sold his place down at Cogg's Crossing to the hippies and retired to Tucson, Arizona, where he's still living, and smoking, to this day.

Some years after the great tobacco battle, the anti-bear-head movement, in a ludicrous miscalculation of relative strengths, decided to test Margaret May's mettle again. Peewee and Julia Overstall led the charge. They're former English professors from the University of Toronto. They bought the old Smith place on the east side with grand ambitions for growing kiwis and ginseng roots. Fibber Miller had told them that there wasn't a better ginseng growing location on the whole coast. Afterwards he'd phoned around frantically, asking everyone what the hell ginseng was and would it grow here.

Like most professors, Peewee and Julia are harmless enough, but everyone wondered back then how they possibly thought they could be a match for Margaret May. Backed up by a few supporters (no one can remember who they were any more), Peewee and Julia entered the store and presented Margaret May with a petition bearing thirty-seven signatures requesting that the bear head be removed on the grounds that it represented "an assault to the aesthetic sensibilities of a significant portion of the island population."

You could have heard a butterfly breathe, it was that silent in the store when Margaret May finished perusing the petition, placed it carefully on the counter, and looked straight into the face of each petitioner present, one after the other.

The few neutral observers on hand fully expected Margaret May to say that thirty-seven signatures didn't constitute a significant portion of the population, because even by then, we were up around two hundred. Thirty-seven was at best an ambitious minority.

Instead, Margaret May, because she was dealing most prominently with professors of English, tailored her response along deconstructionist lines. She restudied the text of the petition and the column of signatures.

"I can't make out this signature here," she said at last, her plump index finger gently tapping the page. "Who's that?"

Peewee and Julia craned their necks sideways across the counter and squinted at the page. "That?" said Julia finally. "Oh, that's Lister Gordon."

"Lister Gordon?" Margaret May seemed enormously pleased.

"Yes, he's very well known," said Peewee.

"Indeed he is," agreed Margaret May. "But doesn't this petition read: 'We, the undersigned residents of Upshot Island?' "

"Well, yes it does," Peewee brushed aside the technicality, "but Lister was visiting and felt very strongly about the bear's head."

"Did he?" said Margaret May. "I see." She paused long enough for an invisible scorekeeper, somewhere up behind the fishing tackle racks, to put up numbers that everyone present recognized as favourable to the shopkeeper.

Another considered perusal of the document. "And who's this?" Margaret May asked, tapping at another name farther down.

"That?" replied Julia, craning again, a little diffident. "Let me see, if, hmm, oh yes, that's Dylan Nosler."

"Dylan Nosler?" asked Margaret May, rising up, beaming like a lighthouse.

"Yes," said Julia and Peewee at the same time, tripping over one another.

"The same Dylan Nosler that comes in here and buys jelly beans after school?"

"Yes, that's him," said Peewee, a bit lamely.

"And how old is Dylan Nosler?" Margaret May was relentless.

"He'll be twelve in March," Julia blurted out, the way kids do when they want to impress you with the weight of an additional year.

"Twelve in March," Margaret May pondered aloud, as though she were pondering a theorem of Pythagoras. "Twelve in March. And the bear head represents an assault to Dylan's aesthetic sensibilities, does it?"

Here I should point out that the neutral observers present at the scene—to whom we are indebted for this entire account—are unanimous in saying that the force of Margaret May's interrogation lay less with the age of the young Nosler than with his unsavoury public habits. These included pulling all the legs off captured daddy longlegs and displaying on his palm to passersby the tiny stumps of the mutilated spiders; also sticking small spears of grass up the rear ends of horseflies so that the only direction they can fly is endlessly upwards. Until this very moment, as Margaret May's insinuation hung like a prairie thunderhead above the petitioners, nobody had ever discerned in young Nosler anything even remotely approximating an aesthetic sensibility, much less any capability of its ever being assaulted.

Several other unfortunate signatures on the petition were deconstructed to equally devastating effect. Julia and Peewee squirmed. Eventually, with Margaret May still beaming benignly, they coughed discreetly, gathered up their petition papers, thanked Margaret May for her time, and, followed by their followers, beat an unequivocally humiliating retreat.

The bear head and accompanying photograph remained in place through another decade without further incident. I suspect that Margaret May was disappointed by the bear head's inability to provoke subsequent controversy. She plainly kept the wretched thing, not because she liked it—nor because, as she claimed, with laughably transparent piety, that it was an important piece of island history—but as a kind of provocation. She liked the dance of dialectic. She had a streak of Margaret Thatcher in her, though none of that lady's cruel egotism.

But now here she is, reduced almost to blubbering, and the bear head vanished.

"What happened?" I ask.

"Theft!" she wails like Medea. "Brazen thievery right here in my store!"

"Who would possibly steal your bear head, and why?"

"Good questions," Margaret May replies, regaining a measure of her customary composure. "Good questions demanding good answers!" She pauses and glances at the ceiling, as though celestial voices might supply an answer any minute.

"There's strange happenings afoot on this little island nowadays." Margaret May sounds like the prophetess at Cumae. "Strange happenings indeed."

"I guess I'll have a coffee," I say, for want of something more profound. I mean, what do you say to a distraught storekeeper who's had her stuffed bear head stolen?

The only person at the coffee counter is Zyrk, a guy in his early twenties, who always dresses entirely in black leather. His head's shaved bare, and his left ear has enough studs in it to decorate a saddle. He's staring into his coffee cup as though it were a black hole in deepest space, while making a low droning noise that might have been a protracted moan or a quiet, mesmeric raga.

"Hi, Zyrk," I hail him.

Zyrk responds with a single raised finger and a subtle tremolo within his chant. There are several extant explanations as to who and what Zyrk is. One version has it that he's deep into astral travel, having journeyed to India and there learned from a renowned swami an ancient technique for projecting one's consciousness out among the galaxies. A second explanation holds that Zyrk has consumed far too much LSD for his own good and is now struggling along on badly scrambled software. For the moment at least, Zyrk isn't telling.

Margaret May pours me a coffee, glances at the astral traveller, throws her plucked and pencilled eyebrows into impossibly gothic arches, and withdraws to her stool behind the cash register.

I sip my coffee and wonder who in God's name would steal the bear's head. Something tells me that its disappearance is linked to the Kumquat business. Almost certainly Elvira will know what's going on, and Caitlin, but do I really want to find out? I'm fascinated and apprehensive at the same time—the whole thing smells rather like what the Brothers of Blessed Columkille the Lesser called "a near occasion of sin" that was best avoided.

Just then the store door clatters open and Waddy Watts strides into the store and across to the coffee counter.

"Hi, Waddy," I greet him, "what's up?"

"Been watchin' the beavers?" Waddy glowers at me.

"No, should I?"

"Just been up to the lake. Goin' like bastards they are, workin' double shift at gettin' in food and buildin' up the lodges. Sure sign she'll freeze early, freeze hard, and freeze often. No way she won't."

"But what about the wasps?" I ask.

"What about 'em?" Oops, wrong question. Waddy's as snarly as a scorpion this morning. At his worst, he has the same scary anger as my dad. Instinctively, I hasten to placate him.

"Did you hear about the bear head?" I ask him discreetly, almost whispering. Margaret May has ears like a bat.

Waddy looks at me like I've just passed wind or something. He takes a swallow of coffee, and you can see it flowing down his scrawny throat, like a goose being force-fed. He stares for a moment at the rows of ceramic cups, white with a green stripe just below the lip, on the counter across from us.

I'm aware of Zyrk's humming beating softly like a tabla against the back of my brain. Waddy still doesn't answer.

"What did you think of Mistral Wind?" I try again, and instantly a change drifts across the old guy's leathery face. "Wasn't she somethin'?" His pale blue eyes flicker with mischief. "If I'da been half my age, boy-oboy, I dunno if they'da been able to hold me down seein' a woman like that. Wow! Just the rump on that big beauty, like a mare waitin' for the stud. Boyoboy." The old lecher's scrawny neck quivers like a rooster's.

"Did you pick up anything from her about permaculture?" I ask him. I couldn't resist.

Waddy's eyes glint with mischief again. "Say, you think that young beauty with her permy culture can grow a bigger pumpkin than me?"

He's setting too obvious a snare. I step tactfully over it. "Nobody can grow bigger pumpkins than you, Waddy," I say. "We all know that."

And it's true. Every year at the fall fair, Waddy takes the blue ribbon for biggest pumpkin. He even built a special wheelbarrow for bringing his prize pumpkins in, because one year he and old Ernie Moffatt and a couple of young guys who were helping them dropped Waddy's entry and it split all to pieces right there in the field, and that was the only year in living memory that Waddy didn't get the blue ribbon, though he did set some kind of record for blue-streak screaming.

One other time he almost got beaten out by one of the Pitfield boys, Dougie it was, whose squash didn't measure quite as much in diameter as Waddy's, but weighed sixteen pounds more. I think it was Geoffrey Munz was on the judging committee that year, and as he bent down to pin the blue ribbon onto the Pitfield pumpkin, he noticed some strange markings on its underside. Turns out Dougie had removed a lit-tle plug, bunged in a bunch of pig iron for weight, then carefully replaced the plug, sealed with contact cement, so that you really had to look close to even see the cut marks.

Of course, Dougie was disqualified and Waddy won as usual, though this chicanery caused quite a ruckus at the time. After the initial shock had worn off, the episode gave rise to a local aphorism used whenever somebody's putting on weight that can't be accounted for. "I got some pig iron in my pumpkin," the failing weight-watcher would say, and there'd be laughs all round.

I notice that Zyrk's mantra has dropped an octave. Margaret May's busy with a cluster of customers at her cash register.

"Tell me this, Waddy," I take the chance of getting the old codger annoyed again. "How come you of all people made that motion the other night? I mean, it's not exactly what folks expected."

Waddy scrunches his face up and squints his eyes, as though he's standing in a sandstorm. Then he scratches the grey stubble on his chin. A road map of blue veins is etched across the back of his hand. "Well sir," he says at last, "I thought I'd seen it all up to then, but that was about the goddamnedest thing ever happened to me." He pauses again.

"Go on," I prod him.

He looks uncomfortable. "I never thought about gardens before, not the way that gal talked about 'em. One minute she has us sneakin' around in the Garden of Eden, hiding from old Jehovah because we've eaten the forbidden fruit and know we're gonna catch hell. She could tell it just like it was actually happenin'. Next minute she has us up in some mountains in Peru or someplace, in the gardens of the gods. I tell you that gal was a magician with words. Just listenin' to her voice was like gorgeous music, like being at the opera or somethin', and she swept me clear away. It was the damnedest thing."

Waddy pauses again, then shakes himself the way a cat does, stretching in front of a fire. He sips his coffee. Zyrk's out in orbit somewhere among the Pleiades.

"And?" I say to Waddy.

My curiosity's piqued. I feel a compelling need to understand what would make an old bull-of-the-woods like him throw in with the treehuggers. It didn't compute. We sit there in silence, with only Zyrk's low droning.

Margaret May drifts over with her coffee pot, this time a single but impeccably penciled eyebrow arched inquisitively. She refills us both.

"You fellas having a good time?" she asks in her best Mae West manner, apparently recovered somewhat from her tremendous grief. Zyrk nods half a dozen times, little ripples skipping across his mantra, and she refills him too.

Waddy stirs a small Matterhorn of sugar into his coffee, musing. I've seldom seen him quite so unforthcoming.

"Waddy?" I probe.

He turns to me, and his watery blue eyes are washed over and murky, the sea against a mackerel sky. I've never seen him shy before.

"I had a vision," he says, and turns away.

I just about fall off my stool. A vision's the last thing I'd ever have believed Waddy would experience. He just isn't the visionary type.

"A vision? Tell me about it."

"I saw my old man," Waddy says, "clear as day. Clear as I'm seein' you. While that young beauty was talkin' about trees and Druids and whatnot, all of a sudden, there was the old man. I don't mean I imagined him, or remembered him—he was there, standing close beside her, real as you or me.

"I shook myself," he continues, "thought I must have been dreamin'. I pinched the back of my hand, hard, but nope! there he was—wearin' his cork boots and that damned old checkered flannel shirt—lookin' right at me, tough as bloody hobnails too. Didn't say a word, his lips never moved, but somehow I heard him clear as a steam whistle."

"What did you hear?"

"About what happened to him," Waddy says, looking at me straight. "Him and all the other little operators up and down the coast. How the government brought in quotas to squeeze out the little guys and give it all to the big companies. And I knew it was right. The whole coast was alive with workin' families back in his day, honest workin' people. There was little float camps all up and down the coast, independents y'know. Guys who knew trees and tides and how to log. No bloody money managers in New York tellin' us how to do it.

"Course, I was just a young buck back in them days, and by Jesus we could whoop 'er up on a Saturday night. It'd come over the radio that there was a party brewin' over at somebody's float camp, and everybody'd pile into boats and head over. Somebody'd have a fiddle and somebody else an accordion, and you never seen such dancin' as that." Waddy smiles, musing, half a century back.

"And then they shut 'em all down," he slaps the counter in disgust, "pushed 'em outta the way, like they was beggars on the street. Gave it all to the big operators. Didn't bother me, I was on the locies by then, but they broke the little guys like the old man, broke 'em hard. They never could make a law for the little guys. That's what the old man was sayin' to me somehow, and all the while that Mistral woman was talkin'. And the old man said to me even though his lips never moved, 'Remember what happened to your mother after that, how she just faded away when we lost the camp, couldn't adjust to life on the outside. Remember her, Waddy.' And somethin' snapped in me just then, snapped like a dry stick you step on in the woods.

"So when that gal says why don't we go over there to Kumquat and kick some company butt, I says, Damn right! Who do these money-grubbin' sons-a-bitches think they're pushin' around, anyway? That's when I made the motion. Speakin' a which," Waddy glowers at me again, "where the hell were you when the votes were counted?"

"Oh," I say, trying to sound breezy, hoping, once more, to have avoided this, "I dunno what happened. I couldn't quite figure out where I stood. So I thought I'd better abstain."

" 'Bout time to figure you're standin' on your own two feet, ain't it?" Waddy seems disgusted with me. "Time to grow some balls, eh? Or you figure it's okay leavin' the shit work to women and kids and old bastards like me with one foot in the grave. Eh?"

At that moment, Zyrk stops humming, and the store echoes with textured silence, the way a cave does.

6

The encounter with Waddy has left a sour taste in my mouth. I'm beginning to feel a hideous primal guilt oozing over me—not guilt about Kumquat or clearcutting and all that, but about letting down my friends, being a disappointment to them.

On my way out of the store, I scan the newspapers stacked near Margaret May's counter. The front pages are teeming with Kumquat stories. Over six hundred people have now been arrested, and blockades are happening on a daily basis. It looks like tempers are running really hot, with accusations of vandalism and sabotage and heated confrontations between protesters and loggers.

Out on the steps of the store, I bump into Davey Rushing.

"You part of this Kumquat thing?" Davey asks me. There's obviously all sorts of talk around the island about who is and isn't going on the garden club expedition. Some of the people who'd gotten swept up in Mistral's rhetoric and voted in favour of the garden club motion have in the interim found they've other more pressing matters on their minds.

I tell Davey I'm not at all sure I am, and ask him where he stands himself.

"It's a crock," Davey snorts contemptuously. "I ain't into civil disobedience any more. Hell, I burned myself out in the Berkeley Free Speech movement twenty-five years ago. I'm still trying to mellow out."

"Burned the rest of us out talking about it anyway," Caitlin quips whenever Davey trots out his standard excuse for inertia. To hear Davey tell it, he just about singlehandedly organized Students for a Democratic Society. Angela Davis had badly wanted to be his lover, Abbie

Hoffman his protégé. "If you weren't in the streets of Chicago during the Democratic convention," Davey'll say, "you weren't anywhere, man."

But somewhere between Chicago and here, the revolution and Davey went their separate ways.

"Alls I know is the timber barons ain't no welterweights," Davey tells me now with a street-smart spit. "These kids think it's some kind of lark, like they're gonna stick it up the company's ass and nobody's gonna care. Bullshit. You challenge those bastards and they'll come down on you like granite blocks. Don't forget: Those guys invented the game. The rules are the rules they like. I know. I been there."

Davey actually raises his fist in a ludicrously pale version of the Black Power salute. For a moment I'm not sure whether or not this is self-parody. But, no. "Take my advice here, pal," Davey stays loyal to his delusions, "pass on the blockade bullshit. And, whatever else you do, don't get busted out there; it ain't worth the price."

Driving home, I dismiss Davey's posturing, but I can't help thinking about what Waddy said. Am I really being a coward, or just my habitual prudent self? Are Waddy and Caitlin and Elvira being brave or merely naive? More than anything I want to distance myself from Davey Rushing's brand of self-indulgence. I can't tolerate Elvira and Caitlin thinking of me the way I think of Davey. Treading a path already well greased with Catholic guilt, I feel myself slip a bit further down a dangerous slope.

I stop to check my mailbox on the way back in. There's the normal pile of junk mail. Flyers urging me to dash off and buy cheap rubbish I don't want or need. The telephone bill. Something from the credit union. And a plain, unmarked envelope that looks like more junk mail.

Back in my kitchen, I set the bill and bank statement aside, and throw the flyers into the recycling basket. The unmarked envelope catches my eye and I fish it out again. I slit it open with a butter knife and inside find a single sheet of paper with a cryptic message composed, like an extortionist's note, of words and letters clipped from magazine headlines. The note reads:

"If you want to find the bear head, talk to the Overstalls." It's unsigned, indicating that it's the work of a schemer with above-average intelligence.

I put the note down and stare through the kitchen window out into my garden. These machinations are getting to be a bit much, even by

Upshot standards. This seems a case less of thickening plot than of thickheaded plotters. Do I care where the wretched bear head is? No. Do I harbour any ambitions of becoming a Greenpeace eco-warrior? No. I want only to go quietly and calmly about my business. I've got a nice little editing assignment on my desk, in which I am certain to find contentment through untangling the mangled syntax of a young writer whose flair and ambition far outstrip his talent. Life is sufficiently complicated as we find it, without having to charge off looking for imaginary windmills to tilt at. How did Blessed Columkille the Lesser put it— "Seek not those things that excite the blood; seek rather to remain in sanctified tranquillity, for therein is found the peace that surpasses all attainment."

I crumple the ridiculous note into a ball and give it a hook shot back into the basket. Then I walk around aimlessly for a bit and eventually fish it out again. I've never received an anonymous letter before, and I do feel an undeniable titillation of excitement about getting one. Who could have sent it? Why send it to me?

After another distracted hour or so, I decide to satisfy my curiosity. I call the Overstalls. Julia answers. When I tell her about the note, she becomes very secretive indeed. She invites me over to join her and Peewee for a late afternoon Jacuzzi. "Not a word to a soul before then," Julia cautions me.

I drive over to Peewee and Julia's place not knowing what to expect. They live on an old farm next to Elvira's on the east side. To nobody's great surprise, Julia and Peewee turned out to be dismal failures as farmers.

"Them two couldn't grow warts on a toad," Waddy had said, early on. Unfortunately, he was right, at least as far as farming went. Their kiwi vines grew monstrously, flowered profusely, but perversely declined to ever set fruit. Their ginseng roots flat out refused to grow at all.

"I warned them at the outset," Fibber Miller confided in a fantastic burst of historical revisionism. "I told them it was iffy trying ginseng in that particular micro-climate; but of course, they were from Toronto and what would a broken-down hick realtor like me know about anything?" Most of Fibber's questions are best left unanswered.

Happily, Peewee and Julia more than compensated for their agricultural shortfalls by launching new careers as co-authors of a string of steamy bodice-rippers with titles like *Lashed by Lace* and *Taken by Storm*. These are published in paperback, in astonishing numbers and without apparent shame, by one of the nation's wealthiest publishing houses.

At first, no one on-island had any reason to suspect that Julia and Peewee were the authors of these masterpieces. They penned them anonymously using the nom de plume Monique Manlotte. As former professors with recognized expertise in the works of Chaucer and Virginia Woolf respectively, the Overstalls could hardly be faulted for circumspection concerning their more recent literary output.

But keeping a secret on Upshot is no facile matter. The cat named Monique got out of the bag one desultory afternoon when Peewee took the galleys of their latest work, tentatively titled *Love Cry Across the Moors*, down to the Preening Peacock. The galleys needed proofing right away, but Julia's parents were visiting from Miami Beach, so Peewee excused himself on the grounds of having a meeting to attend and headed down to the café where he thought he could give the galleys a final going-over in a secluded corner.

Carelessly, he left the manuscript lying open on his table when he went off to the bathroom. Philip, one of the proprietors, and a man blessed with an impeccable nose for the newsworthy, took the opportunity to wipe an adjacent tabletop. Casually glancing over, he was astonished to read the following:

Tiffany wandered in a dreamlike state across the moor. Flowering heathers spread a feathery carpet of colour in soft and subtly undulating curves. Her mind flitted through the memories of these last tempestuous months like a hungry bee among the flowers of gorse.

All of a sudden, she sensed she was not alone. Looking up, like a startled fawn, she saw him: Bradley, standing on a hummock, his muscular legs athwart, his dark locks tossed by the soft moorland breeze.

Her heart leapt, a songbird caught amid the twigs of a hawthorn bush. She felt her breast swell and press against its cambric bodice. As though in a dream, she walked slowly towards him.

Bradley stood unmoving, magnificent against the ochre sky.

And then, at last, they were in one another's arms. Their mouths fused in a scorching, timeless kiss, and all else fell away from her. She was entirely consumed.

With stunning sangfroid, Philip photocopied the page and replaced it before Peewee returned. Within days, the whole island was in on the secret identity of Monique Manlotte. Of course, the news caused an absolute sensation. Peewee and Julia actually bore up remarkably well beneath the weight of this sudden fame, tinted as it was with a distinctly lowbrow blush.

"They're undeniably dreadful," Julia admitted candidly, "but also disgustingly lucrative."

In a grassroots democracy like Upshot, one revelation has a way of triggering others, and it was amazing how many people publicly came forward to admit that they were closet readers of the works of Monique Manlotte. Some of our leading intellects, it soon became apparent, spend the bulk of their winter evenings cozied up around the woodstove amid the swelling breasts of Monique's beleaguered heroines.

In a wonderfully ironic twist, it came to light that Margaret May was particularly fond of these gothic confections. Ever since the bear head battle, she had maintained an attitude of hearty noblesse oblige towards Julia and Peewee. But with the revelation that they in fact were the authors of her favourite literature, her demeanour towards them underwent a noticeable shift, a certain awe now tempering her eminence.

The considerable royalties accruing to Monique Manlotte accounted for Julia and Peewee's fabulous Jacuzzi into which the three of us descend soon after my arrival. Sunk in an extensive red cedar deck, the Jacuzzi overlooks the erstwhile ginseng fields. We sip Perrier. An exquisite alpine garden covers the bank behind the deck. A tiny stream splashes and cascades through a miniaturized landscape of dwarf evergreen shrubs and delicate alpine flowers. Wind chimes tinkle against the sounds of falling water.

Hopeless as fruit and root farmers, Peewee and Julia had quickly recognized that their error was simply one of scale. Tiny people themselves, they were wise enough to shrink their horticultural horizons down to the miniature world of alpines, in which they'd found themselves surprisingly adept and altogether content.

The pale and skinny pair of them, Peewee and Julia look the perfect part of crackpot alpine gardeners, but you'd wonder how they ever come up with the romantic imagery with which Monique Manlotte beguiles her loyal readership. Peewee's barely over five feet tall. He wears tortoise-shell bifocals and his hair is thinning rapidly. He's such a runty, jumpy little chap you'd think there's rodent blood in his ancestry.

Julia's a match—also small, plain as plantain, with mousy grey hair cropped short. Her face is sharply pointed, its force pressed forward in a pointed nose and chiselled teeth.

I like to imagine the two of them creating their fantastic fictional characters—muscular studs with organs stout as billy clubs, pouting maidens with heaving bosoms far beyond the wildest projections of the breast-enhancement industry.

"Fantasy's simple," Peewee will tell you, his nose twitching like a hamster's. "It's reality that's difficult."

We sip our Perrier.

"Now, what about this weird note?" I ask them—I've brought it along to show them.

Peewee and Julia giggle like kids, they both start speaking at once, tripping over one another, then both stop, laughing. "You go ahead," Julia says.

"Well," he begins, "we're speaking here under condition of absolute confidentiality. Is that agreed?"

I agree.

"Then, yes," Peewee says, "we confess; it was we who stole the bear head."

"I think borrowed would be more accurate, don't you, dear?" Julia puts in.

"Yes, of course, point well taken," Peewee quickly amends, "who borrowed the bear head."

"But why would you possibly want to do a thing like that?" I ask.

"It was all Lister's idea," Peewee replies.

"Lister's?" I say, incredulous.

"Yes," Julia jumps in. "Lister had a thing about the bear head from way back when. After we'd faxed him we were going to the blockade, he faxed us back saying: Bravo! Take the bear. Be bold. Lister."

"So you did."

"Oh, yes, we did indeed," Julia sips her Perrier. "We chose early in the afternoon, partly because you know how Margaret May gets a bit dozy after lunch. We decided to strike while she was at her most vulnerable." Julia runs her fingers through her hair. "The kids would all be back in school, and most of the coffeeklatchers would have gone home for their afternoon naps." The indolence of the coffeeklatchers is a choice topic in certain conversations. "I tell you," Julia's fairly sparkling with conspiratorial glee, "we were as cunning as vipers."

"Here was the plan," Peewee can't stay out of it any longer. I keep seeing his balding head floating over the foaming Jacuzzi waters like a buoy bobbing on the ocean. "We took along a draft of our latest Monique Manlotte. It is tentatively titled *Love in the Mists*."

"Aha!" I say, "I perceive the devious device unfolding already."

"Right!" Julia says, "the mighty Margaret May's Achilles heel exposed. So off we went to the store. Sure enough, Margaret May's sitting on her stool behind the counter, nodding over her newspaper. There was no one else about. Peewee made a grand show of having the manuscript under his arm, but not too obvious—Margaret May's nobody's fool."

"No kidding," I interject.

"But we coaxed her into our little trap," Julia says. "We were ever so cunning, weren't we, Peewee?"

"Oh, yes," Peewee chortles, "we planned it that Julia would seduce our sentimental shopkeeper with *Love in the Mists* while I heisted the head."

I'm absolutely amazed at what they're telling me, that these two little English professors would be mixed up in this kind of hijinks.

"Everything went according to plan at the outset," Julia continues. "Margaret May was intrigued by the manuscript. We downplayed it, of course, pretended we were looking for gumboots or something, but all the while dangling the manuscript in front of her.

" 'Your latest?' she asked us at last. Poor thing, she couldn't help herself." Julia's plainly savouring her moment of revenge. I never quite realized how galling it must have been for her to have been bested by a shopkeeper in their previous encounter.

" 'Oh, yes,' we said, nonchalant as anything, 'just finished it. *Love in the Mists*. It may be the best we've ever done.' " Julia acts out the conversation with elaborate gestures and intonations, as though she's been watching too many Meryl Streep films.

Peewee jumps in. "Margaret May told us she was still partial to *Love Cry Across the Moors*. I could feel her great bulk already stumbling into our little trap."

" 'Oh, yes,' I said to Margaret May," Julia gives herself a theatrical voice, " 'but we think this is far more richly textured, don't we, Peewee?' Peewee was better than Olivier. Such consummate indifference."

Peewee's head bobs in the Jacuzzi like a seabird in the surf.

"Eventually," Julia continues, "ever so reluctantly, I offered to read Margaret May a brief passage, so she'd see what I meant about it being the best work we'd done. But I cautioned her! Not a word of it was to get out, the publishing business being what it is, and the manuscript not even at the printers yet. Oh, we had her in our nets by then."

"I can hardly believe what you're telling me. Do you still have this conspiratorial text?" I ask. "I'd love to hear the passage too."

"Seriously?" Julia asks. "Well, yes, we still have the manuscript somewhere, don't we Peewee?"

"I think it's on my desk," Peewee says. "I'll go fetch it." He climbs out of the Jacuzzi, his teal trunks clinging. He looks like the skinny guy in the old Charles Atlas ads who'd have sand kicked in his face by bullies.

"I should be utterly embarrassed doing this." Julia puts down her glass, dries her hands on a towel, and takes the manuscript from Peewee. "Thanks, dear. But somehow I'm not."

She leafs through the pages quickly and finds the section. "So this is what I read to Margaret May," she says, and begins reading:

Heather stood alone upon the headlands and wept. The sea mists drifted in veils of grey, and moisture condensed in microscopic droplets against her flesh and upon her long, flowing dress. A thin wind blew the mists this way and that. The very earth seemed to be weeping with a forlorn and melancholy sadness.

Hot and salty tears ran down Heather's cheeks. She could taste their salt commingled with the sea mist. She let them run. She had had enough of holding back. Her disappointments, her heartaches, her hungering for love had at last become insupportable. She could bear them no more, and so she wept.

As the surf thundered against the rocky headlands, she gave way completely, letting the tears flow freely and all the memories that caused them. Sobbing openly, she unleashed the accumulated sorrows and hurts of her twenty years. They washed over her like waves, submerging her soul completely.

How long she stood there, gazing out to sea, unseeing, she could not say. Had mere minutes passed, or many hours? She was at a loss. Her grief had sent time rattling away, like tide-tossed pebbles on the strand.

At last she dried her eyes. She was spent. Suddenly, she felt chilled by the mizzle and soaked to her soul. She turned on the rocks to leave, and there—far, far down the beach, where the mists lifted off for an instant—she saw a solitary figure walking on the sand. Walking, she thought, towards her.

Could it be . . . ? She dared not even frame the question. Then the mists closed in again and the world was a pitiless grey. She stood there, cold and miserable, yet trembling with a splendid agitation. Was that lone figure on the beach Lance? And was he even now striding towards her, unseen, amid the drifting mists?

Julia lays the manuscript down on her towel, blinks like an owl, and giggles. Peewee giggles too.

"Beautifully read, I thought," Peewee says.

"Isn't it too delicious?" Julia chortles like Lady Macbeth. "Reading that overheated prose to Margaret May and watching her drift farther and farther away into a romantic dreamscape, while Peewee was lifting the bear's head."

"Easier said than done getting the damn thing down," Peewee grouses. "We'd miscalculated how high up it was." Up on his tippy-toes in full spinal stretch, Peewee could hardly have reached the bear head hanging way up over the doorway. Some cunning planning.

"So how'd you manage it?"

"I'd just about given it up as impossible," Peewee says. "Julia was over by the counter deep-breathing in the sea mist, and Margaret May had drifted away nicely, but I couldn't reach the confounded head. Just then, by a stroke of luck, who comes along but Zyrk. I signal him through the window to not make a sound. He slips in through the doorway. I held the door chimes so they wouldn't ring. Then Zyrk boosted me up on his shoulders and I got the head unhooked licketyclick and got it down."

"By this point I had the strapping Lance and tear-stained Heather locked in a passionate embrace," Julia adds, "and I was praying to God that those two would get the head the hell out of there before the chapter came to its ringing close and Margaret May opened her eyes."

"Zyrk slipped out the door with the head while I held the chimes again," Peewee says, "just as Julia finished up with our star-crossed lovers. I tell you, Margaret May was like warm putty in our hands. It was priceless. Then we calmly bid her adieu and left the store without her being any the wiser."

"But Margaret May's really upset, and now I'm getting weirdo notes in the mail."

"Well, that's a bit of a mystery, all right," Julia's suddenly more serious, "but the bigger problem is we don't know what's become of the bloody bear's head."

"What?" I exclaim.

"The damn thing's disappeared," Peewee explains. "By the time we got out of the store, Zyrk had vanished. So had the bear head. We searched all over the place, but we couldn't find him anywhere."

"We even went down to Zyrk's cabin." Julia makes a face. "What a peculiar little place he's got. There was no sign of him about, but the door was ajar, and we did stick our noses in for a moment, didn't we, Peewee?"

"Most remarkable," Peewee says. "He has a tremendous collection of books on herbs and mushrooms and wild plants. The rest of the place looks like a hermitage, no creature comforts at all."

"I just saw him in the store a while ago," I say.

"Really? So he's still around. Interesting. Of course, we can't go in the store," Julia shrugs her skinny shoulder blades. "Margaret May would eat us alive."

"So she suspects it was you," I say. "What are you going to do?"

"Oh, we'll carry on over to Kumquat day after tomorrow, same as we planned," Peewee says breezily. "Are you coming along?"

"I mean what are you going to do about the bear head."

"Oh, well, if the wretched thing doesn't show up, I suppose we'll have to buy another one somewhere. Margaret May won't know the difference." The two of them seem entirely oblivious of the firestorm of indignation their little lark might ignite. "Are you driving, or do you want a ride with us?"

"Ride?" I say, playing dumb.

"To Kumquat," Julia says. "Surely you're going. I mean, how could one not?"

7

How could one not? Julia's question trails after me on my way home like a lost mongrel dog. How could one not? Worse, how could one be outflanked in conviction by the likes of Peewee and Julia and retain self-respect? It's beginning to seem simpler to me, less complicated and problematic, to just go along on this absurd junket and the devil take the hindmost. I mean, what's the big deal anyway about going over to Kumquat and pretending to be a rainbow warrior for an afternoon?

Still, I can't shake off a sense of foreboding, a darker form of the strange sensation I experienced on the wharf, waiting with Caitlin for Mistral Wind to arrive. I have a presentiment of menace, an unmistakable forewarning that if I get involved in any of this business—Mistral, Kumquat, Caitlin—I'm in for no lark. I can sniff tragedy in the wind, palpable as woodsmoke.

I know I can't avoid having a clearing with Caitlin. I can't just leave whatever it is between us hanging there like a rotting carcass. Something compels me to get things straight with her.

"Come over for tea," she says on the phone, "and we'll talk."

I force myself not to be anxious about it. I set off down the footpath that runs through the gully between our two places. I dawdle a bit under the huge trees, soothed by just being among them. Sword ferns grow massed together here, their fronds arching as high as my shoulders. I brush the fronds in passing and clouds of powdery rust-red spores spew into the air. In the old days, not knowing about spores, but aware there was magic in the world, people believed that ferns produced seeds on only one night of the year, Midsummer Eve. The seeds were highly prized because they had the magic property of making their bearer invisible. Oberon, king of the fairies, derived his invisibility from them, and would drive off would-be seed gatherers in defence of his secret. I read all this in the paper just the other day, and remind myself to tell Caitlin about it. A good ice-breaker anyway.

I emerge from the woods into the clearing and catch sight of Jenny, Caitlin's daughter. She stands in the middle of the lawn, holding out some lettuce leaves, trying to entice a pair of small fawns to eat them from her hand. The fawns still bear fading traces of their spots, though their coats are already thickening for winter.

"Here, little deer," coos Jenny, dangling the leaves. The fawns are mesmerized by this peculiar small person. Their ears are up, twitching, their tiny black noses and whiskers taste the air constantly for clues, their slender legs vibrate with the instinct to flee. On the far side of the clearing their mother's cropping fresh lawn grass in the shade. "Here little deer," sings Jenny in a crooning voice.

I work my way quietly around behind the vegetable garden, so as not to spook the fawns, and enter the house through the open back door. Caitlin's standing, arms folded, by the big picture window in her kitchen. I can see Jenny and the fawns through the window beyond Caitlin. Framed by the window, with a windowbox of alternating red and white pelargoniums, Caitlin looks splendid. She's wearing jeans and a plain white cotton shirt, open at the neck, sleeves rolled up to her elbows. She's barefoot, as usual in summer, and her mane of frizzy red hair flows wildly in all directions.

The big country kitchen's a bit of a mess. There's an enormous stack of unwashed dishes in the sink, a tea towel on the floor. Jenny's old calico cat, Bozo, is fast asleep in a rocking chair.

"It's a charming scene out there, isn't it?" I say.

"Ah!" Caitlin exclaims, turning, "the prodigal brother returns! How are you, J.J.? How was your trip?"

"I haven't been anywhere," I say, alert to danger.

"Oh, I thought you'd disappeared," Caitlin says, coming up to me. And as she draws close I can feel a force field coming off her, pulling at me like a magnet pulling a paper clip.

I brace myself for a tug-o-war, one that I know I can't win. The best I can hope for is a draw.

"So is Mistral gone?" I ask nonchalantly, looking away from her, back out the window. I can't see Jenny and the fawns have vanished.

"Long gone," Caitlin says, releasing me from her hold, once again my carefree lovely neighbour in her kitchen. She sets a kettle on the propane stove and fetches a ceramic teapot from a cupboard.

"She's quite a character," I say neutrally, sitting down at the big kitchen table. There's a sprawl of Jenny's drawings and crayons, Caitlin's gardening magazines and sketches of jewellery designs scattered across the table.

"That's putting it mildly," Caitlin says, coming over to the table too, sitting down across from me, her bare forearms on the table fine with golden hairs, "but then you like putting things mildly, don't you, J.J.?"

"I looked up Kumquats," I say idiotically, ignoring the barb, "after her talk."

"Really?" Caitlin replies, bright with irony. "How fascinating."

"Yes," I'll just play this straight, "they're quite fascinating fruits really." Not as fascinating as you, my girl, but I won't play it that straight. "The name's from the Chinese, *chin chu*. It means 'golden orange.' They've been cultivated in China for over a thousand years." Am I sounding pretentious? I think so. I skip over my other two fascinating Kumquat facts and clank to a halt. I should have used Oberon and the ferns instead.

Caitlin stands up, smiling. The kettle's boiling and she goes to make tea. As she walks across the kitchen away from me, I can't help but notice the lithe beauty of her body. Not for the first time, of course, but there's something new in how she seems to me now, something urgently appealing. Something, it occurs to me in a flash as Caitlin pours the boiling water, ignited by that Mistral Wind. How I felt my concupiscence stirred the night of her talk. Roused in a way that Caitlin's salacious tales never rouse me.

She comes back with the teapot and two matching ceramic mugs and puts them on the table. Then she sticks out her hip, with her hand on it, elbow bent out, mimicking a slatternly waitress.

"Will that be all, sir? Or would you like a plate of Kumquats?" She laughs and sits down. "So you thought Mistral was quite a character, did you? What else?"

"Well," carefully here, one careful step at a time, "it was pretty amazing what she did with that group. She really dazzled people. I mean, Waddy Watts proposing we all go off and get arrested at an anti-logging blockade? It boggles the mind!"

"But she didn't dazzle you?"

"Well, I wouldn't say that exactly."

"What would you say exactly?" I sense Caitlin tracking me, circling behind in the woods, unseen.

"I guess I felt there was a little bit of the huckster about her."

"A huckster? She seemed insincere to you?"

"No, she didn't seem insincere precisely . . ."

"We all know you don't care for insincerity, J.J."

Does she suspect that I distrust her as insincere? "No, it was more she seemed, oh, I don't know, swept up in New Age pop-mystical claptrap, I guess. I'm sure she believes it herself."

"But you don't?" Caitlin reaches for the teapot and pours two steaming mugs. She places one before me.

"Thanks," I say, venturing no further, apprehensive that maybe I've offended her.

"Didn't she excite you?"

"Excite me? How do you mean?"

"Erotically. Sexually. Sensually. Didn't you find her absolutely luscious and provocative?"

"Well, provocative, yes, sure, she was that all right." I gulp hot tea and it scalds me going down.

"Didn't you want her in the worst way?"

"Not that way, no."

"Poor J.J.," Caitlin makes a face over her raised mug, "such a hopeless liar."

She's right, of course, I am a hopeless liar. I envy people who can lie convincingly. I was in desperate need of facile lying as a child, with my menacing father scrutinizing me from his Cyclops eye, my mother expecting the best of me, always. Then black-robed nuns and priests hanging around all the time, watching, like a murder of ravens. How I could have used a facility at fibbing and dodging and fudging things around to blur the vision of the watchers. But no. The few fibs I ever attempted must have leaked guilt and shame like a rusty bucket leaks water, for they never fooled anyone. "You'll only make matters worse by lying, lad," my father would say ominously.

"A poor liar, perhaps, but no thief," I say to Caitlin, and tell her about my anonymous note.

"How extraordinary," Caitlin says, absorbed by the story. "Any suspects?"

"I thought you might have a notion."

"Not my department." The look she gives me is brilliant with innocence. We sip our tea. A draw so far.

"So you're not going along with us to Kumquat?" Caitlin places the question lightly, as though we're discussing lunch. She cradles her mug in both hands, her long thin fingers caressing the cup's surface the way the potter's fingers might have touched it when it was still spinning clay, her gaze wandering off to the gardens outside.

"I think it'll be quite heroic really," I say blithely, "to resist all the peer pressure and not go."

"Oh, yes," she replies archly, her gaze coming back and settling on me like a great bird of prey, the faintest hint of a sneer around her lips, "that would be heroic all right. A true warrior chieftain of superior courage and strength. I'm impressed."

There it is again, her jeering at me. It's not just what she says, but how she says it sometimes, with a tone of mocking contempt. I hate it. This is part of what lies between us, her ridicule. I can't trust her not to make a joke of me. So I'm never sure that I can drop the clever game we play together and just be myself with her, my real self, without her making a mockery of that too.

On some level, she holds me in contempt, I know she does, and it's one thing I can't stand. My father did it to me constantly, from when I was just a little kid. He was always watching and judging and finding fault. Nothing I did was good enough. He told me so often what a damn fool I was, I still carry an abiding sense of it about with me. Caitlin's one of the people who can root it out instinctively, like a pig snuffling truffles. When I announced to my parents my decision to join the Brothers of Blessed Columkille the Lesser, my dad called me "the biggest goddamn fool on the face of the planet." Somewhere I suspected he was right. Maybe he was. Even now, years later, whenever I make a mistake, even something simple like nicking myself with a knife or dropping a wineglass, my instinctive reaction is to curse myself for a bloody fool. When she chooses to, Caitlin makes me feel stupid.

"All right, you want the unvarnished truth?" Her low blows have finally got my dander up. "I think these blockades are naive and counter-productive. It's a bunch of middle-class white kids pretending they're Indians and eco-warriors, when all they are is too young to know that ten years from now they'll be sitting in an office tower or selling shoes in a mall, hustling for a paycheque so they can make their rent or mortgage payments just like everyone else. I don't buy the Martin Luther King quotes any more, and the white buffalo pipe dreams and all the rest of it. It's naive romanticism of the most self-indulgent sort, and I'm amazed that someone as smart as you is falling for it. But it's a free country, and if you and the rest of them want to go play at being Gandhi, be my guest. I'm not interested, okay?"

This is tougher than I've ever been with Caitlin, perhaps too tough. Her eyes are shining, looking at me. Is she going to cry? "I'm sorry," I say. "I didn't mean to shout. It's just that . . ."

"Stop!" Caitlin cries, her hand up like a border guard. "Don't apologize. Don't recant. That's the most fire I've seen from you in six years. Don't go snuffing it out as soon as there's a spark."

"I guess I'm feeling just a bit defensive on the issue."

"You know, I read the most remarkable thing in the paper the other day." Caitlin goes glancing off on one of her non sequiturs, rummaging among the clutter on the table, as though we're not having a squabble at all. "I clipped it out. I'm sure it's in here somewhere." From out of the heap she unearths a tattered newspaper clipping. "Here it is! What a filing system. It's a wire service story out of London quoting an article from a science magazine, about spiders."

"Spiders?" What does this have to do with going to Kumquat or not? Caitlin circling again.

"Listen to this," she says, reading from the clipping. "To many people, spiders are hateful and cunning creatures. We're so frightened of them, we even have a special name for the fear: arachnaphobia. Now a new study by Australian scientists confirms that the habits of some spiders are even more revolting than we thought. The scientists report that some so-called social spiders survive as babies by gradually cannibalizing the body of their living mother."

"Good grief," I say.

"The young begin by chewing off her legs," Caitlin's still reading, "eventually rendering her immobile. Within a few weeks she is completely crippled, then her offspring devour her entirely."

She puts the clipping down. "You'd wonder why she does it, wouldn't you? Why she sticks around and lets the little bastards chew her to pieces."

"Yes, you would."

"The scientists speculate that she deliberately sacrifices herself to prevent her babies from cannibalizing one another. It's a species survival thing."

"I suspect a parable in the making," I say.

"Better still," Caitlin says, "it's two parables. One's about sacrificing ourselves for our children."

"Let me take a wild guess: like by going to Kumquat?"

"Absolutely."

"And the second?"

"You know for years we've heard these graphic descriptions of the female spider killing and eating her mate right after copulation."

"Yes, black widows and all that."

"Suicidal monogamy they call it, from the male perspective, of course. Isn't that great?"

"The female devours her mate, and is devoured in turn by her off-spring. Ergo, we should go to Kumquat Sound and get arrested. Doesn't it worry you to be so blatantly losing your grip?"

She bursts out laughing at that, and I have to laugh myself, though the parable's not played out yet.

"Do you see yourself as a hermit, J.J.?" Caitlin asks me as she pours more tea.

"A hermit? No, I wouldn't say so at all. A solitarian, perhaps. I enjoy my seclusion."

"I know." She pauses. Sips her tea. Then looks at me full bore. "You've never been with a woman, have you?"

"No, I haven't," I admit, putting a bold face on it, muscling my way straight into the question I've dreaded her, or anyone, asking.

"Nor with a man either?"

"No."

"Have you wanted to? Make love with a woman, I mean."

"Of course. Who wants to be a forty-three-year-old virgin? I feel like a freak, or like the last surviving member of an extinct species. The last passenger pigeon dying in a zoo."

"But you took a vow to be chaste."

"A long time ago. And had it annulled."

"Maybe it can't be annulled."

"Of course it can. The Pope does it."

"But you don't believe in the Pope."

"No. And I don't believe in chastity either. At least not for me."

"Don't be silly, you're the most chaste adult male in the western hemisphere, how can you not believe in chastity? Surely you're not ashamed of it?"

"Yes. No. I don't know."

"But it's wonderful."

"Oh, sure. Fine for you to say."

"It's rare and wonderful. There's virtue in it, J.J., a condition full of soul-force."

I don't believe she's fooling any more. It's discombobulating hearing this woman whose love affairs are the stuff of local legend lecturing me about the virtues of virginity. Like Conrad Black leading seminars for street people on the merits of frugality.

"Well, I suppose it beats suicidal monogamy," I say.

"Or being eaten alive by your babies."

"Yes. So I'm best off staying quietly at home by myself after all."

"Perhaps you are. It's only that . . ."

"Yes?"

"Maybe the rest of us aren't better off. That soul-force of yours—it's really what we need on this Kumquat expedition. You know I believe completely in civil disobedience."

"I'd say in disobedience generally."

"Gandhi says non-violence means pitting one's whole soul against the will of the tyrant. I guess I feel your soul has been tempered by your vows, in a way that the rest of us haven't. It's what we need just now."

I feel my great "soul-force" being dragged across the kitchen like an old futon.

"I guess I'm being selfish." Caitlin looks a bit lost.

"What is it?"

"Only that I'd feel so much better if you came along. Safer somehow." She looks at me with plaintive eyes, heartbreakingly innocent.

"You really will get a best supporting actress nomination if you keep this up," I say. But she's casting her power again. I can almost hear my heels scraping against the floorboards as I'm pulled towards her.

"You do know, J.J., don't you, that I'm not the type to cannibalize a mate after copulation?"

"I'm relieved to hear it."

"So you're not afraid?"

"Good God, you're as bold as brass, as my dear old mum used to say. No, I'm not afraid." Holding a leaky bucket.

"So what about it?"

"About what?"

"Kumquat."

"Oh, for God's sakes, all right! I'll go along, see if I don't."

"I'm so glad!" She claps her hands with glee and bestows on me a smile of dazzling beauty.

Illuminated by that smile, I see myself in heroic terms, a knight errant, pure as Galahad, champion of Caitlin Slaney, riding off to Kumquat Sound to do battle with the tyrant.

Just then Jenny bursts in through the kitchen door, startling us.

"Mommy!" she cries excitedly. "Mommy, guess what?"

"Hi, Sweetie," Caitlin says, turning to her, but reaching across the table and tenderly touching my hand as she does so. "I give up, what?"

"The little people are here again!"

"No," Caitlin cries, "are they really? How marvellous!" She claps her hands in delight. "Then we must go visit them at once." She turns back to me. "So I'll see you tomorrow, then?"

"Yes." I have forgotten the tug-o-war entirely.

She smiles again. "Thanks, J.J., you won't regret this, I know." She and Jenny disappear outdoors.

Getting up, I notice on the table several magazines lying open with pieces cut out of their pages. She wouldn't, would she? I resist the urge to try to determine what words have been cut out.

As I'm leaving their yard, glancing back from where the footpath enters the forest, I see Jenny and Caitlin on the far side of the clearing, hand in hand, tiptoeing into a little alder glade and whispering together. Lingering at the edge of the ferns, I feel reluctant to leave. A vague longing, touched with melancholy, brushes past me. I'm conscious that the choices I've just made, my awakened knight-errantry, have set me on a new path, and one I do not care to travel alone.

8

On a brilliant early September morning I wander about in my garden, feeling intoxicated with its beauty. The Japanese anemones are especially thrilling. Just as you suppose the fall garden is collapsing completely, that all the best is now over for the year and only bitter death awaits, these slender beauties emerge into bloom and linger through autumn, tender as children, sweet as a September love affair.

I grow as many different varieties at my place as I can get my hands on. All are exquisite. I got started with anemones thanks to Elvira. She brought me a clump of alba with small white flowers on elegant stems. I liked them so well, their carefree grace and late-blooming beauty, I determined to make them a feature of my fall garden. I bought a rosy carmine variety called 'Alice,' and a gorgeous semidouble pink named 'Queen Charlotte.' These two beauties I call by name and whisper sweet nothings to when I'm alone with them. Then a heartbreakingly lovely semidouble white called 'Whirlwind.' They took a couple of years to get themselves settled, but now they've spread into generous clusters with clouds of flowers that seem to float above their foliage like ethereal pink and white veils.

With a start, I spot Caitlin's red hair emerging from the woodland path.

"Hi, Caitlin!" I hail her. "Come on in!"

She strides across the lawn, wearing a backpack.

"Ready to go?" she asks from the garden gate.

"Yes, I'll just get my pack."

"Your place looks beautiful," she says, coming in.

"Thanks," I say, then clumsily, "and so do you."

She gives me a cockeyed glance. She's wearing a rust-coloured smock that brings out the green of her eyes and the coppery red sheen of her hair.

"Aren't the anemones grand?" I ask, dodging discomfort.

"No grander than you!" Caitlin laughs, saucy as a schoolgirl. "Yes, I love anemones. Back home we call the spring-flowering ones windflowers. From the Greek, you know."

"What Greek?"

"Anemos. The wind."

"Oh."

"There's a tragic legend goes with them, of course. About the beautiful nymph, Anemone, who was banished by the jealous wife of Zephyr, the west wind, and left to the crude caresses of Boreas, the north wind, who could not win her love." She pauses for a moment, gazing at the flowers, and I think to myself that Caitlin sounds heartsore. There's the sadness in her again, that I do not understand, that remains outside the circle of the dance she and I do together. I feel for her, but know no way to touch her melancholy.

"It's strange, isn't it," she says, "how lovely they are, but still forlorn somehow?"

I look away from the flowers and don't answer.

We stash our packs in the back of my truck and drive down to the wharf together. Caitlin tells me how Jenny is staying over at her little friend Alonzo's while we're away, and talking about Jenny seems to disperse her gloom. The sky is a soft cerulean blue. A fresh blush of green colours the rumpled hayfields. I imagine that the vivid beauty of the day bodes well for our expedition, then laugh at myself for fishing in pathetic fallacies.

As prearranged, we gather at the ferry wharf down at Rumrunners Cove. Elvira Stone's already there, standing on the wharf gazing across the water towards the big island. Peewee and Julia are there too, in Tilley hats and Birkenstocks, fussing over their new van. They have one of those customized van conversions that does everything but mix your martinis before supper. It has a video monitor suspended over the bed, and a microwave oven. By contrast, Elvira and Caitlin will travel in Elvira's old beater, an ancient station wagon of questionable endurance. Waddy insisted all along on driving his own pickup, and by default I've been assigned to ride with him. Waddy drives a new import four-by-four pickup with a crew cab and long box. He's got a canopy on the box, and that's where I stash my backpack.

Jimmy Fitz has come down to see us off, though he's the only one. He's wearing a frayed tuxedo jacket over his coveralls, to mark the solemnity of the occasion. Jimmy shakes each of our hands in turn and tells us how it was real nice getting to know each of us during our sojourn on Upshot. "You folks take care of y'selves now, y'hear?" Jimmy addresses us all in final farewell, as though we're pilgrims sailing to a New World, never to return.

On board the ferry, we cluster in a tight knot on the open car deck. We're a peculiar-looking bunch at best. Waddy's telling us how it used to be with the old ferry.

"Hell, it weren't no more'n a scow lashed to a tugboat with loggin' cable back in them days," Waddy says. "Gigolo Miller was captain, Fibber's old man. Gigolo's boys we used to call the crew, ain't that right, Elvira?" Elvira verifies this historical nugget, and Waddy carries on. "Some days a deckhand'd stand at the prow with a big pike pole, pushin' deadheads outta the way. Nowadays they got the deadheads on deck, not in the water," Waddy snorts like a horse. Here he goes, I think to myself. "Oh, hell yes, back then they had a rip roarin' time of it. But Jesus you took your life in your hands with that crew. Christmas, New Year's, Hallowe'en, any excuse a'tall, they'd be pickled. Gigolo'd have to take three or four runs at the wharf just to get 'er in!"

Waddy and I are last car off, but we're barely up the ferry ramp before Waddy hits the gas, taking a run at the steep hill ahead. The ferry road winds down a couple of miles from the highway. Within minutes, he's tailgating Peewee and Julia's supervan, going uphill. Waddy switches smoothly from nautical to terrestrial transportation issues. "Only trouble with them fancy vans," he says, nudging out into the oncoming lane as though he planned to pass, across twin yellow lines, on this impossible hill, "is they got no guts. Too much weight. Oh, they're fine and dandy for crawlin' along freeways," he ducks back into our lane as a car swooshes past going downhill, dashing needlessly for the ferry, "dawdlin' from one KOA to the next, but why would anyone call that camping?" He gears down impatiently into first, almost nudging Peewee and Julia's rear bumper.

"Waddy," I say, "you know we got all day."

"Gotta stop in Port, for one thing," Waddy says, again poking out across the line, "and for another I hate like hell wastin' time on the road." At that, he zips out into the opposite lane, roars past the van and nudges his way back into the uphill lane, without benefit of any signals, forcing Peewee to brake on the hill. We barely miss getting creamed by an oncoming truck. It rumbles past, horn blaring, and we see it's the Happy Honeydipper septic tank pump-out truck heading down to the ferry.

"Least he's empty," Waddy crows. "That's one truck you wouldn't want to hit when he had a full load!"

I retract my toenails from the soles of my boots.

"That honeydipper reminds me of one time," Waddy launches into a new tale, "that time a big old Climax locie went runaway down-island. I wasn't runnin' 'er, it was some Polish guy. Couldn't hold 'er on the grade though. Four per cent slope for over a mile in there. Eighty tons them old Climaxes ran, plus ten loads of logs she's haulin'. No sir, that Pole couldn't hold 'er, not on that grade. Down the track she comes thunderin' like old glory. Course even a Polack's got enough sense to get the hell off. He takes a flyin' leap into a thicket of devil's club, and the Climax she keeps a'comin' and finally she smashes into another train-load of logs parked at the bottom. Whooee! Now that was loggin'!"

Waddy slaps his hand on the steering wheel so the horn blares and scares us both. "Haw haw," he crows.

Pretty soon we pick up the main highway and swing south. We have to track south along the east coast for a bit, then cut across to the west side of the island, another eighty miles or so. The morning sun hangs over the strait like an incandescent orange. Waddy flips on his sunglasses. Back along the shore, a great blue heron perches on a rock, balanced perfectly on one long, slender leg, its elongated beak poised sharp as a stiletto. "It looks straight from a Japanese etching," I say. Waddy only grunts and kicks the truck into high gear. The water lies flat and golden, as though waiting for whales to breach.

"Hot day comin'," Waddy says, studying the sky. We streak south-ward through patches of woodland and past derelict farms, their weath-ered barns and outbuildings sagging with neglect and age. Fenceposts wobble drunkenly across meadows gone to wild grasses and saplings.

We pass a huge new clearing alongside the highway. A month ago it was a forest of big second-growth fir trees, but now they're all logged off, and two D-8 cats are grinding around in the dirt, like enormous yellow beetles, nudging tree stumps and slash into burn piles. Alongside the highway a billboard proclaims: "Future Home of Sea Wind Estates—Luxury Living by the Sea."

"Jesus Christ!" Waddy says, but nothing more.

At Bollyhocks Beach we swing inland. A quaint little seaside town, Bollyhocks Beach has for years been a comfortable retirement mecca for old money. It boasts a couple of nouveau Tudor inns, a golf course with spectacular ocean views, even a road called Ambassadors Avenue. The little town is bustling with building activity, the way an anthill does when you've poked it with a stick. Driving past new slapdash condos and sham Dickensian shopfronts, Waddy shakes his head and grunts something under his breath.

Pretty soon we're rolling back out into countryside, past large and prosperous dairy farms and patches of dark woodlands. A few miles on, we pick up the road to the west coast. The traffic's already heavy, lots of RVs and big trucks rumbling in both directions. Although grandly named the Highway to Heaven, it's actually a two-lane road with periodic passing lanes. The kind of road visiting Americans fresh from the Interstate shake their heads at, as if they were in Mexico or someplace. The kind of road that says where you're going isn't all that more important than where you are. The route wiggles its way through the mountains following an opening called the Bollyhocks Divide, under the sloping shoulders of Mount Hammersmith.

Tourist traps and roadside attractions cling forlornly to the edge of the highway, dreaming of better days.

If it hadn't been for Waddy's driving—several times already I've made my last act of contrition and prepared to face death head on—I'd be perfectly happy. I love just booming along a highway, windows down, tape deck wailing, yapping away about whatever the landscape throws up for examination. Even Waddy's Dwight Yoakum tapes don't sound all that bad, which is a pretty good sign that I'm mellowed right out by now.

"Good to get off that goddamn rock once in a while, ain't it?" Waddy says. "Guy could go nuts stayin' too long in a place like that."

We shimmy our way along Young Lake and into Gothic Grove. Here the road cuts through a stand of old-growth trees preserved in a small park. Traffic slows to a crawl, and Waddy's jumping around the road like a water beetle. Motor homes and camper vans and sporty cars with kayaks on the roof are nosed in all along the road. There's tourists wandering around dressed in Bermuda shorts and T-shirts and pastel designer track outfits.

Over them all the huge trees loom—great ancient Douglas firs, their enormous trunks six or more feet thick. Sheathed in rough reddish bark, the boles rise straight and untapered as if they were the columns of an ancient living temple. Huge western red cedars, silver-grey trunks fluted at the base, towering skywards and drooping fronds hanging like gathered silk from long curved branches. Knotty hemlocks, younger than the others, crusty and twisted in their shade, young at only a couple of centuries, emerging as seedlings when the ancient firs and cedars were already old.

"Used to all be like that around here," Waddy says. "Real trees, not these friggin' beanpoles they're cuttin' now. See them big cedars?" He points to some trees as we work our way along, narrowly missing several pedestrians. "Used to be they'd knock 'em down, big bastards way bigger'n them there, and they'd be hollow in the butt end, most of 'em, so they'd put a charge in the middle and blow 'em into pieces, just so they could handle 'em, they were that big."

"Hmm." I'm barely paying attention. I'm remembering the first time I ever stopped here, when I first came west. I pulled my old VW van into the empty parking lot and stepped into the first ancient forest I'd ever seen up close. I was completely overwhelmed by the sheer enormous bulk of the trees. Trees big in the way that whales are big, or waterfalls. Huge and ancient. I realized in an exhilarating flash that these same trees were already growing before Blessed Columkille the Lesser ran mad across the green hills of Ireland with his sack of snakes. Perhaps even before Jesus of Nazareth roamed the desert hills of Judea. In my mind history compressed and expanded like a wheezing squeezebox. Standing beneath the big trees I became aware, perhaps truly aware for the first time, of how small I was, and alone, and how quickly passing a human life is. Discomfited, I scuttled back to my van and popped on Leonard Cohen.

Waddy and I are lugging up a steep grade leading out of Young Valley towards Zebediah Summit. The locals call this stretch 'the hump.' It's the dividing line between the island's east and west sides. The eastern slope, facing the calm inland sea of the strait, is really a pretty tame place, practically gentrified, a thin ribbon of lowlands long ago cleared and settled. The string of small towns dotting the shoreline could be from Anywhere, USA.

But once you cross the spine of rough mountains running down the length of the island, over to their western side, things change dramatically. The wild west side they call it. Out on the edge, where storms roar in from across the open Pacific. Sombre mountains stand in rows like jagged basalt teeth fierce before the storms, in places plunge down sheer into thundering surf. Fabulous rain forests, thick and dripping, impenetrable for fallen logs, mauling salal, and spiny devil's club, and laced by gurgling creeks and streams.

We crest the summit and begin to glide down its long western slope. In the opposite lanes, huge trucks roar and grumble, geared down so low they may never get up again, crawling slowly up the steep grade, slow as old poets labouring up Parnassus. There's a wild look in Waddy's eye as we fly down our side. "Remember the Polack!" Waddy screams against the rush of wind through his window as we whoosh down effortlessly, giddy almost, our ears popping as we drop down out of the pass into the Zebediah Valley.

"Helluva town, this place," Waddy mutters as we near the outskirts of Port Zebediah. "Fight like cats and dogs over here. Always have. Scabs, company goons, rat unions—they got it all in Port."

A classic mill town, Port lies in the bottom of a mountain-rimmed bowl like leftover stir fry in a wok. Looking at the hills all around, you wouldn't think it was a saltwater port, but the Zebediah Inlet, a long arm of navigable water, reaches in through the fabled mountains of the west. From here huge freighters steam westwards, loaded with pulp and lumber from the island's forests, bound for all over the world. Gliding down into town from the east, you see an aging pulp mill belching vapours from multiple stacks. Wood frame houses and small shops sprawl under its sulphurous clouds. The old part of town looks as though some mischievous trickster had ripped out a piece of old rust-bucket Pittsburgh or Cleveland and flung it, smokestacks and all, down among the mountains.

"Fight? Jesus, they're like coons and hounds, this bunch," Waddy savours his simile. "I guess we better load up on grub." We'd agreed back on the ferry that Waddy and I would buy groceries for the whole group to donate to the camp kitchen. As well we've all brought produce from our gardens. Waddy swings the truck into the parking lot of a down-town mall.

Stepping out of the truck, we're assailed by a violent beating of the sun. The parking lot blacktop sizzles. The air is stifling hot and sul-phurous.

"Told ya she'd be hot," Waddy says as we hurry across the parking lot towards the dingy-looking mall. I notice a number of solitary men, bearded or unshaven, each sitting alone in a pickup parked in the lot. They watch us as we walk by. Waddy seems oblivious to their blank stares. "Helluva town," he mutters, more to himself than to me. I'm aware of feeling a faint but persistent tremolo of apprehension. I sense a brooding, sullen resentment hanging over the place, a sourness of spirit mixed in with the mill's stench of rotten eggs.

At the supermarket entrance, Waddy tells me, "You go ahead in, I'm just going to get something at the grog shop, I'll catch you up in a sec."

I hesitate. Should I tell him that the Kumquat Peace Camp is alco-hol and drug free? It isn't the kind of thing you tell Waddy. Oh, the hell with it. "Okay," I call after him. The automatic doors swish open with an asthmatic wheeze and I step into the artificial coolness of the store.

I finish shopping and take the grub back to Waddy's truck, but there's no sign of him anywhere. I stash the groceries in the back, under the blank gaze of the watchers, and head over to the liquor store to find the old guy.

The liquor store is cool and dark inside and almost deserted, a cav-ern lined with glistening decanters. I look up all the aisles, but Waddy isn't in any of them. I decide, since I'm in there anyway, to buy a couple of bottles of wine to take back home as a temporary respite from Elvira's home-brew.

I get in line at the check-out counter behind an enormous man. He looks like Yukon Eric, the professional wrestler who'd "bear hug" oppo-nents to near-death, back in the glory days of pro wrestling at Maple Leaf Gardens. Whipper Billy Watson and Gorgeous George. The das-tardly Miller Brothers.

I'm over six feet tall myself, and not many people make me feel small, but this guy does. He stands like a Kodiak bear, a mountain of muscle run to fat. His thick leather belt swoops down in front, holding up a pair of stained and baggy jeans and supporting a huge beer belly. He has an intricate tattoo on his bicep, and I find myself staring at it, absorbed by the image of an apocalyptic beast breathing fire and clutching a naked woman in its claw.

The giant is wearing a white T-shirt dark with sweat under his armpits. He turns to look at me, exposing a logo on the shirt front. "Save a job—Screw a hugger," it screams in vermillion lettering. Under the motto there's a crude cartoon of a hippie with a huge screw driven through his stomach, pinning him to a fir tree.

Eric looks at me with bloodshot and malevolent eyes. He's got greasy hair and a short ragged beard. I think of Charles Manson. Rasputin the mad monk. Looking away quickly, I become intensely absorbed in a special display promoting a new California spritzer. "Cool Out, Dudes!" the display enthuses. Yukon Eric rumbles like an earth tremor, pays for his three cases of beer, picks them up as lightly as though they were empties already, glances again at me, and shambles out of the store.

"That everything?" the cashier asks with consummate indifference.

"Yes, that's all."

Waddy's waiting for me in his truck. "That booze?" he asks me, as I stash my bag in the crew cab.

"Just a couple of bottles of wine."

"You know there's no booze allowed at the camp, don'tcha?" he asks me, whinnying. "Let's get the hell outta here." He hits the gas and we speed away, out of Port.

I tell Waddy about the liquor store giant. After I've described him, Waddy starts laughing like a jackal.

"What?" I ask him.

"That feller," he snorts, "that's Tiny. Meanest lookin' bastard you'd ever see. And y'know what? There ain't a mean bone in the guy's body. No more hurt someone than you would. Heart of gold, old Tiny. Everybody loves the guy."

And away, away speeding westwards, speeding towards Kumquat.

9

The countryside out west of Port Zebediah is spectacularly scenic. For many miles the highway twists along the shoreline of Lake Centralia, meandering like Gregorian chant through the mountains of the big island's centre. Muscular mountainsides come shouldering down to the lake, braided with long, slender waterfalls that tumble down the rock face and splash through veils of mist into the lake.

"You ever run trains up in this country?" I ask Waddy.

"Nah," Waddy says as though I'd asked him if he believes in the tooth fairy. "Don't need locies when ya got water like that." He cocks his scrawny thumb towards the lake. "Why in hell would ya load logs onto rail when ya can throw 'em in the water and float 'em wherever ya want, eh?"

"Good question," I say.

Waddy looks at me as though I'm being flippant. He really is a cantankerous old fart, but you wouldn't dare say so to him, not unless you were ready for a barroom brawl. He has the same quality my father had, a hair-trigger temper, a readiness to stick his nose in and start swinging at the least provocation. Though he must be well into his seventies— Waddy'll never say his age—and only half my size, and nowhere near as well educated as I am—I think he told me once he got part-way through grade five—I realize that I'm afraid of the old codger, fearful of confronting him if he gets riled up.

Gazing out the window, I probe that fear the way you probe an aching tooth with your tongue. Afraid of what? Not just of his anger, I don't think, no, more than that. More that he does not respect who I am. That he thinks me ridiculous. Effete. And if he gets mad enough, he'll tell me so, confirming my own judgements of myself, the way my father did, ramming his contempt down my throat. You learn to float like a butterfly to keep from getting hit. But I want something more from Waddy than just not to be hit. I'd like him to actually say I'm okay. That he respects my point of view. That I belong. I'd long before stopped hoping for as much from my father, when I stood by his graveside never having heard it. But somehow it's still there for me with Waddy, like an itch I haven't yet scratched.

"Logged these sidehills back in the thirties and forties," Waddy cocks his thumb again, oblivious of my musings. "Knocked the big old-growth down with ballcrackers."

"Ballcrackers?" I laugh, abandoning my thoughts.

"Them first chainsaws. Jesus Christ, they weighed more'n the goddamn trees. Took two fellas just to pick 'em up and drag 'em to the next tree. Quicker'n axes and saws, though, you better believe it. Then skid the logs downhill and into the water, smoother'n a hooker's slit."

"How would they drag them downhill," I ask, ignoring his metaphor, "oxen?"

Waddy snorts and brays like a donkey. "Oxen?" he says. "On them fuckin' sidehills? Look at 'em! Nah, fer Christsakes, they had big A-frame yarders anchored to huge log rafts down on the lake. Haul like hell, them big bastards. Oxen! Jesus Christ!"

Down at the west end of the lake there'd been a huge forest fire back in the sixties, miles and miles of burnt forest, though you can hardly tell any more there even was a fire. Most of it's gone back to scrub alder and young conifers.

"Buncha damn fools caused that fire," Waddy says, as we drive through. "Blastin' rock in here someplace for a road. So the powder monkey puts in way too big a charge and knocks a hydro line down. Real genius, y'know. Then whoosh! the whole goddamn mountainside goes up like a Roman candle. Middle of summer. One hell of a fire, that was, couldn't douse 'er. You could smell it all the way back home for weeks."

As we swing around a corner, I glance out through the window to my right, up a hillside, and I'm dazzled for a moment by what looks like a row of silver spires gleaming against the pure blue sky. Jerusalem, perhaps. Or Camelot. Then I make out what it is: high up on the mountain, along the lip of a ridge, there's a long palisade of dead trees, just their stems left. They were obviously killed by the fire but left standing. I guess they've been bleached by the sun and rain all these years, and just at this moment, they're catching the sunlight at such an angle that each snag looks like a pure silver spire shining against blue sky.

"Can you see those snags?" I ask Waddy. "Up on the hilltop. They're absolutely beautiful."

Waddy just grunts. His notion of beauty and mine lie miles apart. The gentle thunder of his Pacific Shay, the tension of ten carloads of big timber on steel, these are the components of his aesthetic, not dandified appreciation of sunlight on burnt snags. His grunt says it all.

"Gotta take a leak up here," Waddy says when we see a sign for the rest area just below Sudden Pass. Waddy comes off the highway too fast and sends an eruption of dust and gravel spewing into the air behind us. "Whoa!" Waddy yells, braking hard against the gravel, and we come sliding into the rest area like something out of an idiotic television ad for Detroit's latest piece of turbo-charged garbage.

And there, standing in the middle of the parking lot, are Elvira and Caitlin.

I feel a little rush of excitement to see them in this strange place, especially after two hours of Waddy, but I can tell straight off there's something wrong.

"Well, you two are a sight for sore eyes," Elvira says, smiling, as they come up. "We're in a dreadful pickle."

"What's wrong?" I ask them.

"My poor old wagon's packed it in," Elvira says. Caitlin's looking at me in a funny way.

"Have a look at 'er," Waddy says straight off, not even bothering to stretch after the drive, but pulling an enormous toolbox out from behind his driver's seat. "What she been doin'?"

"She been bad," Caitlin says, mocking Waddy a bit. And me. Caitlin's not scared of Waddy's anger the way I am. I don't think Caitlin's scared of much of anything.

"Ain't bad machines," Waddy counters. "Just bad operators."

"Spoken like a true old Wobbly," Caitlin laughs and slaps Waddy on the shoulder, "so let's have a look at her." The two of them walk off to the station wagon parked over by the picnic tables. Even from a distance, there's something woeful about the old wagon, something that says it's too old for climbing these hills any more. Elvira and I drift on behind the others, neither of us willing participants in the arcana of sprockets and universal joints. We stand around, superfluous, while Waddy pokes under the hood, then under the vehicle itself. Lying on his back, his coverall legs stick out from under the chassis, Romeos up, and twitch now and then like he's just been run over.

Caitlin hands Waddy whatever tools he calls for, wrenches and sockets and things I don't know the names of. Waddy's cursing away under there and banging things around. His skinny little legs scissor up and down like spider legs as he shifts around under the motor. Finally he crawls back out. His face is smeared with grease and dirt, and he's dusted all over with flakes of rust so he looks like he's been left out in the rain all winter. "Jesus Christ!" Waddy grumbles as he dusts himself off. "I seen pit privies cleaner'n that piece a shit! Give 'er a try anyways, Elvira."

Elvira gets into the driver's seat and tries the ignition. The car makes an awful sound, like a slaughtered pig's dying breath. Then nothing.

"Sonofabitch!" Waddy snarls and kicks the front tire angrily. "God-damn sonofabitchin' piece a shit!"

The three of us leave Waddy to perform these mechanical last rites, and decide that we'll abandon the wagon where it is and carry on all together in Waddy's truck.

We stash Elvira's and Caitlin's bags in the back while Waddy's gathering up his tools. Each of these he places carefully, almost reverently, back in his toolbox.

Then we're on the road again, Waddy and Elvira up front, Caitlin and I squeezed in the crew cab behind. We're climbing up into Sudden Pass when Waddy bangs the steering wheel with his hand so the horn blares again. "Sonofagun!" he says. "In all that commotion I forgot to take a leak. If you'll pardon my French, ladies."

"We could just go back to the rest stop," I say, but Waddy shakes his head.

"I'll just pull over at the top here," he says. "Gild the lily right there, if you ladies will look the other way."

"Oh, don't spoil our fun, Waddy!" Caitlin teases him, and in the rearview mirror I can see a twinkle in the old goat's eye.

"Now look at that!" Elvira says, pointing. "Isn't that awful?"

At the top of the hill, alongside the road, there's a huge graffiti painted on a rockface in flaming red letters. It says "Save a job—kill a hippie."

Waddy sees it and starts laughing so hard we just about go over the edge.

"Real geniuses, these guys," Waddy crows. "Bunch a real Einsteins. Here, I'll show ya some eddytorial comment."

He pulls the truck off onto the shoulder, and walks over to the graffiti.

"What's the old coot up to now?" Elvira says.

Waddy makes a huge production of unzipping his coveralls, pulling out his mighty penis, and proceeding to urinate on the graffiti. Finished, he shakes himself off, tucks himself in, and swaggers back to the truck as though he's just felled Goliath.

We're laughing our heads off as he climbs back into his driver's seat.

"That'll dampen the bastards down," Waddy says, as he guns the engine and we pull away. "Course at my age ya can't get it over the fence any more, the way ya used to. Couldn't hit the top a the letters, but I gave 'er a pretty good dousin' anyway."

We all clap and cheer for Waddy as we go hurtling down the western side of the pass.

"It's funny," Caitlin says to me after we've grown quiet, "before you guys came along, I was feeling it was very weird back there."

"Weird how?" I ask.

"For the last few miles, I'd had this chilling sensation, a feeling that we were travelling deeper and deeper into a dark, dangerous place. The day's so lovely and the landscape all along here's so gorgeous, and yet I felt this sinister, creepy feeling, as if a stalker was following us, and we were moving further and further away from the light. You felt it too, didn't you, Elvira?"

"Yes, I did," Elvira says, turning in the front seat to look at us. "I don't know why."

"I tried to talk myself out of it," Caitlin says. "I mean, the place was crawling with Winnebagos and tourists, so we were hardly Frodo and Samwise going alone into the dark land of Mordor—and yet that's just how it felt. Weird and ominous. Foreboding in an unmistakable way." She shivers a bit and throws the dark vision off, smiling, as though it were foolish, at odds with her fearlessness.

"Hmm," is all I can say. I don't want to say to them that I have had misgivings about this adventure from the first, that all week I've been prey to foreshadowings of calamity. They'd only laugh and say what else is new with me. But I haven't forgotten what I saw clearly in the eyes of Mistral Wind that first evening down on the wharf, that sense of perilous depths into which one could plunge. And it was her, after all, who set us on the road we're now travelling.

"Do you think Mistral will be at the camp?" I ask.

"She said she'd meet us there." Caitlin seems instantly cheered by the reminder of Mistral, as though that enigmatic character were a talisman against misfortune. "I'm sure she will."

"She better," Waddy says, though I don't understand why.

Just after Sudden Pass, we pick up Nixon River. Its entire length is a short cascading dash from ice melt in the mountains to the vast Pacific. The river flows milky blue-green, ice melt, or molten jade diluted and spun over and around huge boulders, whirlpooling in deep, clear pools of blue green. Entwined serpents, road and river slide together westwards.

We decide to stop for lunch somewhere along the river. Most of the pull-offs are clogged with tourists but Caitlin says she knows a secret spot well off the highway. At a certain point she directs Waddy to pull off the pavement and down an old logging road. It follows a bend in the river. The road runs in twin ruts, as if it hasn't been used for years. Young hemlocks are crowding in on it, so they brush the truck as we go through. A green-fingered tunnel through the forest. About a quarter mile in, there's a pull-off spot, an old landing or something, and Waddy pulls the truck in there.

We climb out and stretch in the cool dappled shade of alders. Elvira says she'll have lunch fixed up in just a couple of minutes. Waddy says he'll have his siesta in the meantime. Caitlin and I wander off together through the glade.

I ask her how she knows this spot—it's so well hidden from the highway. Has she been here before?

"Just once," she says, brushing her hand across the soft leaves of a huckleberry bush. "I wasn't sure I could find it again."

"Why do I sense a scandal?" I try to sound casual.

"Because it's your nature," she grins, and looks out across the river, shimmering in sunlight. "The last time I was here," she muses, "I was in love."

I hesitate. "Jean-Luc?" I ask her finally.

"Hmm."

I believe Jean-Luc was the one great love of Caitlin's life. He was an artist in the grand French mode: passionate, debonair, witty, agreeably eccentric. He'd arrived on Upshot one springtime, half a dozen years ago, not long after I'd arrived myself, fresh from Paris, to paint, he told us, some of our extraordinary gardens. He'd heard about the island from a friend. He descended upon us like Monet upon Giverny.

And descended in consummate style. He leased a large waterfront house in Cascara Heights for the summer. He drove about in a rented BMW. He dressed flamboyantly in tailored clothes.

Like everything about him, his landscapes were exquisite. He had a passion for painting romantic gardens, the wilder and blowsier the better. Impeccable in his own toilette, Jean-Luc was a connoisseur of the romantically unkempt in gardens.

He would remain among us for three months, he declared, and, with our permission, devote each month to painting one of the island's most appealing gardens.

Well, needless to say, once word of his intentions got around, the fur began to fly. If he'd been some starving artist from a roach-ridden Montreal garret, there might not have been such a furor. But Jean-Luc was an aristocrat, and highly acclaimed for his work. He'd appeared, as one wag put it, in more catalogues than Timothy Eaton. People began imagining their gardens immortalized through his art. They envisioned images of their very own flowers hanging on the walls of the Louvre for the admiration of generations yet unborn.

The ensuing courting and wooing of Jean-Luc was a marvel to behold. Geoffrey Munz, of course, was in there like a bark beetle. Living just up Ocean Spray Drive from Jean-Luc's pied-a-terre, Geoffrey was perfectly placed to make connections. He and Rose invited Jean-Luc over for cocktails.

"Splendid fellow," Geoffrey declared at the garden club meeting a few nights later. "A first-rate artist and a true gentleman." Though he didn't say as much, Geoffrey seemed confident that his rose garden would be Jean-Luc's first choice for artistic inspiration.

A lot of islanders thought Angus and Petty MacIvor's rock garden, which was just approaching its peak of springtime brilliance as Jean-Luc was conducting his preliminary assessments, was a shoo-in.

"A most charming garden, most charming," Jean-Luc said to Angus and Petty when taking his leave after an introductory visit. "Thank you so much for permitting me to view it." This was the same spiel, liberally laced with Gallic charm, he gave to each of the gardeners he visited.

"When will you be wanting to start then?" Petty asked him.

"Madame?" Jean-Luc looked genuinely puzzled.

"When would you like to start painting the garden?" Petty said.

"Oh, I see!" Jean-Luc smiled graciously. "Pardon, madame, but for the present I seek only to experience the genius loci—how do you say it?—the genius of the place."

"But . . ." Angus started to fluster.

"And what extraordinary beauty you have created here," Jean-Luc sailed on smoothly. "So in harmony with its surroundings, so comely. I congratulate you on its success." And with that, he bowed and made his exit, leaving Angus and Petty dumbfounded.

Rumours of ferocious jostling for position among the would-be famous gardeners were flying thick and fast, and provoked in Elvira a pressing need for a permanent. Whenever there's a particularly juicy bit of news making the rounds, Elvira likes to schedule an appointment at Wilhelmina's Beauty Salon in order to get filled in. She was into Wilhelmina's chair in no time. It was through Wilhelmina's breathless reportage—with the customary "not a word of this is to leave this room"—that Angus and Petty's dismay came to light. For no sooner had Jean-Luc's silver BMW glided out of their driveway than Angus and Petty had hightailed it over to Wilhelmina and Karl's for a council of war.

"Aye, well, he may have more money than he knows what to do with," Angus concluded his tale of rejection to Karl and Wilhelmina, "and he may be a fancy Frenchman with all his madames et messieurs, but under it all that fella's a fat-headed fop!"

"But he hasn't chosen or rejected anyone yet," Rose Munz tried to say, but everyone ignored her.

Wilhelmina herself had been entertaining high hopes of Jean-Luc painting Karl's dahlia garden. Perhaps foolishly, she confided to Elvira, while fussing with the rods, that she fancied herself in Paris for the exhibition opening. "Just imagine," she'd said, "me in the City of Lights!" But her hopes too were dashed. Karl put it down, not to any lack of charm in his dahlia brigades, but to lingering Franco-Prussian enmity on the part of Jean-Luc. Karl didn't mind at all, Wilhelmina explained to Elvira, because he doesn't like art anyway, and certainly didn't care for what he called "that limp-wristed Frog."

With the dexterity of a foreign diplomat, Jean-Luc picked his way across the minefield of island politics and emerged, unscathed, with a decision that he would paint the gardens of Ernie and Gertrude Moffatt, Caitlin Slaney, and Blackie the Mechanic.

Well, you could have cut the indignation with a cross-cut saw, it was that thick. Nobody could quibble about Gertrude and Ernie's garden being selected because it really is a masterpiece, with its meandering pathways, its cunning interplay of fastigiate and weeping trees, its chain of limpid pools and cascades with thematic plantings around each. Jean-Luc had been completely charmed by its eccentric owners.

"I'm sure your Verse Isles is very grand, right enough," Ernie explained to Jean-Luc, "but why would we want to spend all that time and money going over there, when we got this right here, eh?" Then he twisted his little monkey face into a canny grin and clicked his dentures.

Caitlin's, as well, was a not illogical choice. She's managed to cultivate a wonderfully wild and carefree look while subtly incorporating the classic principles of garden design. Although your first impression is of an almost reckless fecundity, the trained eye can see behind the massed plantings an artistic discipline of exquisite taste. It is an unquestioned triumph, and Jean-Luc saw so right away. "Your gardens," he said, kissing Caitlin's hand in courtly fashion, "betoken a greatness of spirit."

But Blackie the Mechanic's place? This peculiar choice sent a spasm of disapproval shuddering through certain quarters of the community. Not that people disliked Blackie himself. Blackie's little flatbed tow truck and his baling wire brilliance in auto mechanics—although not always up to the contemporary challenges of high performance, fuel-injected microchippery—have rescued most of us, at one time or another, from mechanical collapse. We acknowledge our indebtedness to Blackie, and view prudently our potential for future dependence upon him, pending the whims of a wayward camshaft or contrary alternator.

With his bushy black beard and bald head, his magnificently rotund beer belly, and his grease-streaked T-shirts that may have been white, however briefly, once upon a time, Blackie has never been taken seriously as a gardener. His yard—"And I think in his case that's a more appropriate term than garden, don't you?" Geoffrey asked, upon hearing the news that Blackie's place had been selected by the artist in preference to his own—is adorned with metal sculptures that Blackie fashions in his spare time by welding together salvaged parts from wrecked autos. The only plants to be seen are dozens of red hot pokers scattered amongst the sculptures.

"I like 'em 'cause the deer don't," is how Blackie sums up his attachment to *Kniphofias*.

To Jean-Luc the interplay of metallic sculptures and fiercely red hot pokers was a stroke of genius. "Monsieur Blackie," Jean-Luc bowed deeply before the mystified mechanic, "I pay homage to you as an inferior artiste to his superior."

Jimmy Fitz, who was there at the time getting Blackie to do something with the hydraulics on his backhoe, said that all Blackie could do in response to the dapper Frenchman was to emit a protracted and particularly resonant belch.

Needless to say, Jean-Luc and Caitlin became an item. Caitlin was living alone at the time—this was long before the pedalling poet hove into view—and having the debonair Frenchman in her gardens day after day, eating lunch together, his producing a bottle of expensive champagne to celebrate the day's accomplishments, well, it all added up to the two of them tumbling into an affair. And what an affair it was! I hated to hear it, but everybody agreed that they made a splendid pair—elegant, clever, vivacious. Their infatuation seemed to spill over and bathe the whole island in its intoxicating vapours.

"Oh, yes, that was love all right." Caitlin is gazing out across the river. "Love and lust and art and everything transcendent—I was completely swept away."

"I remember." Trying to hide what I know now was the pain I was feeling back then.

"We only had that one trip off-island together," Caitlin muses. "Jean-Luc wanted to experience the beaches out here on the west side. He'd heard so much about them. We were on our way, our first day off together, when we stopped right here. We found it by accident, the way wonderful things happen automatically at that stage of a love affair. We parked the car and went darting off through the trees. We were laughing and whooping wildly, like kids.

"We scrambled down a rocky bank, somewhere along here, the sun was blazing hot and the light on the river was blinding. We threw off our T-shirts and cut-offs and plunged into a cold, deep pool. And we dove like dolphins." Caitlin's in a sort of reverie, remembering. "I could see large cobbles lining the bottom of the pool, smooth and flecked like eggs. It was exhilarating under water. Even the stones seemed ready to crack open and give birth. I saw Jean-Luc dive down past me, supple as a salamander. His hair streaked behind him like eelgrass in the sea."

Caitlin's face is transformed, glowing in the afternoon sunlight.

"Go on," I say quietly.

"I scrambled out onto a large flat rock in the river, and lay back on the warm stone. I was cold and gloriously warm at the same time. I closed my eyes and listened to the river, felt it swirling all around and through me.

"In a minute or two, I heard Jean-Luc splash up onto the rock as well. I felt his shadow fall across my face, blotting out the sun. It was behind him as I looked up, blindingly intense, and he was silhouetted against the fierce light. Neither of us said a word. He was dripping cold drops of water onto the warm stone. He stood there over me, not moving, not saying anything. Then he knelt and kissed me."

Caitlin stops and blinks away the vision. "Do you really want to be hearing all this?" she smiles. "I mean, it sounds like classic Monique Manlotte."

"I hate that it's about you and him," I say, conscious that my throat is dry and there's a tightness in my chest. I'm remembering how strong that yearning was in me yesterday to not leave Caitlin's place, to not be without her. "But I guess I like that it's about you. Please tell me."

"Well, then we made sweet love right there on the rock in the middle of the river. And what love we made! Pure ecstasy. I like to think that's where Jenny was conceived. Of course, it could have been anywhere, the way we went at it on that trip, but I like to think it was there on the rock. That was special. We seemed to be commingled with the river and the rocks and the sun. I want to call it a miracle, but that's just too corny, isn't it?"

Caitlin lapses into silence, and I have nothing to say either.

What she leaves unsaid, what doesn't need saying, was how Jean-Luc flew back to Paris, as he'd said at the outset he would, after three months, taking his canvasses with him. Several weeks later, Caitlin received a parcel by special delivery. It contained a small portrait he'd painted of her. She'd never posed for him, but he'd spent long hours gazing at her, and he'd taken dozens of photos. The portrait, in oils, was lovely. There was a letter enclosed, full of raptures, but even more full of the dreadful confession that Jean-Luc was a happily married man with three charming children of his own. He closed the letter by bidding Caitlin a reluctant but final adieu.

She never wrote back to him. She never informed him that she'd borne his child early the following spring.

We are sitting perfectly still by the swirling river.

"Poor Anemone," I say at last, both artist and poet in my own right.

Caitlin looks up at me then, and I think she's going to cry. Instead she smiles and says, "Is that you, Boreas, I hear whispering among the leaves?"

Then we hear Elvira calling that lunch is ready.

10

It's already the middle of the afternoon by the time we pull into the peace camp. You couldn't miss the place for trying; there's banners and flags and pennants hanging from trees and poles all along the highway.

"Looks like hippie heaven in there to me," Waddy says.

We pull in on the highway shoulder where there's a whole line of vehicles parked and clamber out of the truck. We stand there staring for a bit. Traffic crawls by, everyone craning to look at what's going on. A big truck thunders past and blasts his air horn at us.

"Up yours!" Waddy yells after him, flipping him the finger.

The camp's set up in the middle of an obscenely big clearcut. The land lies flat along the highway, a sea of blackened stumps, then rises in clearcut mountains farther back.

"Beautiful," Caitlin says.

A big Cadillac with Alberta plates pulls in behind us on the shoulder, and out steps a respectable-looking couple in country club dress. They stand by their car and stare up into the Apocalypse, shaking their heads in incomprehension.

"Pretty awful, isn't it?" Elvira says to them, being friendly.

"How could you people let this happen?" The man says to us. He's got hair like a silver fox and smells of cologne and success. I don't know if he means the camp or the clearcuts. Once more, the two of them shake their silver heads in disbelief then climb back into the Cadillac and drive away.

We walk over to the camp entrance where a makeshift wooden bridge straddles the roadside ditch. "Welcome to the Black Hole," reads a large hand-lettered sign spiked to a stump. A half-dozen ragtag characters are sitting around a smouldering firepit. It's hardly a fire, just a little ribbon of acrid smoke drifting up from charred logs. They're smoking hand-rolled cigarettes and looking sullen. One young guy with a great bushy beard and wearing a skirt is explaining to the rest of them how to cook banana slugs. The rest look bored. Nobody pays any attention to us at all.

We poke our noses into an information booth close by. It's thrown up with rough planking and poles lashed and spiked together. The walls are plastered with maps and pamphlets and newspaper clippings about the blockades.

"Absolutely the weirdest thing happened yesterday," somebody says behind us, and we all turn around. There's the most peculiar-looking character standing in front of us. You can't tell for certain if it's male or female—a girl, I guess, but I'm not really sure. Her head's shaved bald and she's got a ring through her lower lip. No more than sixteen, she's wearing filthy blue jeans and a loose-fitting woollen thing that might have started out as a dress or a sweater or a thermal undershirt. She seems oblivious to how hot the day is. But she's got a goofy smile about ten miles wide and you have to like her right off.

"What was that?" Caitlin says.

"The health inspectors, they show up yesterday afternoon to check the camp out, see if we're up to standards or something. Well, you shoulda seen them, two guys so fat they can hardly get out of their car. Then they smoke cigarettes the whole time they're here. One guy's hacking so much he can't hardly talk. Then they tell us at the end we aren't perfect but they'll turn a blind eye. It was the funniest thing."

She gives us directions where to park the truck, where to pitch our tents, how the camp kitchen works and all that, then off she goes.

We wander up the road a bit, looking around. Waddy's staring at everything like he was in Timbuktu or someplace.

"What a godawfully desolate place," Elvira says.

It looks pretty grim all right. An old logging road runs about a hundred metres from the front gate at the highway up to the camp kitchen. The road's lined on both sides with vehicles—battered old vans and campers mostly, some trailers and a couple of ancient school buses. Radical bumper stickers abound. Some of the old wrecks look like they were at Woodstock twenty-five years ago and have limped across the continent to find a final tribal resting ground.

"Jesus, Blackie'd have a ball with all these old wrecks, eh?" Waddy says. "Elvira, we shoulda dragged your old wagon along. Fit right in here." Of all of us, Waddy seems best adapted to the bedlam of the camp.

There's tents and tipis and makeshift shelters pitched everywhere between the vehicles. Beyond the vans and tents, on either side of the road, the clearcut stretches unbroken, a vast landscape of charred logging debris. Huge tree stumps sprawl like the severed hands of thieves, their fingernails still clawing at dirt and rock. Scrubby willows and red cedar saplings push up gamely here and there among the heaps of blackened debris. Back beyond, a row of mountains looms over the camp like heaped enormous corpses. The slopes have been clearcut from top to bottom. You can see the scars of logging roads and rockslides etched across the mountains.

There's a look of dismay on Caitlin's face as she stares up at the ravaged hillsides. I touch her elbow, to hint at reassurance.

"No matter how often you see this sort of butchery," she says, "it's always just as horrifying the next time, isn't it?"

"It's not a pretty sight, no question," I say.

"So you see why we had to come, J.J.? Why it was important that we all come together?"

I don't see any such thing, but it seems churlish to say so just now.

The road ends at a large circular pavillion, open on all sides. Stout poles lashed with rope hold up a conical roof made from an old parachute stretched over fish net. Inside, the remains of another smoky fire smoulder in a rock firepit in the centre of the circle. Rough wooden benches and bales of straw line the circumference. The ground's covered with straw, old blankets, and sleeping bags. Shaved and woolly heads of sleepers protrude from their cocoon wrappings. A pair of young mongrel dogs cavort in the straw, testing their new teeth on one another. There's several small children, stark naked, tumbling about. Two scruffy musicians sit in lotus position on the straw making desultory music, one thumping a native drum, the other playing a bamboo flute. Across the way a dog lifts its leg and urinates on a Cowichan sweater left draped across a bench.

"Jesus Christ!" Waddy says, shaking his little walnut head. "This is the bunch that's gonna kick company butt?"

Beyond the pavillion, across an open space, there's a rough wooden stage. A small group of people is sitting in a circle on the stage floor listening to a grey-haired woman speaking. Off to the right there's a large covered kitchen area. Half a dozen people are at work slicing vegetables at a big central counter, laughing and chattering together. A barrel-chested character in the corner is belting out selections from *Il Trovatore* in a quite passable tenor. "The Selection Cut Cafe," says a crudely lettered sign nailed up at the kitchen entrance.

I'm feeling a familiar discomfort with all of this, a sense of not belonging here and not particularly wanting to belong. I was never one for adolescent rebellion. Never played at being a hippie. While everyone else was, at least according to *Newsweek*, going to San Francisco with flowers in their hair, I'd already been accepted by the Brothers of Blessed Columkille the Lesser and wasn't going anywhere. No flowers, no hair, no nonsense. I was mortifying the flesh, not indulging it. For all those years, each afternoon before Vespers we brothers would gather in the chapel, lift our habits, and lash our buttocks with a flagellatum. Now I look at these footloose youths roaming the globe and think what might have been for myself but never will. The passionate affairs of youth. Not my affairs then, and surely not now.

We wander back down the road. People are coming and going constantly. There's new people arriving, nudging their cars in here and there, pitching tents wherever they can. Four young backpackers come striding past us, terribly hearty and outdoorsy looking, talking among themselves in animated German. A group of natives are banging on drums and chanting outside a tipi. A brace of Buddhist monks in vivid saffron robes drift past like clouds. Amazingly, the place is already feeling less oppressive to me. There's a buzz of excitement with people coming and going. It's all very young, very international.

"It really does feel like an outpost of community, doesn't it?" Elvira says. "Even in this godawful clearcut."

Then who do we spot coming up the road but Peewee and Julia Overstall in their Tilley hats and cottons. We all hail one another like long-lost comrades.

They've parked their van in an out-of-the-way corner where there's room for us too, so we decide to get our camp set up. We pitch two small dome tents side by side. Elvira and Caitlin will sleep in one, Waddy and I in the other.

"You snore?" Waddy asks me as we're unrolling our sleeping bags.

"Not that I know of," I say, "but there's never anyone else around to tell me."

"Can't stand a snorer," Waddy warns. "Had a guy up in camp once, Zelnick his name was or somethin' like that, Jewish guy, wouldn't eat ham and eggs if he was starvin', but by Jesus he could snore! Bunked with him once myself. First night I wake up and I think there's a goddamn tsunami comin' up the inlet or somethin' there's such a racket goin' on. But it's only old Zelly roarin' away there like a bullmoose in rut. We tried everythin' with him, me and the other guys. Put a clothespeg on his nose. Put a pillow over his head. Tried liquor'n him up, but that only made it worse. Finally, we all walk out on wildcat. Yes sir, we says to hell with it, we ain't bustin' our balls all friggin' day and then layin' there listenin' to Zelly saw wood all friggin' night too. They couldn't fire him 'cause he was the best goddamn steam engineer on the coast, fix a busted donkey so fast you didn't have time to scratch your ass. So they give him his own bunkhouse instead, all to himself. Zelly's rowdydow we used to call it. Haw, haw, good old Zelly. Wonder what ever happened to him?"

It's getting on close to suppertime, and I need to relieve myself first. I make my way over to one of the pit privies—there are four or five of them scattered around in the clearcuts. I make sure it's not in use, then walk up to the privy. Good God! I can't believe it. You couldn't dignify the thing with a word like primitive. Even to call it a privy is a cruel joke, because there's nothing private about it. It consists of a rough plank seat with a hole cut in the planks and an old wooden toilet seat attached. At each corner, a vertical two-by-four sticks up in the air about five feet, with an old sheet loosely draped as a screen around the sides and back. The front's completely open. I peek in. The pit underneath is more like a pothole overflowing with excrement. A wave of nausea and revulsion sweeps over me. But, face it, there are no alternatives.

I don't have a problem with excrement the way some people do, but I like my privacy. I'm sure it comes from growing up in that wretched little apartment on Jane Street. It had only one bathroom, immediately adjacent to the kitchen. The flimsy wall between concealed nothing. You shared your sounds and scents with anyone who happened to be home. The monastery of Blessed Columkille the Lesser was worse. It had washrooms with long rows of toilet cubicles directly across from long rows of sinks and mirrors. The cubicles had no doors, presumably so the brothers would not be seduced by any untoward temptations of the flesh. Brothers washing and shaving and brushing their teeth were free to behold, reflected in the big mirrors, other brothers defecating in the cubicles. I wonder now that I lasted all those years.

I look around to make sure no one's nearby. I check that there's tissue at hand, which there is, and hasten about my business. Despite my briskness, before I'm done I hear someone approaching. I cough loudly to warn them off. Then, my God, a young woman emerges from behind a willow thicket and stands there almost right in front of me. She's decked out in fringed leather, beads and feathers, long blonde hair, the complete advertising copy. I freeze in panic. She smiles at me like a pre-Raphaelite angel and strikes a small Tibetan bell she's carrying. The bell tinkles as though calling us to prayer. I sit there, pants down, like a perfect fool on my makeshift throne. She smiles at me again and disappears behind a stump.

This is too much for me. I want to be home. I don't want to be in this wretched gypsy camp, I wish I'd never listened to Caitlin and the rest of them, that I'd never heard about Mistral Wind. (And where is she, anyway, after all her big talk? The fake.) I hate being manipulated and taken for a fool. To hell with it! I want to shout and flee this crazy place.

"Something wrong, Joseph?" Elvira asks me when I get back to our camp, but I'm too grumpy to talk about it. I can feel Caitlin watching me. What are they whispering about me, I wonder.

Things pick up a bit at supper. There must be two hundred people come crowding in from God knows where when the dinner gong rings. We form a long queue two abreast and inch our way towards the kitchen. There's talking and hailing and hugging going on everywhere you look. Mongrel dogs slink about looking for scraps. Kitchen volunteers dish up food from huge pots. Several different salads, a curried rice, tofu in peanut sauce, several other dishes I don't even know.

"Great food," Peewee says, after we've all settled together on a couple of big logs. And it is. Unbelievably good. My spirits begin to lift. Looking around I have a sense of what Elvira said earlier, that this really is a pretty remarkable gathering. There's all sorts of nuts in this bowl, all ages and sizes and persuasions, raging grannies and aging hippies, crazy characters in oddball outfits, sweet young things who look too tender for the cruel blows of this wicked world. I don't imagine there are any stockbrokers around, or commodity traders, or any others whose careers depend on keeping their mouths shut and their heads down. I try to imagine my father here and can't. The Brothers of Blessed Columkille the Lesser? I don't think so. I begin to actually appreciate the place, weird as it is. I begin feeling a bizarre sense of camaraderie with this lunatic fringe.

After supper, most of us reconvene for the evening planning session. We sit in large concentric circles in the pavillion. Our purpose is to plan the next morning's blockade. Two young women from the Friends of Kumquat Sound facilitate the planning session. It actually goes remarkably smoothly, considering there's two hundred people at it.

One man stands up, sort of a working-class guy who maybe does carpentry or drives a cement truck or something, and says he wants to raise the Canadian flag at the protest and sing "O Canada." He's even brought along a big Canadian flag on a pole. "We're standin' up for our country here, that's what we're doing," the fellow says. He's really passionate about it.

But a young guy with Rastafarian dreadlocks and a Sally Ann designer outfit, pops up and says he doesn't believe in flags or countries or national borders or any of that crap. "This is one world," he says, "and all that nationalist flagwaving bullshit is just to keep the masses distracted while the power brokers go on about their business."

I expect this firebrand speech to be greeted with a lusty round of cheers and applause, but instead all these little fingers start flicking in the air in dead silence. The facilitators explain to us newcomers that this is dingling. You demonstrate approval by raising your hand, with fingers and thumb closed, except for your pinkie finger, which you stick up in the air and then flick up and down. This is dingling. Overwhelming approval is signified by dingling with two pinkies.

"You got that, Waddy?" I whisper to the old guy, and he gives me a glower miles beneath contempt. I'd pay money to see Waddy dingle. I get a sharp poke in the ribs from Caitlin, on my other side.

The discussion soon degenerates into a protracted debate on the problem of nation states and whether or not government isn't the root of all evil, whether anarchy isn't the answer. "I haven't heard this sort of cant since university," Caitlin whispers in my ear. "Those interminable debates with campus Trotskyites and Maoists spitting at each other while everybody else nods off with boredom."

On and on it goes, brash young men mostly, standing firm on convictions set in concrete. Dingling dwindles. Once again I'm wishing I was home in bed with a glass of brandy and a good book. Then, all of a sudden, the place is electrified. The whole group falls silent. We all look in one direction. A rush of elation sweeps across the crowd, like a night wind rising.

"Jesus Christ Almighty!" Waddy exclaims out loud. And there, by the flickering light of the fire, we see a solitary figure standing apart— with a great bear's head on its shoulders! Several of the people closest to it cower back. The savage face of the bear seems real, alive, about to snarl in anger. Its eyes and exposed teeth gleam. The figure begins to sway and twist in the firelight, dancing through shadows. Is it real or not? Alive or not? We sit, two hundred of us in concentric circles, dumbfounded by the bizarre apparition. I notice the figure's dressed entirely in black leather—surely it's Zyrk, it must be. But before I can be certain, it slips away, back into the dark, leaving all of us bewildered.

11

The magic of the apparition soon wears off. The strange surge of elation it stirred in us dies away, almost as quickly as it arose. As we've known all along, Zyrk's an anomaly, a lonesome cowboy. Only fools would pin their hopes to an evanescent character like him.

We've heard there's been trouble at the camp the last few weeks; they've had yahoos busting in at night, vandalizing equipment and threatening people. Security's been beefed up. They say they need volunteers to help with night security. Waddy volunteers right off. "Can't sleep in a nuthouse like this anyways," he mutters to me. "Be worse than havin' old Zelly along."

Then Elvira says she'll take a shift too, later in the night. Each crew has four or five volunteers responsible for a two-hour shift. It's about the last thing in the world I want to do, sit around in the middle of the night waiting for trouble to happen, but after Elvira's volunteered I feel I can hardly refuse. So I volunteer for the shift after hers. Waddy's on eleven till one, Elvira one till three, and me three till five. After that we'll go up to the blockade and get arrested. Terrific.

It's cold and dark and everyone's tired. We trudge back to our tents.

"What do you think Zyrk's up to?" I ask Caitlin as we walk down the road together.

"I don't know," she says. "I don't know what's going on here."

"What do you mean?"

"Well, Zyrk for one thing. Plus there's no sign of Mistral, and nobody here seems ever to have heard of her. That's very strange. I'd thought from how she talked she was one of the main camp organizers."

"Very interesting," I say. Feeling a secret sudden puff of satisfaction that Mistral is falling from grace. Atop this new vantage point I can admit to myself that I was jealous of the influence that charismatic charlatan was having on Caitlin. Exploiting her romanticism the same as that wretched pedalling poet.

"Do you think we should still go ahead tomorrow?" I see a small glimmer of hope for avoiding the hopeless complications of getting arrested. "I mean, we could call the whole thing off. We've done our bit just by being here."

"Have we?" Caitlin says, distracted. "I can't shake off these dark premonitions I keep having, this awful sense of being stalked and watched. I sense it all around us, as though we've pitched our tents and cast a small circle in the middle of a dark and savage land."

We've arrived at our tents. A pale light shines from Peewee and Julia's van. They must be reading in bed. Elvira's shuffling around in her tent with a pallid flashlight. Waddy's gone down to the gate to begin his watch. I don't want to leave Caitlin.

"I'm sure it'll be all right," I say, attempting to be reassuring but managing to sound trite. The way you tell open-heart surgery survivors that they'll be up playing tennis in no time. Why not say: You look like hell, lying there in bed with your chest torn open and tubes up your nose. Why not say to Caitlin: This is ridiculous. This entire thing is so ill-conceived and banal, I don't believe it. The only reason I'm here is because you cajoled me into coming along, and now you're telling me you're not sure what's going on and you're getting ominous premonitions? Let's just go home and get on with our lives!

But I don't. I connive at being agreeable. Contrive amiable lies to maintain peace and good order.

Still, I know exactly what Caitlin's talking about. I can smell malignant vapours in the air here, smouldering among the burnt corpses of the trees. Hear vicious creatures scuttling in the dark all about us.

"There'll be a moon tonight," Caitlin says. "Full moon. It should rise soon."

"Yes," I say, still lingering. There's silver light in the eastern sky already.

"Good night then," Caitlin says, leaning forward and softly brushing my cheek with her lips. I feel an awful need to do what I've never dared do before—to take her in my arms and hold her against me. But I don't. Any more than I say what I really believe about this mad venture we're on. I dance in the wind like a sapling, bent this way and that.

"Good night, Caitlin." I watch as she disappears inside her tent.

I bed down and try to sleep. A vague dread of tomorrow morning besets me. Davey Rushing appears like Marley's ghost to warn me again about not tangling with "the man." I replay the scuttlebutt that was making the rounds on Upshot before we left. About getting a criminal record and how it would mean that you couldn't get travel visas, or get bonded for certain jobs. A lawyer had told somebody that all arrestees would be vulnerable to a civil suit from the company, that we could lose our homes and life savings. That we're putting ourselves at enormous personal risk. And for what? As Davey said, they were going to get the timber one way or the other; nothing we could do was going to stop that. "Best to leave the civil disobedience shtick to kids who don't own anything yet," Davey said. These were the words of my childhood, the well-worn cautions that I'd lapped like mother's milk. The common sense of protecting one's own best interests.

I drift away in a thickening mist of anxiety, vaguely hearing horn noises wailing through my sleep like faraway freight trains, then cries and voices, then nothing at all.

Next thing, I'm jolted awake by something shuffling and growling around the tent. Oh, Christ, it's a bear! I think, but then the front zipper opens with a ripping sound, and Waddy pushes his head in like a snapping turtle poking out of its shell. Moonlight washes everything in spectral light.

"Buncha peckerheads," Waddy grunts, climbing inside on all fours.

"Waddy, what's going on?" I whisper, sitting up. "Is there trouble?" My mummy bag's twisted all around me so I can hardly move my legs.

Waddy's inside by now. He fumbles with the tent zipper and kicks off his Romeos so they hit the side of the tent.

"What's the matter?" I whisper, adrenalin pumping, wide awake. "What happened?"

"Call themselves loggers," Waddy snarls. Boy, he's growlier than I've ever seen him, and that's saying something with Waddy. "Them asswipes wouldn't know real loggin' if it grabbed 'em by the balls and squeezed."

"Who're you talking about?"

"Buncha assholes down on the road just now." Waddy's breathing fire and brimstone.

"What happened?"

"How many of them pansyfuckers you think ever went up a big

Doug-fir on spurs, two hundred feet up, and knocked the crown off for a spar and sat there while she heaved back and forth in the sky? Eh? Loggers, bullshit! All them losers know is pushin' buttons and kissin' company ass!"

Waddy's getting himself really worked up. Plus he's working his chaw like crazy. I need to know what the hell's going on.

"What did they do?"

"Yah, they come bustin' up to the camp gate there, two or three truckloads of 'em, lookin' for a fight. Pissed, o'course, only way they could get up the gumption. Up they come, and I see they all got baseball bats or axe handles. Comin' to pick on a buncha women and kids, in the middle of the night, and they gotta have clubs. Buncha fuckin' losers."

"What did you do?"

"I say to 'em straight out: 'What d'you assholes think yer doin'?' 'Course they're too pissed to know the difference. Then they start pickin' up rocks off the side of the road and throwin' 'em at us. Grown men throwin' rocks at people and thinkin' they're tough guys. Jesus, it got my goat."

Waddy lets a hawker go and I hear it hit the bottom of a tobacco can he carries for a spittoon. I can see him by moonlight, shaking his head and chewing the whole time.

"Then one of the rocks hits this young gal who's with us, hardly more'n a baby, caught her right on the shoulder, rock as big as a baseball. Well, that was it for me. I skedaddle back up to my truck, y'know it's parked just over here a bit, and I get my shotgun outta the rack. I pop in a coupla slugs, scattershot y'know, and head back down to the ruckus. I didn't aim to really hurt anyone, but I figure I'll give 'em a warning shot over their heads and then a blast of buckshot up the ass when they cut and run."

"You didn't, did you?" I'm sure I would've been wakened by gunshot that close.

"Nah. Before I get halfway back, three of them camp people stop me. Say there's no guns allowed in camp. Say it's against their code of non-violence. Well, it's against mine too, I tell 'em, but I'm willing to make an exception fer them assholes down there. Nope, they say, wouldn't have it a'tall. Stayed after me till I unloaded my shotgun and put it back in the truck and promised not to bring it out again."

"Probably wise," I say, thinking to myself thank Christ Waddy didn't blast anybody. Just what every peace camp needs, somebody getting shot. "Then what happened?"

"Them yahoos are still throwin' rocks and carryin' on down at the gate. Pretty soon they run outta rocks and then they just yell a lot. Well, them peacekeepers—that's what they call 'em, them camp people who've taken special training in all this non-violence shit—they just keep talkin' and tryin' to cool things down. 'Course they might as well have been talkin' to the bloody stumps, these assholes are that thick. Gotta admire those camp kids though, ignorin' all that abuse and stayin' at it. I kinda faded into the background, but I tell ya my finger was itchin' the whole time."

"Didn't anybody call the cops?"

"Ffah, bloody cops," Waddy snorts with disgust. " 'Course they called 'em right off. Eventually they show up, took their sweet goddamn time about it too, almost two hours to get here from five miles away. 'Course these cops here are right in the company's pocket, just like the yahoos. Plain as fuckin' pancakes. They don't even pretend they ain't holdin' hands with the goddamn company."

Waddy's into his sleeping bag by now. He's made a pillow from his old down vest and punches it several times before he lies down. His breath is coming in little wheezing grunts. Finally he spits his chaw into the tobacco can. I was wondering if he kept it in all night.

"Cops arrest them or what?"

"You gotta be kiddin'," Waddy says, his wizened face staring up into the moonlight like a corpse drained of its blood. I see his Adam's apple moving back and forth in his scrawny throat like a subcutaneous creature. "Cops didn't do fuck all. Just give them turkeys a free ride home."

"You think it'll be all right? I mean, Elvira's on the next shift, isn't she?"

"Uh huh. I just woke her up, like we arranged. Should be down at the gate by now."

"You don't think those yahoos will show up again?"

"Nah, I think the cops got at least enough moxy to keep 'em away for the rest of the night. Now shaddup and let me go to sleep."

The old guy rolls over so his back's to me, then he turns over again. "Know what?" he asks me.

"Huh?"

"I still wish I'd given them turkeys a load of buckshot up the ass. G'night."

⸻ ❀ ⸻ *12* ⸻ ❀ ⸻

Within minutes Waddy's snoring away like an old dog beside a fire. I lie there in the tent, awake. I don't like any of this. Cops, thugs, shotguns. All of it provokes in me a horrid feeling of anxiety. Nor do I like the idea of Elvira Stone being down at the gate, even though there's others there too, not if a bunch of drunken bozos could show up any minute.

I certainly can't sleep with all this going on. I may as well get up and go keep Elvira company. I shimmy out of my sleeping bag, shocked at how cold the night air is. I put on the warmest clothes I've brought, and slip out of the tent. Waddy's snoring away, oblivious.

Outside the tent, the moonlight is doubly bright. A full moon high in a cloudless sky, the whole landscape shimmering in silvery light. Not a soul moving anywhere. I pause for a moment beside the tents. I'm suddenly conscious of Caitlin, sleeping in the other tent. I feel a troubling urge, resist, succumb to it. I gently unzip the front of her tent and peer in through the opening, holding my breath, knowing this is wrong. I can hear her light breathing, I can smell the vivid scent of her inside the little tent. Every molecule in my body pulls towards her, as the ocean waters are now being pulled towards the moon. I swallow hard. There is a terror here for me, a feeling like the terror of the confessional. Against the tide, I pull back from the tent and gently reclose the zipper. I shall go see Elvira Stone.

The night air is cool and damp, and the night itself eerily silent. Walking down the road alone I wish again that I was at home, that I might be walking in my gardens at this very moment, smelling the night fragrances of late summer, glimpsing the silver ghosts that moonlight makes of plants.

I find Elvira and the others huddled around a small fire at the entrance to the camp.

"Hello, Joseph," Elvira smiles warmly. "What brings you down here already?"

"Couldn't sleep. Waddy woke me up coming in. He told me about the troublemakers. Then he went right to sleep, the old bugger, and of course I couldn't sleep any more for worrying. I figured I may as well get up and do something useful as lie there fretting."

"Waddy told me the peacekeepers did a real good job handling the troublemakers," Elvira sips tea from a large mug, "and the Mounties finally took them away. Seems like everything's settled down for the night."

"I sure hope so," I say. "Is there more of that tea?"

"I'll make you some"—it's the young woman who greeted us when we arrived. She's wrapped herself in a blanket against the night air. Her bald head shines in the moonlight.

"Thanks," I say. "My name's Joseph, what's yours?"

"Starstream," she says, fumbling with the kettle on the fire. Her blanket's dangling perilously close to the flames. My avuncular streak wants to give her practical lessons in life. She makes camomile tea in a big cracked pot.

There's three others in the group: another young woman who seems immensely shy and sad and sits staring into the fire, and two young guys. One of them's from Newfoundland, he tells us, the other from Quebec. The Newfie's strumming a battered guitar and singing a Sarah McLachlan song.

Just then a big truck roars past us on the highway blaring its airhorn full blast. Nobody pays any attention.

"They try to keep everyone awake all night, the truckers," Starstream says, handing me a mug of steaming tea.

"How long have you been in camp?" I ask her.

"Oh, since the beginning, since June."

"You've been here three months?" I've barely lasted my first night.

"Uh huh. Been great. Never thought it'd take off like this though, keeps gettin' bigger all the time. Front page of the *New York Times* last week. It's awesome."

"I bet. Thanks for the tea."

"Sure." She gives me a goofy grin.

"Lord, I had a time getting up again tonight," Elvira says. "It was so nice in that little tent with Caitlin. I've got my foamie in there and my down comforter and I was as cozy as a coddling moth. I was fast asleep, one of those sleeps where you're way down in the depths, but someone was tapping somewhere. I was having a dream, and at first the sound seemed to be part of the dream. Somehow I thought it was Freddie tapping a message to me, but then I realized I was awake and where I was, and that it was Waddy knocking on the tent, waking me up for my shift. But Lord it was cold when I climbed out from under my comforter."

"I don't believe how cold it gets here at night," I say, "after such hot days."

"So Waddy tells me about the yahoos who came in," Elvira says, "though I was still so woozy I didn't register too much about it. I'm so glad Waddy didn't do anything rash."

"It wasn't for lack of trying," I respond. "Thank God those kids intercepted him."

Elvira nods, and I'm conscious of it perhaps being unfair to call these people kids; what they've been doing at this camp for the past few months may be a bit odd, a bit naive, but it's far from childish. They've been doing things I'm scared to do myself.

"I said good night to Waddy," Elvira continues, "and I walked down the road. But I was still half asleep—you know that funny state when you've come out of a dream in a strange place in the middle of the night. What with the full moon and the sky so clear and full of stars, the whole landscape lit up by moonlight. Even these clearcuts look beautiful, don't they?"

"Amazingly, they do," I agree.

"It's funny," Elvira goes on, "I stopped partway down the road and gazed up into the sky. There was a light moving up there. It looked like a satellite or a very high plane, except it didn't move in a straight line. It would kind of dart quickly in one direction, then it seemed to be stationary a while, then dart another way. I know your eyes can play tricks on you, especially when you've been in the dream world; still it made me think about Freddie. Was he really out among the stars on some fantastic adventure, or was I just being completely stupid? I couldn't tell. The night's so cold and bright and very clear, I was thinking, but my mind's not clear at all. The dream was still with me. It still is." Elvira smiles and falls silent, musing.

Starstream's kneeling near Elvira's feet, not saying anything.

"Hmm," I say at last. It's always hard to know what to say to Elvira about Freddie. I'm as unsure about it as she is. Rationally, I don't really believe that alien spaceships swoop down on earth and snatch up humans in trucks. Every other part of me believes as Elvira does.

I sip my camomile tea, which goes down warm and soothing. There's something intrinsically fine about sitting around a campfire late at night in new surroundings, talking to strangers. I feel for a moment as though we could be pilgrims, wayfarers along one of the ancient trade routes through the desert, camped with fellow travellers. Then another truck comes roaring by, horn blaring, the driver screaming obscenities at us, bringing me back to that place.

We stay very calm. The French lad feeds the fire, sending a little shower of sparks into the sky. Starstream pours us more tea and we chat quietly about various matters while the Newfie strums his guitar and hums ethereal tunes.

I'm feeling in a drowsy altered state from being up so late in this strange place. It is an atmosphere conducive to disclosure, and even in my general haziness, I have a peculiar clarity of mind about certain things.

"Elvira," I say to my friend quietly, "I'm feeling very topsy-turvy about Caitlin."

"I know." Elvira smiles with the warmth that makes it possible for me to confide in her as in no one else. "I know it's not simple for you, and not as easy as it seems to be for others. But it's who you are, and who she is, and there's no way of getting around it."

"I'm drawn to her tremendously," I admit, staring into the fire, watching blue-green flames flicker among the glowing embers. "But somehow I can't trust her completely. I can't let myself go."

"What holds you back?"

What does, I wonder. "I think I have a fear of her devouring me in some way."

"You don't trust her? Her goodness of heart?"

"In most things I do. But not this. No, I don't. It's as though my instinct for self-preservation won't accept . . ."

I'm interrupted by a terrifying scream from back up towards the camp. Screaming and shouting. The French boy's on his feet in an instant. "You, you, and you, stay here," he says, pointing to Starstream, the Newfie, and the sad young woman, "and would you please come with me?" to Elvira and me. He speaks with a thick French accent, probably a student, but he seems to know exactly what to do. Incongruously, Starstream pulls a two-way radio out from under her blanket and calls back up to the camp. The screaming and shouting grow louder, urgent and terrifying.

We scurry together, the three of us, back up the road. The screaming scratches the night like tomcats fighting in a midnight alley. I have an awful feeling that a woman's being raped or brutalized, that's what the shrieking sounds like, a scream that goes scraping right down your spine. Angry male voices ricochet like rocks against the screaming. We hurry up the road, and I can see flashlight beams flickering around over in the clearcut to the left. It's where a group of women have their tents pitched; they call it Amazonia. The screaming's coming from that direction.

We pick up a little trail that leads in there through the logging slash. The French guy's got a powerful flashlight, but the moonlight's so bright you can see your way without assistance. I can make out a few other people hurrying down the logging road from the main camp, and back at the camp kitchen a fire is flaring and lights are blinking on.

The screaming is now unbearable.

We get to where all the commotion is. There's about a dozen ruffians there, young guys carrying baseball bats and lengths of heavy chain, standing around the tents.

"Douche bag!" one of them shouts at Elvira as we come up. "Fuckin' douche bag!"

A flash of rage flames up inside me. How dare these people speak to Elvira that way! My body's rigid with rage and fear together. Fists clenched. We stand immobilized for a moment, not knowing what to do.

There's a cluster of young women, girls really, huddled together and one of them—she's Oriental, Japanese I think—is screaming hysterically. The others are holding her and trying to calm her down. The rowdies are sniggering and taunting the girls. We don't know what to do, the three of us, bursting in, we just kind of freeze there.

I'm feeling more scared than I've ever felt before, but also this rage flaming up inside me.

"Well, looky here," one of the troublemakers says, a big fellow with a scrawny beard and a beer belly, "if it ain't the rescue squad!" The

whole bunch of them guffaw and start moving towards us, some bran-
dishing their bats, some dangling short lengths of heavy chain. The
French guy steps forward then and asks them what they're doing. They
all burst out laughing and jeering.

"The question is, what are you doin' here, frog," one of them says,
sticking his face right up against the French boy's face. "Why don't you
go back to fuckin' Quebec and separate if you don't like the way we do
things here?"

I know I should do something, take charge of the situation somehow. But I can't get a word out, I'm that frightened. The violence
silences me. Beside me, I see Elvira's face taut with emotion.

The Japanese girl's still sobbing hysterically, and two of the others
try to lead her away from the scene, but a couple of the punks block
their way.

"Hey, gals," one of them says, leering horribly, "you ain't leavin'
already, are ya? Hey, chinky, don't go yet, the party's just beginning."

Several peacekeepers arrive from the camp, and they try to talk the
hooligans into just calming down and going home. The one big guy's
still face to face with the French boy, daring him to move, swinging a
length of chain the whole time.

They're too drunk to listen to anything that's being said to them.
One of them pushes his bat into a peacekeeper's face, trying to provoke
him. Then another guy puts his great filthy hands on one girl's shoulders and starts moving them down towards her breasts. She tries to pull
away, but he squeezes her shoulders and keeps her there.

"Whatsa matter, honey?" he slobbers at her. "You rather hug trees
than a real man?" and all the rest of them laugh.

I can see how terrified the girl is. Elvira takes a step forward. "That's
enough," she says.

"Fuck you, you old douche bag!" the fellow snarls at her.

I know something awful's going to happen any second, that somebody's going to snap and all hell will break loose. I have to speak, I
know it, I have to stop this somehow, and just as the tension seems
absolutely unbearable and I start to say something, suddenly I look sideways and there stands Mistral Wind.

I didn't see or hear her come up. I don't know where she's come
from or how she got here, but instantly here she is, standing on top of a
big tree stump, six or seven feet up in the air. She's dressed all in white

or silver, gossamer stuff, it looks like. It billows out, and her raven-black hair flows out too, though I swear there isn't a breath of wind.

Silence stuns the group. We all stand there, absurdly, wax figures in some bizarre diorama.

Mistral stands above us, her legs spread wide apart, her bare feet gripping the edge of the stump, as though she were about to leap. She extends her arms up into the night sky, into the moonlight and stars. She throws her head back and begins to keen. A terrible, mournful, eerie keening.

I can't believe any of this is really happening. The hoodlums just stare at her, dumbfounded. They jostle around nervously and try to taunt her, the way they've been taunting us, but there's something terrible and frightening about her, even their sodden brains can see it. The fantastical look of her, the awful sound of her wailing. Her voice soars up above their noise. High and wild it rings, I've never heard anything like it. I can feel a cold shiver running up and down my spine. I'm trembling, mesmerized. I see Elvira's face lit up with an unearthly light. Moonlight and more.

Mistral looks enormous up there on the stump, bigger than life-size. Her calves and thighs ripple with muscles, and her bare arms rise like the sinuous limbs of a winter oak high into the night sky. As her wild keening grows louder and louder, it begins to echo back across the clearing from the sidehills. I hear something else in her crying. The sounds of many voices, thousands of people lamenting, all the women raped and men murdered in brutal wars. The innocents of the ages who've suffered and died at the hands of violent men.

Still Mistral sustains her eerie dirge, her voice rising and rising towards the stars. I hear the same sound echoing back to us from the camp. I hear nightbirds crying out too, and wolves howling from the hills, I'm sure of it. I lose place and time completely. The mangled stumps of trees in the clearcut rise up like corpses on the day of the dead, joining in the terrible lament rising from all the earth, crying to heaven. Elvira's beside me, taking my hand, tears streaming down her face, and she's keening too, wailing with all the ancestral sadness in her soul. Something gives way in me, something so deeply buried I've never felt it before. It lets go, a logjam breaking apart, and I too start crying, sobbing, losing myself entirely.

I have no idea how long this goes on, I'm lost to time. I'm dimly aware at some point of the troublemakers all slinking away, still swearing disheartedly. In the end there's nothing left but Mistral on that stump, Mistral and her mournful lament. Like something out of a dream. I stagger back to the tents, still holding Elvira's hand. Tears stream down her face and down mine too. We hug one another, clinging tight, and whisper good night. I crawl into the tent and into my sleeping bag, vaguely conscious of Waddy's snore. I fall instantly into exhausted sleep, into fantastical dreams, the haunting sound of Mistral's lamentation still ringing in my blood.

13

I awake before dawn to a strange sound. I am in the monastery, rising in the predawn darkness with my fellow brothers to go chant the holy office of Matins and Lauds. No, I'm not, I'm not there any more, I live on Upshot Island now. Dimly, I make out the tent walls close around me in the dark, hear Waddy snuffling into wakefulness beside me. Ah, yes! Kumquat.

I've been dreaming, vivid, crazy dreams. Caitlin was in them, and Mistral Wind, and dozens of other people. Did I dream an attack on the camp last night? Mistral keening? Was that real, or part of the dreaming? I missed doing my shift at camp security last night. Or did I?

"Goddamn worst night's sleep I ever had," Waddy growls, sitting up in his sleeping bag, scratching himself all over, like he's got fleas. "Hardly slept a'tall."

"That's funny," I say, my mind clarifying rapidly where we are and what we're about today, "because you were snoring like a hibernating grizzly all night."

"Horseshit," Waddy says. "Where's my goddamn Romeos? I gotta take a leak."

Waddy climbs out of his bag. He's wearing long johns that look older than he is, greyer than an old dog's blanket. He fumbles with his boots and makes his way out of the tent. Moments later, I hear the splash of him urinating close by.

All around there are sounds of people rising and getting organized. People stumbling into a dark morning. Somebody's playing a flute. Somebody's laughing. Coming out, I feel the night air's bite and I bundle up against it. The moon has disappeared. Flashlight beams slice the darkness like lasers, dart about all over camp.

Caitlin emerges from her tent looking cross and dishevelled, electrified wild hair all over the place. She ignores me. Elvira crawls out behind.

"Morning, Brother Joseph," Elvira says. "How are you?"

"Confused," I say, "and tired."

"Me too." Elvira grins like a kid. "My poor back's killing me. I think we're getting a bit long in the tooth for camping out. They've got the right idea," nodding towards Peewee and Julia's van. There're lights on inside, curtains drawn. You can hear faint music coming from the van. Mozart.

"That really happen last night?" I ask Elvira.

"Oh, yes," she says, "nothing ever more real."

"Need a goddamn cup a coffee, straight off," Waddy interrupts, coming out, hitching up his overalls. "I'm as snarly as a sasquatch if I don't get my mornin' coffee."

"You're as snarly as a sasquatch whether you do or don't," Elvira laughs. "They say there'll be coffee up at the blockade."

"Better be," Waddy says, zipping up his vest.

Caitlin's over by the edge of the circle, brushing her hair distractedly and staring off into the dark. Elvira catches my eye and nods in her direction.

"Good morning," I say, coming up to Caitlin. "How're you feeling?"

She looks at me hazily, almost as though she doesn't recognize me, then smiles lamely. "Sorry. I'm bloody hopeless this hour of the morning. What time is it, anyway?"

"About four-thirty."

"Sweet Jesus!" Caitlin says. "No one should get up this early, ever." Her hair's full of hopeless tangles, and she's pulling a hairbrush through it as though she were carding wool.

"Would you like me to do that for you?" I ask.

She peers at me over her shoulder, surprise and amusement flit across her face. I'm even surprised myself.

"That's a chivalrous suggestion, J.J., chivalrous and perhaps a bit reckless, isn't it? A bit like last night?"

"Last night?" So she knows I looked at her in the tent. She was only pretending to be asleep.

"Howling at the moon with half-naked women," she says.

"Oh," relieved. "Elvira told you?"

"She told me some of it. I've no doubts you could tell me more. If you were of a mind to."

What exactly's going on here? I wonder. I'm treading water, looking for something to grasp, something clever to toss back to Caitlin. Luckily Waddy tells us it's time to get going. The four of us pile into his truck, Caitlin and I again squeezed into the crew cab. The plan's to line up along the highway, then follow a lead vehicle up to the bridge where we'll mount our blockade.

We sit on the highway for a while with nothing happening. Waddy's getting itchier by the minute, drumming his fingers on the steering wheel and muttering to himself. Caitlin's staring off through the window into the darkness.

"What about last night, Joseph?" Elvira turns in the front seat to face me. "What did you make of it?"

"I really don't know what to think." I don't want to talk about it. I'm feeling tired and out of sorts and, like Waddy, jittery for a cup of coffee. But I make an effort for Elvira. "I'm still trying to process it. First Zyrk showing up with the bear head and then disappearing again, then Mistral popping up like that. Every time she shows up, things tend to get crazy and unreal."

"I'm so glad Mistral's here," Caitlin says, turning away from the window towards us. "I was beginning to doubt her, to doubt this whole bloody escapade. But having her reappear like that, the way you described it, Elvira, I'm more convinced than ever."

"Convinced?" I ask, disliking this renewed preoccupation with Mistral. Though I must concede that Mistral's performance last night makes it hard to continue discounting her as a charlatan. "Convinced of what?"

Caitlin considers for the briefest moment. "That Mistral and Zyrk are in this together."

Waddy snorts in the driver's seat. Elvira and I look at Caitlin, waiting for her to say more.

"I suspect they've got something in mind for this morning," she says. "I don't know just what, but something."

"Goddamn cup a coffee's what I got in mind," Waddy says, "and if this traffic jam don't get movin' soon, I won't be held accountable for my actions."

Just then, a pickup truck pulls past the line of vehicles, its emergency lights flashing, and we all pull out in single file behind it. We drive, far too slowly for Waddy, in a solemn cavalcade up the highway, dozens and dozens of vans and cars and pickup trucks moving deliberately through the dark.

"It's a marvellous sight, isn't it?" Elvira says. "Like an ancient candlelight procession."

"It makes me feel far braver," I say. "Strength in numbers and all that."

Peewee and Julia are a couple of cars back. The vehicle in front of us is a classic old hippie van, an ancient VW with more rust than paint, plastered with anarchist bumper stickers and reeking with disrespect. I'm feeling better by the minute.

A few miles along, the cavalcade pulls off the highway onto a gravel logging road. We bounce and rattle along the washboard, and you can't see much of anything except car lights ahead and behind and the dust we're kicking up. Dark silhouettes of trees and bushes loom along the road edge, moving as huge dark shadows around us.

We sit quietly, each of us separately preoccupied.

"Do you feel it here, the strangeness?" Caitlin asks after we've bounced along for a bit. She's in a very abstracted mood this morning, not her normal incisive self at all.

"Yes, I do," Elvira says. "It feels just like that time the psychic and I went looking for clues about Freddie, that time up at Dark Creek."

"Yes," Caitlin says. "I'm sure a dark spell has been cast about here. You can feel it all around us, can't you?—a dark malevolence, as though we're being watched and stalked."

Waddy snorts in derision, but Caitlin ignores him.

"There's evil in the world sure enough," Caitlin says, "and for reasons I don't think anyone understands, evil pools in certain places, like drifts of leaves heaped together by a wind, so that humans living in those places will do the vilest, most despicable things and think them normal and acceptable. And who knows why evil pooled so deeply in that place, at that time. Bosnia, Burundi, East Timor."

I think we each know that Caitlin's fears are real, only she's speaking her fears aloud, voicing what we each feel. I can certainly sense a landscape laid waste all about us; malignant forces seem to lurk just beyond the windows, crouching in dark shadows. It takes no great imagination to invest the landscape with the legions of darkness, the servants of the evil one: fallen Lucifer, Asmodeus, Beelzebub. Still we go on. Our cavalcade of light and dust pierces deeper and deeper into the gloom.

"An expeditionary force of angels," Caitlin muses aloud.

"Are you afraid at all?" I ask her.

"Of course I am," she says, lightening up. "I may be a fool for love, but I'm no bloody Joan of Arc."

"Here we are!" Waddy sings out. "Now we'll get some fat into the fire."

We pull into a crowded parking space jammed with vehicles. There are people bustling around in the darkness, building a campfire and setting up banners and signs. A crew erects a huge banner over the road, just before the Nixon River Bridge. We cheer as it goes up, lit by Coleman lanterns. "Kumquat Shall Not Be Clearcut!" the banner reads in large letters. There are a couple of TV crews clattering around with cameras and microphones, and other press people scribbling notes by flashlight and taking flashbulb photos.

We form a big circle on the road, there must be two or three hundred of us in the circle. All sorts of characters and costumes. Some are holding lighted candles. The person standing next to me is disguised completely as a raven, feathered head with a great blunt beak and all. Its arms are feathered as wings, and it flaps them, making guttural raven croaks in its throat. Having the bird-person beside me is, absurdly, reassuring.

One of the camp leaders, a woman who looks too young to be out of junior high, goes over the action we've planned for this morning and the nonviolence code of conduct. How we must treat everyone, including opponents, with complete respect. When she's finished, everybody dingles. The raven person beside me flaps its wings.

An enthusiastic gnome covered in enough rings and feathers and beads to open his own trading post leads us all in a Navaho blessing. His accent is pure Brooklyn.

Over by the firepit, by the flickering light of a fire, I can see Waddy Watts in animated conversation, no doubt concerning coffee.

We sing some songs, rounds and goddess chants, not terribly well, in fact almost as slowly and drearily as the old Tantum Ergo we used to drone away at, my mother and I, attending Benediction in a near-deserted church each Sunday evening of my childhood. As the songs grind on, I'm thinking how weird it is to be standing here, how cold and dark and austere it is out here in a wild forest in the middle of nowhere just before dawn. The whole experience—rising in the dark, the solemn procession of vehicles in single file, our voices raised in sacred song— the whole scene has carried me back to my monastery days. The great bell tolling early in the morning. Stumbling sleepily from our cells down long dark corridors guarded by saints in life-size statue, down to chapel. The abbot rapping on his wooden lectern, we monks rising as one body to intone the solemn chants. Our antiphonal chanting, each side of the chapel answering back and forth, praising the new day, mesmerizing and exhilarating. And here I am now, thousands of miles away from all that, light years away really, chanting at dawn with a group of mad dreamers on this godforsaken logging road.

"And now the monster comes," Caitlin says. She is standing beside me, facing down the road into the darkness, where I can just pick out the distant gleam of headlights. The circle is dissolved, people are running around, calling that the loggers and cops are coming.

Elvira joins us and hands me and Caitlin each a sign. Caitlin's says "Earth First! We'll clearcut the other planets later." Mine says: "Kumquat Forever. Clearcut Never!"

Excitement flashes like sheet lightning across the crowd.

Waddy comes bustling through the crowd towards us. "Jesus Christ," he says to us, "is it time to get busted already? I didn't get my goddamn coffee yet."

Peewee and Julia scuttle up too, looking terribly pleased with themselves. "Look here," Julia bubbles excitedly, and the two of them unfurl an elaborate cloth banner stretched between two tall poles. Against a forest green background, bold red lettering declares UPSHOT ISLAND GARDEN CLUB EXPEDITIONARY FORCE TO KUMQUAT SOUND.

Elvira claps her hands with glee, as Julia and Peewee hoist the banner aloft.

Now the lights of the approaching vehicles are drawing closer, and a man's voice is booming out over a loudspeaker.

"The voice of Moloch!" Caitlin cries aloud. She seems transfixed by the approaching company, as though in a trance. "The minions of the Dark Lord!"

I can't tell whether she's joking or whether she actually sees herself as a Celtic queen leading a ragtag army into battle.

"I fear Caitlin's been reading too much Tolkien," I whisper to Elvira, but she doesn't smile, or acknowledge my jest.

"And here we stand to meet them," Caitlin cries again, "with our banners unfurled, cherubim and seraphim, ready to do battle with the Prince of Darkness!"

I really think Caitlin's gone over the top, but by now the whole scene's kind of frenzied and crazy. Headlights are shining in our faces. There are company men scurrying all over the place with video cameras and walkie-talkies. They stick the video cameras right in our faces, bright lights on the cameras shining blindingly. There are enough cops to break up a Stanley Cup riot.

A company guy climbs up on the back of the lead pickup truck, right in front of us. He fumbles with his microphone and it makes a piercing squeal. He tells us good morning and tries his best to be jovial. Certainly not Beelzebub. More like a kindly but incompetent uncle. He reads the court injunction forbidding anyone to interfere with the logging crews getting to work. We all stand absolutely silent in front of him, as we'd agreed the night before, to listen respectfully, even though we know the injunction deserves no respect at all. Everyone except Waddy, that is.

"Never heard such a piss-poor bit a readin'," Waddy grumbles, close beside us. "You'd think the guy would put some umph into it, bein' his big moment and all. Sounds like he's reading the goddamn telephone book."

We try to ignore Waddy. I'm not entirely confident that Waddy's fully grasped the nonviolence code. The injunction reader's just getting to the end, telling us we'll be arrested and charged if we don't clear the road, when Waddy yells back to him, "Clear your snot pipes!" and we all have to laugh, even the cops and the guy on the truck. All except Caitlin, who's staring ahead with a blazing intensity.

The guy with the big Canadian flag raises it aloft and begins singing "O Canada." We all join in, singing lustily. I've never sung our anthem with such feeling before. The cops look sheepish, not knowing whether to sing or stand at attention or what. We end up singing mightily "O Canada, we stand on guard for trees."

Suddenly the whole crowd breaks into another song about saving Kumquat Sound. The singing grows louder and stronger, there are people clapping, drums beating underneath with a primitive, powerful drumming, flute music over top, fluttering like birds. The song builds and builds, hundreds of people singing ecstatically, I'm singing myself— to hell with it! I'm singing and waving my sign, feeling wilder, crazier than I've ever felt before. People are whirling like dervishes around and around, flaring out from the blockade, weaving past the cops and the company men, swirling around the loggers standing there.

Swept up in the middle of it, I suddenly feel the hair on the back of my neck begin to rise. I start to tremble all over. I'm up near the front of the crowd. From somewhere behind me there comes a dull roaring sound, the way you hear a waterfall from a ways off in the woods, before you actually see it or know just where it is. I turn around to see what's going on. All behind me the crowd's swaying crazily, like a wheat field in the wind. The swaying ripples up towards us and across us.

The roaring grows louder. I can't believe it, because everyone seems to be smiling and swaying, but there's this roaring sound coming from the crowd. I feel as though I'm intoxicated, having bizarre hallucinations. Everything's a swirling confusion, like when you're a kid, whirling to make yourself dizzy. It breaks over me as a wave breaking, sweeps me away, then I'm roaring and swaying with the rest.

Like the Red Sea parting before Moses and the Israelites, the crowd parts down the centre, and I see her, standing alone: Mistral Wind. I know instantly it's her. She's wearing the bear's head, so you can't see her face, but there's no mistaking her, how she moves, her raven dark hair. She advances slowly through the divided crowd. Her hands clasp the bear head, holding it so it tilts skyward, and the roaring and the swaying of the crowd grow and grow as she advances. The drums are beating wildly, somewhere off to the side, a jungle rhythm. We all fall in behind Mistral as she advances to the front, hundreds and hundreds of us swaying and roaring like wild beasts in a trance.

The company guys and the cops fall back in dismay. I'm hardly aware of them, except to know they're in retreat before us, recoiling in confusion. And everything else seems to fall away too. The darkness is dissolving. There's light dawning across the eastern sky. Big spruce and cedar trees stand tall all about us, enormous ancient ancestors, as we dance behind the bear's head. We become the bear, unbelievably, miraculously, all of us together become the enormous body of the bear. We twine our arms and bodies together and the whole mass of us interlock, roaring and moving in unison, roaring behind the head of the bear, while the drums beat wildly and dawn breaks over us as though it is the first golden morning of Creation.

I am Ursus. Musquaw. Thick-furred and fierce. Shaggy and savage, shoulders rippling with great muscles. My eyes are bleary in the light. Wind ruffles the fur along my neck. I shamble forward snarling, claws striking the earth, the scent of human fear vivid in my snout.

We turn as one body, lost entirely inside the bear spirit, all of us together turn and part a second time, and the bear-woman Mistral runs through our midst and we close again behind her and surge in one body towards the bridge. We stop short, and Mistral stands alone on the bridge, enormous, her legs spread wide, her arms reaching into the dawn, holding the bear head aloft. The drums suddenly stop. We cease roaring at the same instant. Wordless, with one loping bound, Mistral hurls herself off the bridge into the river. The whole crowd gasps. We stand there, stunned to quiet. Then someone cries "Look!" pointing downriver. There we see, not Mistral Wind, nor any other human, but a great black bear swimming with powerful strokes towards the opposite shore. Emerging from the river onto land, it shakes the water from its coat. It rears up on its hind legs, scenting the air, then drops to all fours and disappears into the bush.

14

Everybody is off the road except our little group from Upshot. We're the only ones standing for arrest this morning. The rest of the crowd lines up along the sides of the road. I'm still reeling from the business with the bear. I feel as if I haven't stopped reeling for days. Caitlin and Elvira are on my left, holding up their placards, resolute as rocks. Waddy's on my right, full of piss and vinegar. Peewee and Julia are just behind us, with their banner stretched wide. I turn around to look, and there, between them, under the banner, with a faraway gaze on his face, stands Zyrk.

I don't even bother being surprised. You just never know with Zyrk. I'm sure Caitlin's right about Zyrk and Mistral Wind working in tandem. I mean, could it all be pure coincidence that Zyrk shows up at the store at the very moment when Peewee and Julia are lifting the head, and then makes off with it, reappears at the peace camp with it on the same night that Mistral Wind reappears out of nowhere, then they both disappear and she shows up as a bear this morning and he's standing under Peewee and Julia's banner?

Zyrk's dressed as always in black leather. He assumes a lotus position on the road beneath the banner. Peewee and Julia stand holding their poles like noble standardbearers of old. Zyrk takes up his mantra as the cops come up to us.

"You guys Mounties or company guards?" Waddy asks them, feisty as a fighting cock.

The cops aren't amused. They go right up to Waddy and ask him his name.

"Waddy Watts," says Waddy.

"How do you spell Waddy?" the head cop asks him. There are about four other cops taking notes. Then there's a bunch of big ones, who all look like clones of Hulk Hogan, standing in a row behind. Three different video cameras aim right into Waddy's face.

Waddy spells his name out for them, sarcastic as he can be.

"Is that your real name?" the cop asks Waddy.

I can see Waddy workin' up his chew like he's gettin' set to let a real good ringer go. He looks down at the cop's shiny black boots. The cop sees it too. He's no dummy, this cop. So he says to Waddy, "How old are you, Mister Watts?"

Waddy tells him he's eighty-one.

"Eighty-one!" the cop says, all smiles, trying to ingratiate himself, diffuse the situation by being the nice guy. "My, my."

I can see this cop's digging himself into an awful hole. Waddy's working his chaw like crazy. There's a little rivulet of tobacco juice dribbling from the corner of his mouth down to his chin. I feel a small tingle of alarm looking at Waddy. He's getting too wound up; at his age he could easily pop a gasket.

The cop explains how he's going to have to arrest Waddy, as though he's talking to a three-year-old.

"Well, fer Christ's sakes get on with it!" Waddy just about bites his head off. "I ain't got all friggin' day!" That's Waddy all over.

So the cop puts his hand on Waddy's shoulder and arrests him. They've got an old school bus pulled up along the road to put us in, and the cop asks Waddy if he'll walk to the bus or does he want to be carried.

Waddy just about blows his chew. At some of the blockades, arrestees refused to move off the road and the cops had to carry them off. That's why they got the gorillas in back. But Waddy doesn't know that. He thinks the cop means he's too old to walk that far.

"Whaddya mean, carried?" Waddy barks at the cop, real snarly. I can see Waddy's dander coming up like applejack. "You listen to me, sonny," he says and sticks his nose right into the cop's face. He's working his chew the whole time, so there's a spray of tobacco juice landing all over the cop. "The day anybody carries me anyplace," Waddy says to him, "I'll be in a goddamn coffin. What the hell's the matter with you anyway, ain't they teaching respect for your elders at cop school any more?"

Then Waddy lets a gob go out of the side of his mouth. It sails right past the cop's ear, just misses him. The whole crowd on the side of the road cheers like crazy, and Waddy walks over to the bus just like he was walking up to his Pacific Shay fifty years ago. I almost cry just watching him. Waddy's not someone you think of in terms of poignant moments, but this is one. Something about his age, his long history in the woods, his fierce defiance of convention, and, strangely, I realize, his old man's vulnerability, despite the spring in his step.

The cop takes out a handkerchief and wipes the tobacco spray off his face. I feel bad for the poor stiff. "Jesus!" he says, and comes up to me next.

"What's your name, sir?"

"Joseph Jones."

"Age?"

"Forty-three."

"You live on Upshot Island too?"

"Yes, I do."

"All you folks from Upshot?"

"Yes, we are."

"You know if you refuse to leave the road, I'll arrest you for disobeying an order of the court?"

Here I stand at last. How I got to be here. Who I came with. Whether anyone talked me into it. Whether it will make any real difference in the end. None of this matters. Here I stand. My mother would weep to see me, my father curse me for a fool, the Brothers of Blessed Columkille the Lesser shake their tonsured heads in shame that one of their own should fall so far from grace as to become a common criminal. Yet here I stand. A coward born and bred. A compromiser. Conflict-avoider. Chronic placater. Yet here I stand. One syllable will put me across a borderline I've never dared even approach before. With one small word I can unlock the door of my cell and walk away, absolved of the sins of my fathers, shriven, redeemed.

"Mr. Jones?"

The syllable hangs on my tongue, a droplet of dew on the lip of a leaf. I glance across to Caitlin and Elvira. I am not afraid. I say the word quietly.

"Yes."

"Very well," the officer says, placing his hand on my shoulder and reciting his "I arrest you" formula.

I don't hear what he's saying. I don't hear or see anything. A tremendous surge of exhilaration comes sweeping across me like a warm wind across the aromatic hills of Greece. I am lifted, as though by the wind, as though by a wave. I stride over to the bus as giants must once have walked upon the earth, as Hercules and Goliath must have walked, the crowd's cheers ringing behind me.

"That's the stuff, Joey-boy, that'll fix the bastards!" Waddy greets me in the bus. There's a gawky young cop with rampant acne sitting there, assigned, I guess, to keep an eye on us. The cop smiles at me awkwardly. I'm sure he's been getting an earful from Waddy.

I sit down and exhale. Breathe deeply. I can see the blockade through the window. The cops are talking to Elvira or Caitlin, I can't tell which. My mind is swirling. Everything's off slightly, distorted from normal. As though on a wild carnival ride. Everything topsy-turvy, nothing coheres, nothing logically follows what precedes it. All wild peaks and plunges. Not life at all, not my well-measured life, at least. And yet those peaks, those moments of exaltation—Mistral keening to the moon, our dancing into the body of the bear, my standing my ground just now before the law—how to measure those against the careful composure of a well-ordered existence?

"What's all this about a bear?" Waddy intrudes on my musings. "The kid next to me kept yelling about a bear, but I didn't see no friggin' bear, did you?"

"Yes, I did."

"Remember the time I fell on a black bear down island," Waddy says. "Dunno what the hell I was doin', crashin' around in a cutover down that way. Salal up to your armpits, so ya can't see the ground in front of you. Well sir, I take a step and whoosh! down I go like a load of coal, into this big hole. Only I don't hit bottom, see, I hit this bloody big lump of fur. Yep, a great smelly black bear, musta been sleepin' in there. It jumped up, snortin'—scared the livin' bejeezus outta me. I tell you, I was outta that hole quicker'n a gandydancer with hot pepper on his pecker. And the bloody bear's outta it too, in the opposite direction. I musta scared the bejeezus outta him, same as he did outta me. Haw, haw." Waddy snorts and crows over his story. He seems completely indifferent to having been arrested. The cop drops his guard and starts to laugh, as though he's a kid and Waddy his grandpa telling him bushwacker's tales.

A round of cheers outside, and I see Elvira walking towards the bus, chatting with a female officer. Elvira climbs into the bus, grinning broadly as Waddy and I greet her.

"Surely you're not going to put me in here with these hardened criminals?" Elvira says to the gawky cop. He looks sheepish, like he'd prefer us to be drunk and disorderly. Elvira sits beside Waddy.

Cheers and applause erupt again as Caitlin comes striding over to the bus. The policewoman escorting her is giving Caitlin a wide berth. When Caitlin bounds into the bus, you can see sparks flashing off her, smell gunsmoke in the air.

"Well done, Caitlin!" Elvira cries, and a glint of mischief softens Caitlin's face for a moment, but she's seething with energy. She strides up and down the aisle of the bus a couple of times, not saying anything.

"You'd better sit down, miss," the cop who's watching us says to her.

"Better than what?" Caitlin flashes at him from halfway down the aisle. Oh, oh, I can see the poor guy's in for a drubbing. "Better than you? Is that what you mean? Hah! You know what you're doing, don't you?"

"Just doing my job, miss." The cop's trying his best not to look terrified. And who wouldn't be? Caitlin's doing her spitting Irish vixen turn to perfection.

"Just doing your job? Now where have we heard that before, eh? Was it Nuremburg? Or was it Never-Never Land?"

"When you deliberately break the law, you get arrested, it's real simple," the cop says with a thick voice. "This isn't Nazi Germany, and you know it."

"That's what I thought too, beforehand," Caitlin flashes back at him, points right at him with a lethal index finger, "but when those truck lights were coming up the road at us through the dark, and that awful man's voice booming through the loudspeaker like the voice of Baal, and the video camera lights in our faces—then I knew this wasn't dear sweet polite Canada any more. This was more like Belfast. More like El Salvador. This was men with guns arriving in the dark to do their master's bidding."

She's glaring at the cop with ferocious intensity. I hope, for his own sake, the cop has enough smarts to just be quiet. "I don't care what anybody says about the rule of law," Caitlin bores into him, "or our precious right to dissent, and all the rest of it—I saw you guys, coming at us through the gloom, the way you've been coming at the innocent for centuries, with your guns and bright lights and your 'just doing my job' excuses. You're the henchmen of darkness, no matter what uniforms you wear or what justifications you have."

Caitlin sits down with an umph! I've never seen her more fiery. Her green eyes gleam like green embers. The poor gawky cop squirms with anger and embarrassment.

I'm bursting to talk to Caitlin about what happened out there, about Mistral and the bear, but her fierceness keeps me at bay. A lioness guarding her cubs. Silence in the bus, like when an angel passes. But broken by more cheering outside. Peewee and Julia join us, and we applaud them too.

"I think the press got some shots of our banner," Julia announces triumphantly. "Let's hope the wire services pick it up. I'd kill to see them all back in T.O. if the pic runs in the *Groan and Wail.*"

"Caitlin's right," Waddy says, ignoring Julia. "These cops are just tryin' to yank our chains. Coulda give us citations right there on the spot. But, no, figger they're gonna teach us a lesson by holdin' us for hours and draggin' us all over the fuckin' country." The cop with the acne's turned his back on us, looking through the windshield. "Hell," Waddy says, sticking the skewer in, "there's serial killers out there they pay less attention to.

"Course it's water off a duck's ass to me," Waddy's got us as a captive audience, and looks us over to be sure we're paying attention. "Remember them dust-ups we used to have down island when we come outta camp. We'd be in bush camps, workin' shifts of eleven-hour days, seven days a week on some shows. When there was free time, we'd all head to town and boyoboy she'd get pretty wild by Saturday night. You'd have sixty or seventy loggers—fallers and whistle punks, bull buckers, chokermen, chasers, the whole shootin' match—all jammed into them beer parlours whoopin' 'er up like Aunt Matilda's panties."

Everyone hoots at Waddy. Looking out the window, I see there's a commotion still going on out on the roadway. Zyrk's in the middle of it. The cops are probably trying to get him to talk, not realizing Zyrk's in deep incommunicado mode.

"I wonder if one of us should go out and help Zyrk," I say.

"You're not goin' anywhere, fella," the cop up front says.

"Never knew where you'd wake up in the mornin'," Waddy carries on, "chances are it'd be either the whorehouse or the local lock-up. Either way you wouldn't have a penny left in your pockets. After they'd cleaned us out, we used to say them girls will be fartin' through silk underwear this winter. Haw, haw." We all hoot at Waddy again.

More shouting and clapping outside, and I see four cops big as linebackers carrying Zyrk towards the bus.

"Crazy bugger," Waddy mutters.

Zyrk enters the bus with an expression of absolute serenity. His mantra flows out as unperturbed as ever. He bows slightly towards us, then sits in the driver's seat, and starts the bus up.

"Hey, you!" the guard cop shouts, freaking out, lunging at Zyrk. He pulls Zyrk away from the wheel and shoves him down the aisle. "Get back there!"

"That's what I mean," Caitlin says, calmer now, and Zyrk sits down beside her.

We watch out the windows of the bus as the logging crews pass by. Pickup trucks and crummies full of loggers, some of them waving to the crowd, some glowering, some flipping the finger. The crowd, lined along both sides of the road, waves and smiles as logging trucks and grapple yarders and other huge machines grind past.

We sit in the bus for about an hour. Waddy tells us camp tales. By unspoken common consent, we do not talk about Mistral and the bear. Not in front of the cop. Though it's all that's in my mind; the arrest is nothing. What happened with Mistral? Was that real? Impossible! I need to dissect that improbable, thrilling vision.

A cadaverous driver with skin the colour of last night's dishwater climbs into the bus and starts it up. We're moving at last. We drive through the twin lines of protesters. The whole crowd cheers and waves. The raven person flaps its wings. I see Starstream standing beside the road, tears streaming down her goofy, lovely face.

The bus carries us back down the logging road we'd driven up in the dark, through a desolate landscape of scrub brush and dust. Then down the highway into Ubiquity, a forlorn little town huddled under the grotesque face of a clearcut mountainside.

We pull into the RCMP substation. The cops ask each of us a series of questions, photograph and fingerprint us. The women are put together in one cell down a corridor and us men in another. This is the first time I've ever been in jail.

The cell's a windowless box of concrete and steel, about ten feet square, lit with jaundiced fluorescent lighting. The only adornment, a stainless-steel toilet bowl, juts out from one wall. By comparison, the camp privies now seem charming structures of secluded luxury. I guess each of us is secretly relieved that we've had nothing to eat or drink all morning.

Still, I'm hungry and thirsty as hell.

The cell's a desolate hole. It stinks of disinfectant, excrement, and failure. There's nowhere to sit except the floor. A filthy blanket spread on the floor. The place is crawling with awful ghosts.

They keep us in there for three or four hours, and you can feel our spirits sag under the accumulated tragedies that have hardened like a crust upon the concrete. Even Waddy's colourful tales of camp life and cathouses can't sustain us that long. Poor Peewee fidgets like a gerbil in a cage. Zyrk alone seems to sail along with complete equanimity. He sits in the lotus position on the filthy floor, fixes his gaze upon the toilet bowl, and hums an elaborate raga. After several hours I begin to see Zyrk as the only sane person in that wretched hole.

My faith in this adventure is draining away. Without Caitlin's passion or Elvira's gentle strength close by, I realize, I don't feel half so bold. I may have walked as a giant only a few hours ago, but now I'm as small as I've ever been, and fraught with misgivings. Doubt. Faith and doubt. Always it comes down to faith and doubt. I look at my companions, each of them lost in private reverie: Waddy, Peewee, and Zyrk. And me. Our revolutionary cadre. A band of bold adventurers sallying forth to do battle with multinational timber giants and the governments they control? Good grief. Who's kidding whom? Davey Rushing's warnings come back to me. These guys invented the game. They'll come down on you like granite blocks. You could lose everything. Fear creeps like a furtive rodent into a corner of my soul, hides there, a wounded creature in its lair.

The cops call us out, one by one. I'm the last one, left alone in the cell. I picture myself the Birdman of Alcatraz. Before any birds arrive, they bring me out and get me to sign a document ordering me to appear at court in the city next March and to refrain from further law-breaking. Then they release me. I tell you, sunshine never shone more sweetly, grass never glistened more brilliantly green, than when I step outdoors from that vile little lock-up into the delicious autumn breeze of freedom.

$$15$$

After only three days back on Upshot, the bizarre happenings of our Kumquat escapade are already beginning to blur in my memory, to lose their clarity and force, the way you start forgetting the textures and details of an exotic vacation soon after returning to familiar places and routines. I am relieved to be back to my tranquil, predictable island existence, no longer tossed about like flotsam by events and emotions I do not understand and cannot control. I haven't seen or heard from any of the others since our return. As if by tacit understanding, we have stepped back from our reckless fellowship.

I'm admiring the coneflowers in my garden, purple and white, thinking how I should really get myself organized to start processing their roots for echinacea tincture, when the telephone rings. I catch it on the fifth ring.

"Hello?"

"Brother Joseph," it's Elvira, "are you rested enough for round two?"

"I don't like the sound of this, Elvira."

"Sound and fury both," Elvira says. "How's about a coffee at the Preening P.? Say in an hour?"

"Fine. I'll see you there."

As anxious as I am for peace and quiet, I feel a sudden surge of interest around our expedition and its consequences. I can't imagine what Elvira's come up with, but from her tone on the phone it's something hot.

Forty-five minutes later I hop in my truck and zoom off to the Preening Peacock. I pass Angus MacIvor driving north in his four-by-four. A florid Scot, Angus usually salutes me in passing with a firm nod of his head and a grimace halfway between a scowl and a smile. But not today. He speeds past without even a feint at a nod.

A mile or two farther on, I draw a similar reaction from Elsie Pitfield, puttering along in her Geo. Elsie's never exactly loose, but she's usually at least civil. She doesn't even give me the flutter of a finger, just a smile set in stone.

Davey Rushing comes gliding by on his mountain bike and flashes me the Black Panther salute.

Then Jimmy Fitz comes whizzing past—at least his truck does. I can't spot Jimmy at all because, seeing me approach, he's ducked below his dashboard to avoid eye contact. Better death by collision, Jimmy seems to have concluded, than confusion over the appropriate wave to be employed.

And there are appropriate gestures, oh, yes! One of the subtler rituals of modern rural life involves the body language of acquaintances passing one another in their vehicles. Attractions, flirtations, fallings-out, rejections, recriminations—the automotive-age rustic can communicate any of these, and more, through a wave or a wave withheld, a nod so short as to be a snub. A tribal feud that has simmered through generations can be condensed, in a momentary passing on a country road, into the faintest flicker of a finger.

Approaches vary. There's one group I think of as the cheerleaders, who are given to exuberant waving and toothsome smiling whenever you pass them, no matter how frequently you pass them. These people seem to believe that all the world and they are on waving terms, the way all Volkswagen van drivers used to be. Cheerleaders afflicted with myopia are a special menace; they'll smile and wave extravagantly at complete strangers—leaving carloads of dumbfounded tourists or taciturn tradespeople wondering who is that peculiar person waving to them like a long-lost relative. Elvira's one of them. "It's nice that people smile and wave that way," she'll say. "It makes a person feel liked."

Stonewallers, on the other hand, give barely any sign of recognition at all. Eyes fixed firmly on the road ahead. Both hands gripping the steering wheel. Mouth pursed puritanically. Passing by, you might be blessed with the faintest nod, or perhaps a lone index finger rising briefly in austere acknowledgement. Seldom both together, and never more.

Between these two extremes pass a grand panoply of possibilities. The indifferent and carefree flourish of the playboy. A regal wave like the Queen of England's. The Pope's stiff Pinocchio hand-on-a-rope. Perhaps an enlightened smile reminding you of the Dalai Lama. The gruff and knowing nod of tough old duffers. All of these are standard issue on the rural byways of the nation.

Secret meanings lie hidden in these rites of passage, subtle undertones and subtexts that can only be divined by recognizing minute variations in delivery. The toothy exuberance of a cheerleader's salute might seem to denote a hale and hearty fellowship uncluttered with complications. But the practised passer might detect in the gesture an initial hesitation, a moment's pause before the gladsome gesticulating breaks out, and in that split second of uncertainty, of momentary holding-back, whole volumes might be read.

A habitual stonewaller's index finger, on the other hand, might in passing leap to life with unaccustomed alacrity, indicating that the taciturn chap attached to the digit is in fact in unusually high spirits at the moment.

In desperate times, or if one is in disgrace, there may be no sign whatsoever given, and this is the most damning sign of all.

Thus the prevailing mood of the community, and one's own status in it, can be determined simply by driving around for a bit. You don't need to speak a word to anyone to get a precise reading of which way the wind's blowing on any given day.

Today it's perfectly clear to me the wind is up and blowing fiercely in several different directions.

Which makes me glad to be meeting Elvira. Nobody has a finger more deftly placed on the pulse of the community than she does. The woman has a remarkable capacity to be right in the thick of things, dust and spittle flying in all directions, and still calmly reconnoitre.

Arousal runs along the sinuous rails of rumour. Rumours and gossip, of course, are the lifeblood of island culture, oozing like slime moulds across the rotting logs of conversation, diverging and reconverging, splitting off into fragments, then reassembling in new and fabulous configurations.

One time a sociology professor from the city came to Upshot for the express purpose of trying to plot the spread and progress of rumours through a small community. Naturally, he kept his profession and his purpose secret. Pipes his name was, which everyone thought was pretty funny once we'd discovered what his game was. Pipes would amble into the general store or the Preening Peacock or wherever, idly engage in general conversation, calculatingly plant a specific rumour, then sit back and see what would become of it. He had, we later learned, a grant from the National Research Council to conduct this work.

Some of his ersatz rumours just died on the wing, like turkeys. For instance, he cooked up a story that the Anglican church was going to be painted fuschia with aquamarine trim, but nobody picked up on that at all. He did much better with a tale that somebody on-island—he wasn't at liberty to disclose just who—had unexpectedly come into an inheritance of several million dollars from a recently deceased relative.

Well, that one caught fire all right. Money and sex, Professor Pipes eventually concluded, have the best shelf life among rumours. Everyone started trying to figure out who the instant millionaire was and whether it was somebody who owed them anything. Within a week, the inheritance had multiplied in the popular imagination to more than 10 million, and somewhere along the line it became established fact that the recipient lived down at Cogg's Crossing.

Within days, the field had been further narrowed to two possibilities, and then to just one: the enigmatic Zyrk, whose mantras were reliably reported to have risen at least one octave right around the time when the inheritance was first heard of.

Every morning since he'd arrived on Upshot, Zyrk had walked from his cabin at Cogg's Crossing up to the general store for coffee. People would drive past him on the road, the way you'd drive past an elderberry bush, without further thought.

But not any more. Now that Zyrk was the putative possessor of (by this time) perhaps 20 million dollars, people took an interest. Jimmy Fitz took to parking his pickup behind a big cedar down near Miller Drive and waiting for Zyrk to appear on foot. Once his prey had passed, Jimmy'd hop into his truck and drive up and offer Zyrk a ride. But Zyrk had other things on his mind—investment portfolio stratagems, no doubt—and ignored Jimmy's blandishments.

"It's him for sure's got the money," Jimmy'd splutter, "but what the hell good is all that cash gonna do somebody like him?"

This very question occurred to Fibber Miller too. Ever the opportunist, Fibber worked out a little land development scheme for which Zyrk would supply the capital and Fibber the expertise. They'd develop a world-class destination resort and retirement community right here on Upshot with a golf course, an airstrip, a big marina, and then retire wealthy men. Fibber laid out these plans to Zyrk in the general store under the watchful eye of Margaret May. This new development instantly took on a life of its own and became an integral part of the overall rumour. Fervent committees were formed to oppose or support the alleged development. Fibber even invited Zyrk to dinner at his house, which nobody had ever done before, so they could discuss the deal in detail. Throughout all this commotion, Zyrk said not a word, preferring, it seemed, to contemplate the folly of human ambition in the depths of his coffee cup.

Eventually Professor Pipes, safely back in the city, sent a letter on university stationery addressed "to the residents of Upshot Island," explaining what he'd been doing amongst us and why, and promising to forward a copy of his monograph on the function and form of rural rumours once it was published. But by then nobody could quite remember who Pipes was, and a firm belief still persists in some quarters that Zyrk is a multimillionaire.

So it's not at all surprising that our expedition to Kumquat has generated lots of imaginative rumourmongering. And what better person than Elvira, what better spot than that hotbed of gossip, the Preening Peacock Cafe, to find out what's going on?

I arrive at the café ahead of Elvira and take a table out on the terrace in the dappled shade of a ginkgo tree. The café derives its name from the flock of peacocks and hens that the owners have strutting around the grounds. They came from Elvira's place originally and, like all peacocks, are unimaginably stupid. I find the screeches they make— nothing as poetic as a cry or call—excessively loud and grating. Elvira once talked me into taking a pair from her, a few years back when Freddie was still around, and I tried my darndest to like the birds for Elvira's sake. But, by God, they're stupid! And then for the cocks to have that magnificent plumage! It's all wrong, perverse, like a person you meet who's undeniably attractive and thoroughly repulsive at the same time.

Philip and Charles are the proprietors of the Preening Peacock. Philip is our sole black resident, Ethiopian I think, tall and lithe and strikingly handsome. Charles is shorter and less elegant. He crops his hair close across his scalp and wears a single gold ring in his left earlobe, so he looks like a Robert Louis Stevenson pirate. They were the island's first unabashedly gay couple. One might have expected there'd be great consternation, at least in certain quarters, when they first came ashore a few years back. But no, it fell out that Philip and Charles manifested a level of eccentricity perfectly attuned to community standards. They slipped seamlessly into the social fabric of the place. Their establishment, peacocks and all, soon became a cornerstone of the community.

They took over a decrepit old fish and chip shop, gutted and renovated and expanded it so thoroughly you can't recognize any of the original structure. Where before there was only greasy gloom, all is now spacious, airy, and tasteful. A semi-tropical jungle of houseplants thrives indoors, and Charles fusses over the plants with the same meticulous attention he brings to his butter tarts and caffè lattés.

Philip is charged with the public interface end of the business. He is a scandalous gossip, but a wonderfully subtle one. A quick wink or a sotto voce murmur from him, a lifting of his large dark eyes to the ceiling, might reveal secrets of astonishing indecency. Professor Pipes had straight away recognized Philip as a meistergossiper and had endeavoured to exploit him as a conduit for his bogus rumours. But Philip is a maestro where Pipes was little more than a post-doctoral Peeping Tom, and he blithely evaded the professor's clumsy overtures.

But if you want to know what's happening on Upshot, or what various factions believe to be happening, other than the partisan perspectives available at Wilhelmina's Beauty Salon, Philip is your man and the Preening Peacock is the place.

I tell Philip I'll wait for Elvira to join me before ordering. He and I sit together on the terrace, chatting for a bit. He trolls delicately for details of our Kumquat expedition, and I drop tantalizing fragments. After a few minutes Elvira arrives. Philip adores Elvira, he dotes on her and fusses about whenever she comes in for coffee.

"No need to order!" Philip declares, after holding Elvira's chair for her. "Something very special awaits!" He winks at us, flaps his little waiter's towel across his arm and strides back to the kitchen as though he's John Gielgud playing the butler.

"What's up?" I ask Elvira. "I haven't seen a soul since we got back. Haven't wanted to."

"I was over to Wilhelmina's this morning," Elvira says, "for a bit of a trim, though I really didn't need one."

"And?" I can see Elvira's busting to tell all.

"Well, she was behaving very oddly right from the start," Elvira begins. "She didn't really want to talk to me, and that's saying something for Wilhelmina. So I had to ease her into it. Eventually she gets going, on about eggs and chickens and the weather and her sister's arthritis and everything else she can think about to keep the talk from turning dangerous. I just waited her out." Elvira smiles disarmingly, like a crocodile.

At this point Charles appears, with Philip alongside, emerging from the kitchen carrying a silver tray which he bears solemnly across the patio as though it contained the sacred relics of a saint. He places the tray on our table while Elvira and I make faces of amazement to one another and Philip beams with proprietary satisfaction. Charles, I should say, does not wait on just anyone; this presentation represents a mark of the highest deference on the part of the Preening Peacock management.

"Voilà!" Charles exclaims, removing the tray's cover to reveal the makings of a splendid tea, including Elvira's favourite little cakes and scones, whipped butter and various jams, and a tea service of elegant china. Nothing about the presentation is ordinary.

"Charles!" Elvira exclaims, "this is so sweet of you."

Charles bows profoundly and withdraws to his kitchen without another word, followed by Philip. This is Charles and Philip acknowledging our adventure, the way the Preening Peacock might do it if the lieutenant governor popped in for tea.

As we fuss over the tea things, Elvira picks up her story. "It was obvious from even the little bit I could squeeze out of Wilhelmina that there's a plot being hatched," she says.

"A plot?"

" 'Well, Elvira, dear,' Wilhelmina says to me, 'some people are quite upset, you know, and you really can't blame them.' I ask her which people—as if I didn't know—but she won't say, not right off." Elvira sips her tea, holding her pinky finger out at a swank angle just to be funny. "I gradually wheedle out of her that there was a brunch yesterday morning."

"A brunch?" I say. "Has any good ever come out of a brunch?"

"Geoffrey and Rose Munz, Elsie Pitfield, the Muhlbachers and the MacIvors got together at Wilhelmina and Karl's yesterday morning to have brunch and, it sounds like, to plan an insurrection."

"I wouldn't think that bunch could plan a dogfight."

"I couldn't get any details out of Wilhelmina, try as I might. She was extraordinarily secretive. I couldn't crack her, no matter how hard I tried. But one thing's certain," Elvira sips her tea again, "they're planning a revolt of some sort."

"What sort?"

"Not sure exactly."

"What's got their dander up? Kumquat obviously."

"Have you seen the papers?"

"No."

"Look here." Elvira pulls a newspaper clipping out of her jeans' hip pocket and hands it to me. It's from one of the big dailies. A photograph showing Peewee and Julia holding their garden club banner aloft, with Zyrk in full leather smiling between them. "Garden club members arrested at Kumquat," reads the cutline.

"Yeah, that would do it, I should think," I say.

"It's done it all right," Elvira says. "The pot-banging's really going to begin now. And you know who'll they go after, don't you?"

"Caitlin."

"Of course. Geoffrey's revenge. I think she's going to need some help." Elvira takes a sip of her tea and looks at me as though waiting for robust volunteers to step forward.

"Elvira," I say, and pause.

"Yes?"

"I'm not sure where I stand with Caitlin just now. I'm still really confused about her."

"I know. All the more reason to go see her, I should think."

Elvira's right, as usual, but I have no great desire to visit Caitlin, quite the reverse, in fact. When I think of her now, I picture her at the blockade, incandescent·with rage, a burning ember you don't want to touch. The tumult of Kumquat and my turbulent feelings for Caitlin are entangled together. There is no tranquillity in either.

Strangely, Elvira and I don't discuss any of what happened at Kumquat, as though that's a spot still too tender to touch. I leave Elvira in the parking lot, feeling my restored equanimity already slipping away.

16

I stop at the general store on my way home, to see if the newspapers have anything more on our expedition. I find Margaret May at her customary post behind the counter engrossed in one of the daily tabloids.

"Lovely day, isn't it?" she greets me. There's a hint of something in Margaret May's tone, an insinuation that things are not entirely right with us.

"Indeed it is," I say. "What's going on in the world?"

She shows me the tabloid headline: SCHOOLS KICK BUTTS it shouts in enormous block letters over top of a photo showing school kids skulking outdoors puffing on cigarettes.

"About time too," Margaret May says. Any advances, however small, in the war against the killer weed come as welcome news to Margaret May.

Somehow it seems to me wise not to ask Margaret May if she's come across anything about Kumquat. I drift over to the newspaper rack. The headlines shout of wars and atrocities. I scan one of the dailies quickly. There's a small item on page three about more arrests at Kumquat yesterday.

I remember that I need to buy twine for tying up my tomato vines. I find a big ball of good brown twine and charge it, and the newspaper, to my account.

"Will that be all?" Margaret May asks laconically.

I hesitate. I glance across at the door and the bare spot above it where the bear's head hung for so long. The spot's a different hue from the rest of the wall, lacking forty years of texturing by the smoke and soot and scandals of the store. The framed photo hangs there still, though it's carelessly aslant at the moment. Nothing, so far as I know, has been said directly to Margaret May about the head's disappearance, though its alleged role at Kumquat is by now common knowledge.

All this is uncharted territory. According to Elvira, Margaret May has said not a word about any of it, nor indicated to anyone her feelings on the issue. Her uncharacteristic silence is, in its subtle way, far more disconcerting than any raging could have been.

I vacillate. Margaret May rattles her tabloid noisily. Then I take a step off a high cliff.

"Margaret May . . ." I begin.

"Hmm?" she replies distractedly, perusing her paper.

"About our Kumquat expedition."

"I've heard something about it," Margaret May murmurs, still absorbed in her tabloid, "not that you've mentioned it yourself, of course."

Aha. So Margaret May's feeling sore that no one's talked to her. Or does the resentment in her tone have more to do with the bear's head? I suspect Peewee and Julia committed a more grievous sin in hoodwinking Margaret May through the passionate prose of Monique Manlotte than in heisting the head. I'm in a minefield.

"Well?" Margaret May raises her hooded eyes to me at last. I can't help noticing she is wearing a tad too much mascara. She seems to loom in front of me like an enormous spider with compound eyes, trembling in her web, waiting for me to take another, perhaps fatal, step.

"I just wondered about the bear's head," I say, barely inching forward.

"Ah, yes, the bear's head," Margaret May exhales mournfully, as though we're speaking of Chernobyl or Tiananmen. "That's a pity, isn't it, that things should come to that?"

"To what?" I ask her.

"To what?" Margaret May feigns genuine astonishment. "To theft, that's what. Robbery. Larceny. Call it what you will, it was the wrongful taking of personal property, wasn't it?"

I briefly consider advancing the hypothesis that the bear's head is, in fact, collective property, transcending the comings and goings of individual storekeepers. But you can't stand against Margaret May when the winds of indignation fill her sails.

"Yes, I suppose it was," I say instead.

"Never so much as a word of explanation or apology. And where is it now, I'd like to know?" Margaret May asks, plaintive and defiant, a storekeeper's rendering of Medea.

Why did I start this conversation?

"Well," I venture, "the whole thing was so bizarre, I don't think anyone would expect you to believe it."

"Do you mean to say it's less believable than theft and deception right here on Upshot?" Margaret May's indisputably in command of the moral high ground. I'm feeling uncomfortable being cast as an apologist for thievery.

"I think it started out as a bit of a lark," I say.

"I'm sure it did," declares Margaret May, her great bosom swelling as she warms to the strength of her position. "I'm sure the whole sordid episode was a grand lark for certain persons."

I feel I should distance myself from the knaves responsible for this enormous suffering. "But it turned into something else part way through," I add, weakly.

"Into what, may I ask?" Margaret May looks down on me like the Queen of Hearts, from a great height.

"Well, into a bear," I say. Without conviction.

"What?" Margaret May positively bulges with disbelief.

For a moment there's no sound at all in the store, just the humming of the freezer units. The tableau we strike, Margaret May and I, is perhaps a bit theatrical, perhaps a little absurd. A truck rumbles by outside. A car door slams.

"Are you trying to tell me," Margaret May rises on the rhetorical question like a rum-soaked senator, "that you of all people believe that cockamamy story—that a mangy old bear head that's hung on this wall for forty years or more actually came back to life?" Her incredulity seems to swell before me, a thunderhead above foothills.

"I know it sounds a bit strange," I admit feebly.

"Strange? Strange you call it?" God, she's magnificent.

Just at that moment, the store door clatters open. Margaret May releases me from her magisterial glare. We both glance across to see Waddy Watts standing by the door, blinking like a barn owl.

"Bright enough out there to blind a bat," Waddy says, shattering the tension. Then, looking at the two of us, "What the hell's goin' on?"

"Tall tales the lot of it," huffs Margaret May. "A bear indeed! I'd like my head back, gentlemen."

"Oho, it's the bear truth we're after now, is it?" Waddy's puns always stink.

"I'll say no more," sniffs Margaret May, "except that I've been wronged. Sorely wronged."

" 'Course you been wronged," says Waddy, sticking his bony little head and beady eyes towards her. "We all been bloody wronged some way in this one, ain't we?"

"Well," says Margaret May, fluffing herself a bit.

I'm amazed at how quickly she subsides under Waddy's influence. She's smart enough to avoid an open clash with the old curmudgeon.

Waddy grins slyly at Margaret May. "Listen now," he says to her, his pale blue eyes shining with mischief, "that bear head of yours will go down in history, don'tcha see? So will you. Just leave it to clever fellers like Joey-boy here, and we'll all end up like Looey Reyell or somebody, eh?"

"You mean hanged?" Margaret May asks. She glances at each of us, apparently uncertain whether a prominent place in the historical record doesn't in fact hold greater attraction than the delicious moral indignation of the moment. Then, gradually, the footlights of immortality begin to illuminate Margaret May. She fluffs herself again, the way a broody hen does, and straightens her tabloid.

"You're a pack of dreamers and fools," she chides us, but with her customary warmth. "If my head's returned in good order, I'm willing to overlook the whole sordid episode. But you should all be locked in jail for a bit and learn to behave yourselves."

The three of us laugh together.

"You want a cup of coffee?" I ask Waddy.

"I didn't come all the way down here to buy bobby pins," Waddy says. "You buyin'?"

Waddy and I settle at the coffee counter. Margaret May makes a grand production of pouring us each a cup of coffee. She still retains about her a trace of the great soul bruised by cunning fools, and in this guise retreats to the solace of her tabloid.

"Been watchin' the dragonflies?" Waddy asks me.

"No I haven't. They doing something special?"

"Boyoboy, never seen dragonflies like this year. Clouds of the bastards everywhere you look. She'll be dry and tight this winter, you just wait and see."

I don't bother comparing this augury against the conflicting evidence already presented by wasps and beavers. Nor does it matter with Waddy. He'll just hop onto his next train of thought, and you can do whatever you want.

"Check your mail today?" he asks me.

"Not yet, I'm just heading home now."

"Flyer come around. Boyoboy, she's a scorcher all right."

Bulk mail flyers are as much a part of life on Upshot as rumours. For about thirty or thirty-five bucks in postal charges you can have a single-sheet flyer delivered to every household on the mail route. With no community paper, this is by far the most efficient way of announcing important events to everyone on-island. Like guns and other useful inventions, it has, over the years, sometimes been employed for questionable purposes. There was one time, a few years back, a flyer came around under the banner of something called the Cannabis Crackdown Committee. This bunch of crackpots wanted to set up a neighbourhood-watch-style operation in which people would spy on their neighbours to see if they had any pot plants growing in behind the Jerusalem artichokes. The person reporting the most illicit plants would win a free ride in the RCMP's dope-spotter helicopter. Well, that one got certain folks smoking mad all right. A counter-flyer hit the mailboxes the following week threatening public disclosure of certain sexual indiscretions on the part of two leading Cannabis Crackdown Committee members unless the snoop program was immediately cancelled. Which it was.

"What does this one say?" I ask Waddy.

"Margaret May!" Waddy calls out. "You got a copy of that flyer come around today?"

"I haven't had a chance to look," says Margaret May, "things being the way they are," slipping off her stool with the weighty grace of a sea lion sliding from its haul-out into surf. She rummages around over at the mail counter.

"Here," she says, handing Waddy a sheet of paper.

"That's it," Waddy says, passing it to me.

I scan the flyer. "UPSHOT'S SHAME!" it says in bold letters, then:

As most islanders are aware, a handful of people from this community have recently participated in illegal activities at Kumquat Sound. These persons have been arrested and charged with criminal contempt of court.

We the undersigned believe that every citizen has a right to his own opinion. However, in a democracy the accepted method of advancing one's political opinion is through the ballot box, not through breaking the law or mob rule. We do not believe that any of us has the right to take the law into our own hands. In that direction lie anarchy and civil disorder.

The persons now charged with contempt of court perpetrated their crime claiming to be official representatives of the Upshot Island Garden Club and Horticultural Society. News reports identified them as such. We the undersigned believe their illegal actions are not supported by the majority of the community nor by the garden club's full membership.

We request that all members of the club and all other interested parties attend the next general meeting of the garden club (Oct. 12, 7:30, Community Hall) to make your views known on this important issue.

Lacking any signatories, notwithstanding the several references to "We the undersigned," the announcement was identified as emanating from "The Committee for a Non-Partisan Garden Club."

"Well, that's a pretty definitive throwing-down of the gauntlet," I say to Waddy.

"Shit's gonna hit the fan's what you mean," Waddy clicks his dentures. "Body snatchin'll begin good and earnest."

Body snatching is a local euphemism for packing a public meeting with supportive hordes. The idea is to round up as many warm bodies as possible, convince them by any available means of the urgency and legitimacy of your point of view, and ensure that they're at the hall en masse for any public meetings on the issue in question. Shouters and abusers are especially prized, with one good shouter generally reckoned to be worth six polite supporters.

"Old Moffatt seen Karl and Geoffrey headin' into the Dreeb place yesterday." Waddy clicks his teeth. "That's a sure sign."

Whenever a controversy erupts on Upshot the Dreebs achieve a dazzling rise in popularity.

The Dreebs constitute what might be called an extended family, made up of old Doris and Charlie Dreeb, their four sons and their miscellaneous mates and offspring. The whole pack of them live together in their own private shantytown of ramshackle sheds and trailers up at the north end, next door to the Moffatts. Black bindweed infests the Dreeb landscape, and they have a large area of wetland given over to purple loosestrife. Ernie and Gertrude Moffatt are forced to maintain constant vigilance to prevent this twin menace from leaping the property line into their gardens.

Notwithstanding the squalor in which they live, the Dreebs are far from penniless victims of a vicious economic system. Quite the opposite. Several years ago, shortly after Doris and Charlie retired to Upshot, Doris hit the jackpot on the 649 lottery and the Dreebs became instant persons of wealth. This is when their kids migrated to Upshot too, all having experienced a profound new inclination to be closer to dear old mom and pop.

It was Margaret May herself sold Doris the ticket, and though she never said as much, I suspect Margaret May considered a small token of appreciation from the Dreebs to be in order, but no such token was ever forthcoming.

Fibber Miller, forever in quest of investment capital, made one and only one sortie into this enclave of the nouveau riche. Rufus Dreeb— the eldest and most imposing of the sons—grabbed poor Fibber by the lapels of his blue blazer ("Just dry cleaned too," Fibber complained to Margaret May following the altercation), shook him the way a terrier shakes a rat, and told Fibber if he ever set foot on the Dreeb estate again Rufus wouldn't be responsible for what harm might befall him.

Every winter all three generations of Dreebs break camp and head south to Las Vegas where they're installed with great ceremony at Caesar's Palace and proceed to spend the better part of a month gambling, drinking, and smoking with reckless abandon. Nobody knows for sure, because the Dreebs maintain no confidante beyond their own compound, but the word is that young Crispin Dreeb is a wizard at blackjack and that his winnings alone more than finance this annual junket.

Crispin's a mild-mannered fellow, but his three older brothers—big Rufus, Slade, and Hunter—are holy terrors. Luckily they keep to themselves most of the time and seldom get involved in community affairs, unless busy body snatchers get them involved. If someone can convince them that their own interests are being threatened by a particular initiative—there was, for example, the time a proposed bylaw sought to limit the number of trailers permitted on any one piece of property—the

Dreebs rise up like the bile of Beelzebub and, once roused, are formidable adversaries.

With the crucial garden club meeting imminent, Karl and Geoffrey are obviously courting the Dreebs and other combative personalities. This is the insurrection Elvira had sensed coming. The trick, as all sides know, is to stack the hall with heavy hitters who are riled up enough to disrupt a meeting and throw all into confusion. It's probably what the old Greeks had in mind talking unenthusiastically about democracy as "rule by the mob."

No mistaking it: the flyer gives fair warning that our beloved garden club is about to be split down the middle, rent like the curtain in the temple of Jerusalem in the darkness of the Crucifixion hour.

For decades the club has survived revolts and schisms, tyrannies and coups d'état, scandals and divorces and fierce internecine skirmishing. It's endured several tempestuous flower shows like the one in '69 when Eulalie Fitz, Johnny's wife, became enraged at what she took to be the judges conspiring to deny her tuberous begonias a blue ribbon on the basis of some imagined slight delivered when she herself was on the judging panel the previous year. Voices were raised. Tempers flared. Suddenly, Eulalie started throwing her begonias at the startled judges and screaming at them to the effect that they were whores not horticulturists. Somebody dragged Johnny in from the back porch where he was trying to enjoy a cigarette in peace. Several vases were smashed and bouquets ruined in the ensuing melee.

But that was all par for the course, and pretty soon things were patched up and the club kept rolling along on its only occasionally tempestuous way.

Our Kumquat caper, though, appears to have put a different spin on things altogether, having opened up the club's very ground of being, like the great rift of Africa, threatening to leave us members stranded awkwardly on one side or the other.

"Shit gonna fly for sure," Waddy says, putting down his cup and wiping his lips on the sleeve of his flannel shirt. "You maybe better warn Caitlin."

Every event in this saga, and all expert commentary upon these events, appear to be specifically designed for driving me into the dangerous embraces of Caitlin Slaney.

"Yes," I say, "maybe I better."

17

Caitlin and I are sitting on her deck, eating sugar plums. Jenny's crouching on the wooden steps just below us. She has a tiny tree frog squatting on the palm of her hand. No more than an inch long, the frog's a brilliant iridescent green. A thin dark band runs from cheek to cheek, giving the impression that the frog is smiling broadly over some arcane amphibian joke. You can see its throat bulge out and in, expanding and contracting with air, and Jenny's trying to do the same thing with her cheeks, passing a bubble of air back and forth.

I've come to warn Caitlin about the garden club troubles. That's what I tell myself. The afternoon sun is sumptuously warm, and Caitlin's wearing a thin cotton blouse and scandalously short skirt, vaguely Indonesian. I can't seem to prevent myself from glancing at her bare legs. Long and exquisite, they have me entranced and I keep catching myself ogling them slyly, a dirty old man in the making, pretending not to, to be studying something fascinating in the patterns of the deck's cedar planking. Does she notice, I wonder? Is she even conscious of how fine she looks? With Caitlin I can't tell. Her lovely legs softly cross one another, enfolding my idiot's imagination between them.

"So how are you, J.J.?" she asks, and glancing up I catch a mischievous look in her eyes and smile.

How am I? Infatuated? Spellbound? Bewitched?

"I'm worried," I say.

"Oh, alas!" Caitlin laughs. "I thought you were going to say something more . . ." She lingers over her adjective, archly.

"More what?"

"Oh . . . risqué?" The sugar plum she's nibbling oozes tantalizing juice across her lips and fingers.

"Risqué?" She's leading me on again, but I'll be too quick for her this time. "I think we've run more than enough risks in the last little while, don't you?"

"Not a bit of it," Caitlin thickens her brogue a touch as she hopscotches across to her countryside colleen charm. "We've only been splashing about in a wading pool."

"Glub, glub," Jenny says, trying to talk tree frog, then, "Mommy," she says, looking up.

"Yes, sweetie?" Caitlin leans forward in her chair so that I see the lovely movement of her shoulders, suntanned arms, her breasts beneath thin cotton. "What is it?"

"Frodo the frog wants to splash in the wading pool too!"

"Does he?" Caitlin laughs, "the cheeky little bugger! He's worse than J.J. here."

"J.J.'s not cheeky," the little girl giggles, smiling at me, "he's nice."

"Thank you, my dear," I say, bowing to her.

"Indeed he is," Caitlin says, leaning back in her deck chair again, stretching her long legs forward, "that's why he's come to help us today. Is it not?" she turns to me impertinently.

"I'm worried about the garden club," I say, my lust well tucked behind the respectable breastplate of duty. "That flyer was really nasty, and I know they're going to get the Dreebs and all that bunch out. I'm afraid it'll be really unpleasant, especially for you."

"Dear old Upshot," Caitlin grimaces and shakes her head of wild red hair. "Isn't it funny, after all we've just been through, to be back home in the real world where a garden club insurrection's the biggest news of the season. Isn't it just too silly for words?"

"I guess I worry about you," I say. "Waddy and Elvira both think they'll go after you especially."

"Yes I know, they've both called."

"You don't seem very concerned."

"Well, I'm not."

"I guess I feel you maybe should be."

"Why on earth for? I mean, what can they possibly do? They'll rant and rave and go home and have a few drinks and that will be an end to it. A month from now, no one will even remember what happened."

"I think they'll do more than that. I think they'll try to destroy your reputation."

"My reputation?" Caitlin laughs heartily. "The only reputation I've got in their minds is as a saucebox."

"What?"

"A hussy. A woman of easy virtue."

"That's not true."

"Don't you think so, J.J.?"

"Not at all."

"Not even a little bit? Not even when you're looking at my legs?" She poses her legs coquettishly, like a fashion model, and I feel myself blush. Damn the power this sex thing has!

"You don't care what people think, do you?"

"Of course I do," she breaks her pose, "especially you. But if you do anything at all, there's somebody not going to like it, particularly when you live in a fishbowl like we do."

"Glub, glub," Jenny says again.

"Yes, darlin'," Caitlin says to her, "Frodo's welcome to stay in the fishbowl for as long as he likes." Then to me again, "If we only do what won't offend anyone, we won't do much worthwhile at all. You know that."

"But isn't it important what other people think of you, how they see you, isn't that what Kumquat's about in the end, getting more and more people involved because they admire and respect the people already active there?"

"You sound terribly concerned, for someone who was just going to play rainbow warrior for an afternoon," Caitlin takes a little jab. "You're partly right, but the true measure of what we do is the values we hold, not how other people see us. We don't do what we do for approval, we do it because we must." She pauses. "Can I say something to you, J.J.?"

"You've seldom hesitated before." I play it light, but inwardly fearful, gulping like Frodo the frog.

"Just this: you don't need to keep looking at your life through other people's eyes. You don't need anyone's permission to be who you are."

"I know." I'm mortified she sees my pusillanimity so clearly. "At least, my head knows it, but the rest of me carries on the same as always. Afraid of being caught, I guess, afraid of being punished."

"But who's going to catch you? Who's going to punish you? Not Geoffrey Munz, surely, not the Dreebs."

"No."

"Who then?"

"I don't know. Myself, I suppose."

"Yes."

We both fall silent. I don't know what's more excruciating, these intimate disclosures or the dreadful inner force pressing me towards Caitlin. She bites into another plum, its thick sweet juice moistening her lips and teeth. A glistening dribble runs down towards her chin. Smiling, she wipes it away with the back of her hand.

"That's what was weird about the blockade," I say, holding firm against the allure of her wet mouth, "that we were actually caught, that someone is going to punish us for it. In some ways it's my worst nightmare come true."

"But not so terrible really."

"I can think of more terrifying things." Like making love to you. Like falling in love and being tossed out, the way you tossed your defrocked poet.

"Yes," she says again, wistfully.

"Being in the group made it different; there's no guilt or shame when it's shared that way."

"Um. Bloody Catholics. Even when we know there shouldn't be guilt or shame, when we know what we're doing is right."

"But if you don't know? Or if you suspect it's not right?" Like loving you, perhaps.

"Or maybe we've just been told so often what's right and wrong, we don't know unless we're told."

"Funny, you know. All those years in the monastery, we lived strictly by the Holy Rule of Blessed Columkille the Lesser. It told you precisely what was permitted and what forbidden. Yes, it was absurd and oppressive in some ways, but it was also strangely comforting, because it was absolute and unmistakable. I miss that, the scrupulous objectivity."

"Absolute truth," Caitlin nods. "Yes, I wouldn't mind a dash more of it myself. I think that papal infallibility malarkey must be permanently imprinted on us."

"I mean look at this whole Kumquat thing," I spread my hands like a rug merchant. "Thugs showing up with clubs in the night, that crazy blockade and the bear, Mistral appearing like the angel Gabriel every time you turn around. I mean the whole thing's incredible."

"I know. It seems foolish even talking about it now, doesn't it? As though it were all a dream and not real at all. A movie you'd seen years ago. Sometimes I wonder if we haven't made half of it up. I've been thinking about it a lot since we got back. I can't quite decide if we embellish these experiences in hindsight, you know, make them far more fantastical than they actually were, or if in fact certain experiences really are much fuller and richer than we're accustomed to, more interwoven with subtlety and magic than we're normally aware of. Maybe it's just at certain times we break through the membrane—what do they call it? the cloud of unknowing—and suddenly there we are: caught up in some wonderful, frightening, vivid intensity that later on we can't quite believe really happened.

"That's how this whole thing was for me." Caitlin's very concentrated, exquisitely intense. "Like I'd been bumped into a different plane of experience. My senses were keenly alert, my connections with other people were direct, everything seemed more vibrant and alive, more real somehow. But then, as I say, I wonder if maybe I'm just romanticizing everything."

"Not you!" I exclaim and Caitlin smiles.

"Glub, glub," Jenny says again in tree frog.

"Can you remember it at all clearly?" I ask. "Because I really can't."

"Not really," Caitlin shakes her head, "not the way I'd like to, anyway. It's like seeing it through filters now."

"On the road you called us 'an expeditionary force of angels,' remember?"

"Glub, glub."

"Yes, darlin'," Caitlin says to Jenny, "you're an angel sent from heaven cleverly disguised as a frog."

"Glub, glub, glub," Jenny says, and Caitlin exclaims with delight.

"It's funny you should have said that," I continue, "about the angels, because that whole morning I was having incredibly vivid flashes of my days in religious life."

"How so?" Caitlin spits a plum stone out. It arches across the deck and onto the lawn.

"It started in my dreams, that night in the camp. I was back in the monastery, full of anxiety about whether to leave or not, whether I'd lost my vocation, turned my back on God's calling."

"God, you did get a dose of it," Caitlin says. "You make me feel like a Catholic wimp for my few scrawny years with the nuns."

"Then there was that cavalcade in the darkness, like a candlelight procession on Good Friday, and the chanting. The whole event carried me back. Until the bear. Then it was just out-and-out crazy."

"That's when it really got a bit thick, didn't it?" Caitlin smiles wryly. "You know, apart from little Jenny here coming into the world the way she did . . ."

"How did I come in, Mommy?" Jenny asks, suddenly interested.

"Like a storm off the sea, darlin'," Caitlin reaches forward and touches her daughter's head tenderly, "like wind and waves and seagulls screaming, that's how you arrived, missy."

"You mean like a frog?"

"Yes, just like a frog!" Caitlin claps her hands with glee. "Just like a little green frog with suction pads on your fingertips, you clung to me that tightly, you little tadpole grown too big for its pond!"

"Glub, glub," Jenny says, and Caitlin laughs again.

"Apart from that," Caitlin turns back to me, "and maybe apart from the first time or two that a boy and I actually did it right, what happened at the bridge that morning was about the most powerful experience I've ever had."

"So you believe it really happened? That Mistral Wind transformed herself into a real bear?"

"I have to say I do. I saw it as clearly as I see you now. I know it's loony tunes material, but there it is. I have to believe what I saw."

"What's become of Mistral, do you think, is she gone forever?"

"I have no idea."

We pause for a moment, so the only sound to be heard is Jenny's soft conversation with Frodo. Caitlin picks up a plum distractedly, but does not bite into it.

"Have you ever been lost in the forest?" I ask. "Really lost, where you don't have a clue which direction to go to get out?"

"Yes, I have, several times. Picking chanterelles, where you wander from patch to patch, and at last look up, and your whole sense of direction is gone."

"And how scary that is," I add, "how you have to fight down panic, beat back the surging fear that you're lost forever, that somehow you'll never find your way out?"

"Yes."

"That's what my life feels like now."

"Hmm. Mine doesn't, touch wood. But it has, believe me, it has. And it's okay when that happens. Don't you see, J.J.? It's how you leave your old skin behind, how you slough it off, by getting lost for a while, then finding yourself again, alive in a whole new world."

"A leap of faith, you mean."

"I guess."

"And where does all this leave us now?"

"Us who, you and me?"

"And me too, Mommy!"

"Yes, you too, darlin'. We'd never go get lost in the woods without you along."

"Yes," I answer.

"Is there someplace you'd like it to leave us?"

Is there? I cannot and do not deny that I am slipping gradually, fearfully, ecstatically into loving this woman. We have been friends, allies, for years. But kept apart by something vaguely dangerous that I did not understand but feared enough to keep myself safely in my world and she in hers. I thought the danger lay only in Caitlin herself, in some tragic flaw within her personality that condemned her to a tumultuous sequence of passionate debacles. Which I did not want to be one of. Poor Caitlin going down in flames again. Poor Joseph, falls in love for the first time in his life and look who he chooses.

Now I'm not so sure. Not so sure of anything at all.

"I don't know," I say. "Do you?"

But Caitlin doesn't answer right away. I see that wistful smile drift across her face again, and I realize that she may feel as lost as I do, that for all her bold talk, she may be as confused and unsure of where she is, as vulnerable even, as I am.

18

As I enter the community hall, I'm assailed by a tremendous humming tension, as though the place contains an enormous nest of hornets. The old hall's packed, probably 160 people where we'd normally have 30. Pausing just inside the door, I scan the room. A lot of these people are definitely not club members, some of them I've never seen before. I get an awful queasy sensation in my stomach, like motion sickness, stirred by cowardly fear of conflict, but also protectiveness for Caitlin, who must face this mob.

The four Dreeb boys are standing in an ominous line-up against the back wall, looking as though they can't wait for a fistfight to break out. I spot Jimmy Fitz nearby, studiously poring over a new copy of *The Automotive Buy and Sell*, his body language plainly saying that this is the last place in the world he wants to be. Blackie the Mechanic—who I don't believe I've ever seen at any meeting on any topic ever before— sits next to Jimmy, reading over Jimmy's shoulder while cracking his knuckles and scowling through his thick black beard the way he always does. Up in the front row, wearing taupe, Elsie Pitfield sits stiffly on the edge of her chair with an adamantine face. She's even got her enigmatic brother alongside. "Pits," as he's called, is very seldom seen straying this far afield from his wet bar, and appears to perch on his chair like an exotic bird spotted far from its normal range.

I pick out Peewee and Julia sitting near the back, and take a seat next to them, glad to have allies close at hand. I notice that the chief conspirators have scattered themselves strategically around the room, presumably in order to orchestrate subsections of the crowd. Fibber

Miller and Ernie Moffatt are dragging in additional stacks of chairs for the overflow crowd.

"Do you think they're all here to discuss saving their own seeds?" Julia asks me, archly, leaning across Peewee's lap. The meeting is supposed to feature a discussion on propagating favourite annuals and perennials by collecting and storing our own seeds.

"Absolutely," I say, "especially the Dreeb boys. Very big on seeds."

Julia and Peewee giggle like schoolkids.

At 7:30 on the dot, Caitlin and Elvira enter from the side door and walk to the dais at the front of the hall. The hornet hum intensifies. Caitlin, as president, will chair the meeting. Elvira's recording secretary.

I have a lump in my throat thick as clotted cream.

Caitlin calls the meeting to order, but there's no light-flicking or gavel-banging or shouting above the crowd noise for her—no, she just stands there in front of us and the noise subsides like a rustling of aspen leaves gone still after a gust of wind. Absolute silence. Then Caitlin smiles, one of her brilliant peaches-and-cream, sweet-innocent-colleen smiles.

"It's a marvellous thing," she announces to the crowd in a voice as clear as uillean pipes singing across the hills, "a marvellous thing indeed to see this grand rebirth of interest in horticulture."

A nervous titter ripples across the room. You can feel the tension in the place begin to shift, the way a morning mist lifts off a bog.

Caitlin waits, as poised as a veteran stand-up comic working the crowd. "I assume," she resumes at just the right moment to catch the crowd in free fall, "that the many new faces here tonight have paid their club membership dues." Here she pauses again, and you can hear a little serpent of uncertainty slither into the crowd. "If not, our treasurer, Gertrude, will be happy to relieve you of the fee."

Gertrude smiles from her card table by the door. A murmuring of doubt swirls around, as part of the crowd senses its moral outrage being somehow outflanked.

"Now," Caitlin announces, smiling benevolently all the while, "I should like to call this meeting of the Upshot Island Garden Club and Horticultural Society to order. We'll begin, as always, with a reading of last month's minutes. Elvira."

Elvira stands up and reads the minutes in a voice that seems to tremble on the brink of a deep precipice. Several times it slips and almost falls. Elvira's as tough as oak roots in her own way, and not afraid of much. But she hates public speaking, and even having to read her minutes aloud to a crowd this size is a challenge for her.

She gets to last month's motion about the club sending a delegation to Kumquat. Just at that moment a fierce male voice bellows out "Bullshit!"

Silence stuns the room. Elvira stumbles to a halt. Heads turn in the crowd and a confused murmuring breaks out. It's Hunter Dreeb who's yelled.

Caitlin smiles directly at Hunter. "We'll accept additions or corrections to the minutes after Elvira's finished reading them," she says, ever so sweetly.

Hunter says "Bullshit!" a second time, much quieter though, almost to himself, and subsides against the wall, apparently prepared to await another provocation before erupting further.

Of all the Dreebs, Hunter's the worst. Not as big as Rufus, and nowhere near as smart as Crispin, poor Hunter kicks and curses his way through life, as though all the earth were entangled in the familial black bindweed. Waddy once summarized Hunter's situation pithily: "Feller's got his pecker on backwards."

The disruption has raised the tension in the room to a terrible tightness. Elvira resumes reading the minutes at an accelerated pace. She finishes up with a breathless dash to the wire, so that the latter minutes seem more like seconds and none of them make very much sense, which is the destiny of most minutes anyway. Elvira sits down with an Umph!

"Thank you, Elvira," Caitlin says, still calm as a Bodhidharma. "Now: any corrections or additions to the minutes?" She looks straight at Hunter, pinning him to the wall with her gaze the way an entomologist might pin a collected beetle. Hunter squirms but says nothing.

"Nothing?" Caitlin's gaze sweeps the room.

The minutes are accepted as read, much to Elvira's evident relief. "I hate it when the Philadelphia lawyers get after my minute-taking," she told me once, "as though we're amending the Canadian Constitution, not having a little garden club meeting."

"Now," Caitlin says, one hurdle cleanly leapt, "business arising from the minutes?"

Geoffrey Munz rises with great solemnity from his chair, as though the College of Cardinals had just elected him Pope. He's wearing his country squire tweeds.

"Yes?" Caitlin recognizes him, the picture of innocence.

"Madame Chair," Geoffrey begins, clearing his throat, "concerning the Kumquat issue." (There's that "iss-yew" again!) "I should like to move a motion."

"Please do," Caitlin smiles, as though she's been awaiting no greater pleasure all day long.

"I move," Geoffrey intones solemnly, like Winston Churchill over the BBC, "that the Upshot Island Garden Club and Horticultural Society deplores and renounces the illegal actions of certain of its members at Kumquat Sound, and that it rescinds and holds null and void its earlier motion authorizing any member to commit illegal acts as official representatives of this organization."

Geoffrey sits down to a round of vigorous applause, foot stamping, whistling, and shouts of "Right on!"

"Thank you," Caitlin smiles at Geoffrey. "Do you have the motion, Elvira?"

"I'm not sure I've got it just right," Elvira says. "Was that 'deplores and renounces' or 'deplores and denounces'?"

"I believe, Madame Chair," says Geoffrey, rising again on a point of clarification, but looking rather absurdly like Count Dracula rising from his coffin, "that the motion reads 'deplores and denounces.' "

Peewee, sitting right beside me, instantly shoots his hand into the air.

"Yes, Peewee?" Caitlin says.

"Madame Chair," Peewee always talks fast at meetings, "I believe the mover said quite distinctly 'deplores and renounces' when the motion was moved. And this makes far more sense than to say, as he now does, 'deplores and denounces,' because deploring and denouncing are somewhat redundant, whereas deploring and renouncing indicates both a judgement about the activity in question and an actual withdrawal of support for it, which, unless I'm mistaken, is the intent of the motion."

A muttering of dissatisfaction arises, indicating little patience for Peewee's nitpicking. But Peewee is a student of semantics, and sits down with an air of having made an important distinction. Truth to tell, Peewee has a leaning towards the Philadelphia lawyerism that Elvira grouses about.

"Thank you, Peewee," Caitlin says. "Does the mover of the motion agree that it read 'deplores and renounces,' or would you like to stick with 'deplores and denounces'?"

You can hear scattered groans across the crowd.

"Madame Chair," Geoffrey's back up again, twitching in his tweeds, "I believe the intent of my motion is perfectly clear. Frankly, I'd like to both denounce and renounce this whole sordid affair." A smattering of clapping accompanies this sally, though plainly the complexities of the case are already beginning to muddy the previous clarity of certain people's convictions.

"Am I to understand," Caitlin asks, still smiling beatifically, "that you would like to amend the motion to include both renounce and denounce?"

Geoffrey's momentarily nonplussed, and Peewee leaps to his feet in the breach.

"Point of order, Madame Chair," Peewee calls.

"Yes, Peewee?"

"Madame Chair, the motion has been duly moved but not yet seconded, and I don't believe the rules of order allow us to discuss amending the motion until it is seconded." Peewee sits down with a wonderful gravitas, as though he's just been awarded the Nobel Prize in physics.

"Quite right. Thank you," Caitlin says. "Is there a seconder for the motion?"

Several arms shoot into the air. Elsie Pitfield's recognized as seconder.

"Now," Caitlin says, "it has been moved and seconded . . ."

"Point of order, Madame Chair!" This time it's Fibber Miller on his feet. Fibber has never been known to set spade to soil, but his many land transactions have given him a certain expertise in legal matters.

"Yes, Mr. Miller?" Caitlin seems to be enjoying herself in this procedural quagmire.

"How can the motion be seconded," Fibber asks, "when we haven't yet determined what the wording of the motion is?"

Another round of groans, louder this time.

"Thank you, that's a point well taken," Caitlin says. "Is the seconder clear as to the wording of the motion?"

"Oh, for God's sakes," Elsie Pitfield snaps from the front row, "let's get the wording settled and get on with it!"

Caitlin runs us all around the track a few more laps, entertaining motions to amend, to withdraw, to table the motion, ruling that only the mover of a motion could move that it be tabled, that no new motion could be moved, seconded, or discussed while an existing motion is on the floor. Elvira gets herself into a complete muddle as to what's being moved by whom. Elsie Pitfield keeps calling "Question!" trying to force the vote forward, but at every turn a new procedural hook snags us, as though we're trying to beat our way through a copse of thorny brambles. Arms are shooting up and down as everyone scrambles to grab a bit of turf through points of order and procedural refinements. In all of the hubbub, we never quite get around to addressing the gist of Geoffrey's original motion, which is by now amended beyond recognition.

The sweet irony in all of this is that it was Geoffrey himself who had, while he was president of the club, introduced the cumbersome rules of order that are now throttling his motion. Back then he'd called them a more civilized manner of proceeding than the conversational and occasionally chaotic forms that had been the norm before.

My anxieties are quietening down. I no longer feel as though I should be sheltering Caitlin from the storm. She says she's no Joan of Arc, but she is, I think, wonderfully strong and courageous. I see her as Ingrid Bergman staring into a floodlit future, unafraid, buoyed by a faith far stronger than the vapid one I once had and lost.

You can't exactly call what's happening here manipulation on Caitlin's part—it's more like she's orchestrating the collective nuttiness in the room so that it continues to fold back upon itself, like the mythic snake in a self-consuming coil. Peewee and Julia start giggling part way through, and then I start too. A few hotheads storm out in disgust.

All of a sudden, the big front door of the hall swings dramatically open and, astonishingly, in steps Mistral Wind. I see her straight away. I'd expected never to see her again, after her transformation—or pres- tidigitation or whatever it was—on the bridge. But here she is! It's unbe- lievable how the woman can enter a place—whether it's the Black Hole or the blockade or, now, the packed Community Hall—and every eye goes immediately to her. A hush descends across the room, and every- one turns to look at Mistral.

She stands by the doorway, dressed in the rough brown tunic she wore the first time I laid eyes on her. She turns to look at Caitlin. Sparks and flashes seem to fly between the two women, like fake static electri- city flashing between electrodes in Dr. Frankenstein's B-movie laboratory.

"Seeds, I believe?" Mistral says, in that husky voice of hers that's never loud but always heard.

"Yes," Caitlin answers her, luminous with mischievous glee, "it's seeds indeed tonight."

Did Caitlin know that Mistral was on-island? Surely she'd have mentioned it to me.

"I've brought some *Meconopsis* seeds from China," Mistral announces to the room in a heroic tone that implies she's journeyed to China herself, perhaps crossing the Gobi desert by camel, and carried these precious seeds away with her especially for us. "They're such a gorgeous sky blue in the shade," she rhapsodizes, "I wanted to give you all some. May I distribute them, Madame Chair?"

"Please," Caitlin waves her arm across the crowd in invitation. "We're all crying out for a few moments of sober second thought."

Mistral proceeds around the room, carrying a large spruce-root basket from which she takes packets of seed, giving one in turn to every person in the room. The packets are handmade of rough fibres and imprinted with arcane symbols.

She speaks quietly to each person as she presents the packets. I'm reminded of the priests dispensing holy communion. People accept her seed packets with a kind of bemused reverence, the way I used to take the sacred wafer on my tongue when I was no longer certain that it was in fact the Body of Christ. The Dreeb brothers squirm like guilty urchins when Mistral stands before each of them in turn, looks at them without distaste or fear, speaks softly to them, giving them her blessing and her seeds. Even the insurrectionists—Geoffrey and Elsie and Karl and the rest—seem disarmed, and accept her offering, however coolly, without incident.

She gets to where Julia and Peewee and I are sitting near the end. By then there's a buzzing and humming in the room very different from the hostile swarming sounds at the outset. Mistral stands before me and hands me her packet. "A blessing upon you and upon all that grows," she says to me, looking straight into my eyes.

What precisely my feelings are at this moment I cannot say. I'm unconscious of myself and my surroundings, lifted out of myself in some way. I seem to be floating, suspended in transcendent bliss. All is benign and sublimely peaceful. I feel suffused by ecstasy, as when you close your eyes and sniff the perfect fragrance of an aromatic rose.

I remain in that blissful state for what seems like a very long time. Gradually, reluctantly, I come back to a sense of the here-and-now.

Mistral is still before me, smiling. "I'm sure we shall meet again, Joseph," she says to me, as she said once before, in what now seems a long, long time ago.

I want desperately to talk to Mistral, to ask her about the bear, and other things, things I had not wanted to see in her before. But she moves on to Julia. I'm aware that the room, so shortly before seething with tension and anxiety, is now relaxed, breathing peacefully, floating like a basking shark in the ocean.

Her tour of the room completed, Mistral pauses again by the doorway where she'd entered. Just then the door swings open again and who walks in but Zyrk, carrying the bear head. The whole room gasps in astonishment. Zyrk walks up to Margaret May, who's sitting beside an aisle. He places the head on the floor alongside her and bows profoundly. Margaret May fluffs herself like a hen that's just laid an egg.

Back at the door, Mistral scans the room. "Farewell," she says to all of us. "You are gardeners. People of the Earth. Protect her. Give her your protection as I now give you my blessing." She bows once and steps through the door, out into the night, with Zyrk close behind her.

19

The rains begin. Relentless rain for weeks on end. A lowering sky so leaden and oppressive you sprint to the outhouse, stooping as though under helicopter rotors. Southeasters come thumping up the strait like sloppy drunks, slapping your spirit with wind and rain, scouring your soul of its deepest secrets, leaving it bleached and cracked as a weather-beaten log on a beach. Gumboots line the hallways of houses in which desperate parties are thrown against the sopping darkness. I sit alone in my house, considering, half reading books that do not hold my interest, chafing against the appalling predictability of days.

I sometimes rise in the mornings now with a vague dread that life is slipping past me, that I've become like the hapless Polack of Waddy's tale, trying to hold an enormous locomotive against the grade, against the awful forces of inertia that hurtle one along to certain doom. When I look in the bathroom mirror, my cranky old father looks back at me.

I take to writing gloomy poems about regret and loss. About openings through which there may have existed a chance for happiness, not seen or perhaps carelessly passed by. Occasions for extending kindnesses, for nurturing affection, left unattended. Not saying words that must be spoken until it's too late and there's no one left to hear. I am awash in bathos.

For Caitlin's gone. She and Jenny have flown back east to attend her ailing mother. Waddy too—he's in Arizona for six weeks, staying with Johnny and Eulalie Fitz. The excitement of last summer is fled. Our little company of adventurers is dissolved. Even Elvira is toppling. She and I spend many a winter evening together, drinking perhaps more blackberry wine than we should. She is beginning to doubt that Freddie will ever return, and it's awful to see that doubt creeping like a fungus over her stout soul. Sturm und Drang we call ourselves after several glasses.

We are sustained a bit by following the antics of the new Upshot Island Horticultural Society. After Mistral's dramatic intervention, which has become legend, the meeting settled down to a reasonably civilized discussion of options. A divorce was hinted at. I think it was Margaret May herself—flushed with the celebrity of her prodigal bear's head returned—first broached it, saying something to the effect that it's better to part while you can rather than linger when you can't. The possibility of separation was discussed without rancour, and amicably arranged. A new club, with Geoffrey Munz as founding president, was severed from the old. Someone, I believe it was Jimmy Fitz, said, in an uncharacteristically metaphoric outburst, that this severing was much like dividing perennials for the ultimate good of the plant. The Dreebs filed out at that point, back to their northern stronghold.

Following considerable, and slightly less amicable, discussion, the name too was broken up. Henceforward the old club was to be known as The Upshot Island Garden Club. The new offshoot was christened the Upshot Island Horticultural Society. "After all," as Geoffrey Munz put it, "I do believe that the preponderance of horticultural expertise resides in the organization I have the honour to represent."

Perhaps. But Elvira's information, gleaned from subsequent visits to Wilhelmina's Beauty Salon, is that things have in the meantime not gone as smoothly as had been hoped for in the new horticultural society. Deprived of the cohesion achieved through fighting a common enemy, the group—never large to begin with, and shrunken considerably since—has apparently degenerated into intramural bickering. At one point, if Wilhelmina can be believed, Petty MacIvor goaded Karl Muhlbacher into an appalling shouting match triggered by Petty's description of dahlias as "the kind of thing some people grow to go with their pink plastic flamingoes." Perhaps the preponderance of horticultural expertise weighs too heavily upon them.

"But what about Mistral's departing words," I asked Caitlin the evening before she was to fly away from us, "about gardeners being the guardians of the earth? Buy it or not?"

"Absolutely," Caitlin didn't hesitate, "so long as you throw in the artists too."

"And mothers and kids," Elvira added. The three of us were cozy in Caitlin's kitchen, and my heart was heavy that she was leaving us for what could be a long stay with her mother. We had not been together, she and I, spoken together the way I'd hoped we would. I don't know what prevented it. After that day on her deck, eating sugar plums together, we somehow pulled away, as the days grew shorter, other concerns came crowding in, and before I knew it, that opening was closed, sealed up tight, like a tree awaiting winter.

"Of course," Caitlin agreed, "poets and mystics too."

"You would put in the poets," I said.

"I'll miss you both while I'm away," she said, then she and Elvira hugged. Then she and I, awkwardly, no longer just friends, but not lovers either. But the touch of her, the scent of her, in that awkward embrace!

Caitlin phones on Christmas Eve to say her mother's suffered another heart attack. Caitlin will stay on to close up the house and settle her mother in a nursing home.

I write to her, clumsily, as one does around tragedy. I enclose a maudlin poem about love and death. She does not write back. I am left, bleached and cracked, awaiting a spring tide.

March brings a hint of warmth, softening the sharp edges of the wind. Yesterday I saw the first hyacinths breaking from cold ground, wonderful tumescent nubs erupting from soil cracked and fissured from the force of their green surge.

The telephone rings.

"Hello, J.J.," Caitlin's voice, fresh as buds breaking. "How are you?"

"Oh, Caitlin!" is all I can manage.

"Not angry at me, are you?"

"Angry?" My mind's misfiring; I don't know what she means.

"For not writing or phoning."

"God, no. Not at all. Don't be silly. Where are you?"

"What, didn't think of me at all?"

"Just once or twice, in a slow moment. Where are you?"

"I'm here. Home. And I'm ever so glad."

"I'm so glad too. How's your mum? Can I see you?"

"Oh, I've got about a million things to do with Jenny and school and the house. We're still due in court on Monday, are we not?"

"Yes, that's right. We planned to all go down together on Sunday. We have to meet our lawyers Sunday night. There's billets arranged for us. Do you need a hand with stuff before then?"

"No, I'll be all right. Thanks. I need to just be here and do what I have to do. Okay?"

"Of course. Are you bringing Jenny with you?"

"No. She's going to stay with Alonzo at his mum's. She needs to be settled someplace while this court stuff goes on, and in case they lock us up."

"You don't think it will come to that, do you?"

"It might. This is still tragedy as well as farce."

"I know. I'm sorry about your mother."

"Thanks. J.J.?"

"Yes?"

"I am anxious to see you, you know."

"Good. I actually thought of you a lot."

"I'll see you Sunday then."

"Yes."

I'm one of the apostles on Pentecost Sunday, a tongue of fire licking above my head.

Riding to the city in Caitlin's old Volvo, with Waddy riding shotgun—he won't drive in the city, Allah be praised—Elvira and I in the back, riding to trial, I feel both apprehensive and absurdly joyful, as happy as I've ever been.

We are due in court tomorrow morning. Tonight we are meeting, by prior arrangement, two lawyers assigned to us by Legal Aid. The meeting is at a place inauspiciously called the Sliced Pear, immediately across the street from the provincial courthouse.

We've not met these lawyers before and we had no choice in their selection. They are part of a large pool of lawyers that has gathered around the ongoing Kumquat mass trials "like gulls at a garbage dump" in the inelegant phrase of one tabloid columnist. Two members of our group—Waddy and Zyrk—are eligible for free legal assistance, and were assigned a Mr. Goukas and a Mr. Chang by Legal Aid. Since we are being tried as a group, the two lawyers offered to represent the rest of us as well for, as Mr. Goukas put it, "no additional emolument." All these arrangements were concluded by telephone. Now we're about to encounter our champions in the flesh.

Waddy hadn't wanted to be represented by a lawyer. Over winter he began preparing to defend himself by watching lawyer shows on television. But shortly after getting back from Arizona he let it out of the bag that he was already experienced in the finer points of judicial self-defence.

"They nicked me down-island one time for drunk and disorderly," he told me one gloomy afternoon at the general store. "So they bring me up before the circuit judge, me and a coupla other fellas, and there was somethin' about that judge just rubbed me the wrong way. Snooty bastard, y'know. Anyways, I guess I got a bit obstreperous-like, told the bastard what his judgin' was worth in my opinion, and instead of some piss-ass little fine, I end up in the slammer for a week! Haw, haw!"

This tale, coupled with the announcement that Waddy was preparing to represent himself, sent alarm bells ringing in my brain.

"Waddy," I said to him, "you're a steam man. You're not cut out for that fancy talking. Maybe best leave it to the ambulance chasers." I got Caitlin to tell him the same thing, and somehow I think she was more persuasive than me. He finally consented to pitch in with the rest of us. Peewee and Julia meanwhile hired their own lawyer, a hotshot attorney from back east recently relocated. Nobody's sure what, if anything, Zyrk is going to do.

Waddy, Caitlin, Elvira and I enter the Sliced Pear, an undistinguished establishment wobbling, in the Canadian way, somewhere between a restaurant and a beer hall. Moving like a school of minnows through a haze of tobacco smoke and beer fumes, we make our way to an alcove where the two lawyers await us.

Mr. Goukas is an enormously corpulent customer who doesn't bother about rising to greet us. Mr. Chang, on the other hand, leaps to his feet at our approach, smiling radiantly.

"How do you do," Mr. Chang says, shaking hands and bowing slightly to each of us in turn. He's as slender and precise as his colleague is lumpish.

Mr. Goukas waves a plump hand towards the chairs, indicating we might sit, and sips from a brandy snifter that could have doubled as a fish bowl. Mr. Chang is drinking tea.

"What'll you have?" Mr. Goukas asks us, glancing around the table as though we're a gaggle of peasants gathered in the unaccustomed splendour of a great country house, and he the lord of the shire. He reminds me of Charles Laughton in his latter roles—amplitudinous and suety, oleaginous and shrewd in the pursuit of dissipation.

Mr. Goukas tosses back the dregs of his brandy and waves his fat hand in the air. A stunning young waitress glides across the room to our table on over-exposed and breathtakingly-elongated legs. She leans towards Mr. Goukas, with whom she seems very familiar, revealing a set of preternaturally ripe breasts.

"Do you think the old lecher's having it off with that barmaid?" Caitlin whispers in my ear, reading my mind the way she does, exciting me by just being close.

It's pretty apparent that Mr. Goukas has a soft spot for spirits, and perhaps for barmaids too. Why else would he be taking penny-ante legal aid cases? He doesn't give the impression of someone who's in it for the principle of the thing. Mr. Chang, on the other hand, seems entirely punctilious and honourable. He kindly orders tea for us from the statuesque waitress, once she's withdrawn her chest from Mr. Goukas' appreciative gaze. Caitlin kicks my shin under the table.

Replenished snifter firmly in hand, Mr. Goukas calls our pretrial conference to order. "My friends," he says to us, looking gravely around the table, his great jowls quivering with the importance of his message, "you face conviction for criminal contempt of court. This is a serious matter, a very serious matter indeed. But before you can be found guilty of that charge, the Crown must prove beyond a reasonable doubt four elements, namely," here Mr. Goukas sips again from his snifter and refers to a document placed in his pudgy hand by the attentive Mr. Chang. "Namely, that there existed a valid court order; that you committed an act or acts prohibited by that order; that you had knowledge of the order; and, lastly, that you committed these acts in such a way as to constitute criminal contempt."

At this point the waitress returns with a large pot of herb tea and cups for each of us. Mr. Goukas glowers at the teapot as though it holds steeping mare's piss. Mr. Chang sips his own tea approvingly.

"How can the silly bastards call that criminal contempt, standin' around on a roadway for a coupla minutes?" Waddy snorts. "I'll show 'em contempt if that's what they want!" Waddy's wearing an ill-fitting shirt and a ridiculous tie for the pretrial conference, and seems not at all sure about the tea.

"The Crown," continues Mr. Goukas, his fleshy wattles quavering, "must prove beyond a reasonable doubt that you knowingly and willfully disobeyed the order in such a way as to bring the administration of justice into scorn."

"Not us, surely," Elvira quips. Mr. Goukas glowers at her.

"Or in such a way," he reasserts his authority, glancing again at the document, "as to impair public confidence in the integrity of the court or of the administration of justice."

"I'd say they'd pretty well impaired that themselves with these monkey trials, wouldn't you?" Caitlin asks.

Mr. Goukas studies her for a moment, his great bushy eyebrows undulating like hairy caterpillars engaged in a chase across the folded flesh of his forehead. He seems to realize that Caitlin, for all her beauty, is no barmaid awaiting his salacious attentions. He refers to his manuscript again.

"Or in such a way," he concludes, his gravity sustained, "that demonstrated a public and blatant defiance of the authority of the court."

"Well, that's not us at all," Elvira says, matter-of-factly. "I think they've got the wrong people."

"Whoa, hold on there, honeybunch," Waddy interrupts her, spilling tea on the tabletop. "Speak for yourself. I got nothin' but contempt for them bastards. What about them assholes threatenin' women at the camp. How come they ain't been charged with anythin'? Ain't that kinda crap bringin' the administration of justice into scorn, eh?"

"Ladies and gentlemen," Mr. Goukas is not about to let things get away from him, "it pains me to have to tell you this," he doesn't look the least bit pained, "but your personal opinions on the matter are, frankly, irrelevant. Your political convictions are likewise irrelevant. Your motivations for blocking the logging road are . . . what's the word, Mr. Chang?" He defers to his junior partner.

"Irrelevant," Mr. Chang chimes like a clock.

"Precisely," Mr. Goukas bangs the table with his hand, as though he's just ordered massed battalions into battle against an invading army. "I have outlined the four elements of the case. Now, let us consider the elements of our defence. We shall, of course, plead not guilty to these preposterous charges."

This unilateral determination on the part of Mr. Goukas falls like a failed soufflé in our midst. We've previously spent several tortuous and inconclusive evenings back on Upshot wrestling with how we should plead. The Kumquat trials already concluded have shown the likely consequences of various possible pleas. We can, as Mr. Goukas has already decided we will, plead not guilty and fight it out in court, employing whatever legal manoeuvres our learned counsel can devise to beat the rap.

"Well, as I see it, there's a problem or two with that angle," Caitlin tells Mr. Goukas. "For one thing, it essentially involves denying what we did. And it involves at least a three-week trial with very little chance of winning." Mr. Goukas bristles noticeably at this insubordination and Mr. Chang looks alarmed. "And it will probably piss the judge right off."

"All of these considerations," Mr. Goukas replies, after a pregnant pause, "are . . . what's the word, Mr. Chang?"

"Irrelevant," Mr. Chang says again, smiling broadly at us all.

"I can see pleading not guilty to criminal contempt," Caitlin presses on, "because what we did obviously wasn't criminal behaviour . . ."

Mr. Goukas is rumbling like a volcano.

"But none of us wants to deny that we were there or that we blocked the road. We did it publicly and purposively and we're proud that we did."

No sooner has she finished than Goukas rises from his chair, slowly, and waddles off across the room without saying a word.

"Is he leavin' or what?" Waddy asks. We're all a little disconcerted by the fellow.

"I believe my learned colleague needs to relieve himself," Mr. Chang smiles apologetically.

"What do you think, Mr. Chang?" Elvira asks. "About how to plead, I mean."

Mr. Chang pauses, considers, then says at last, "A very difficult question. If you enter a plea of guilty, the judge will probably go easier with you, because it saves the court a lot of time and money."

"And goes smack against what we stand for," Caitlin adds. "It amounts to abandoning our principles just to get a lighter sentence. I'm against it."

"Or you could take the path of the Mahatma—"Mr. Chang is still smiling broadly, "plead guilty but without any remorse whatsoever. This does not involve abandoning any principle, but it will get you a heavier sentence."

"Well, I'm still in favour of pleading guilty to civil contempt," Caitlin says. "We admit we were there and did what we did, but we had no intention of bringing the court into disrepute."

"And that we were civil in what we did," Elvira adds.

"Not me," Waddy pipes up. "No sir. I ain't givin' these clowns no easy way out. Reminds me of that time we come outta camp into town for a blow-out. Little gyppo show up near Loon Lake. There's this big donkey-puncher, name of Koslowski, takes us all over to a cathouse he knows. I never been with a whore before that, I was just a kid. So before we go in, Koslowski and the others nip into an alley and they all whip out their peckers, see—you ladies will pardon my French here, but I ain't describin' somethin' none of you ain't ever seen—and they start havin' at it."

We all whoop at Waddy, so that people at the other tables turn to see what's going on. "Waddy!" I exclaim, but there's no stopping him now.

"I ask 'em what the Sam Hill they're doin' and Koslowski looks at me like he's part-way through peelin' a banana. 'Hell's bells, sonnyboy,' he says to me, 'fer six bits she ain't gettin' the easy one!' Haw, Haw!" Waddy roars like an old bull sea lion.

"Anyways," Waddy settles down from his ribald tale, rubbing tears from his eyes, just as Mr. Goukas waddles back across the room, "the way I see it, it's the same thing here. The bastards ain't gettin' the easy one. I'm for not guilty."

"Well spoken, sir," says Mr. Goukas as he lowers himself ponderously back into his chair and resumes control of the meeting. "So we have one stout citizen here in Mr. . . . what?" He can't remember Waddy's name.

"Watts!" Waddy snaps at him like a Jack Russell.

"Indeed, Mr. Watts, a person prepared to exercise his full rights before the law. Now what of the rest of you?" Goukas frames the question in such a way that any plea other than not guilty will be viewed as tantamount to treason. Caitlin, Elvira and I exchange glances, and it's Elvira, steady as always, who speaks.

"I don't think I can plead not guilty," she tells the lawyers, "because I do believe that civil disobedience is a symbolic revolt against the state."

Mr. Chang smiles benevolently, but Goukas is plainly not pleased. He drinks from his snifter with elaborate indifference to what Elvira's saying.

"But pleading guilty doesn't really fit either," she continues. "I'm in a bit of a muddle. But I guess Gandhi figured it out about right. It seems to me what's closest to the truth is to plead guilty to civil contempt."

Mr. Goukas is staring off across the room at the long-legged waitress.

"That's my decision too," Caitlin adds, "guilty to civil contempt, and absolutely no remorse."

"And you, Mr. . . . ?" Goukas has lost my name as well.

"Jones," I say. I glance around the table. Waddy's got a combative glint in his eye, and you can almost hear him sharpening his weapons for the scrap ahead. Elvira and Caitlin seem perfectly serene about their decision. Mr. Chang is smiling at me broadly, and Mr. Goukas watching me shrewdly from the corner of his eyes, like an enormous toad studying the flight of an approaching insect.

"Well," I say at last, recognizing that my decision's based less on firm conviction than on a desire to stand alongside Caitlin and Elvira, "I guess I'm for guilty of civil contempt with no remorse as well."

"Fine," Mr. Goukas says with finality, and raises his arm for the waitress again, "now what'll you have?"

20

We enter Courtroom Number Two of the provincial courthouse in single file and sit, as instructed, on a long wooden bench at the front, immediately before the officers of the court. We are an even half-dozen—Peewee and Julia, Waddy, Caitlin, Elvira and I. Zyrk is nowhere to be seen.

A few spectators are scattered in the benches behind us. The arresting officer is there too, dressed sloppily in civvies, looking like he just rushed in from a game of squash. The company man who read the injunction to us is there as well, and a couple of other suits. It feels weird seeing these characters from that phantasmagorical morning at the blockade now sitting here like ordinary mortals with pock marks and dandruff.

The courtroom is clammy with stale air. The bench seats are upholstered with red leatherette that quickly becomes hot and sticky to sit on. I am reminded, uncomfortably, of old church pews and over-long sermons. There's nothing alive in here, except maybe dust mites. The only sound is a low hum coming from an unseen and unnecessary heating unit. There are no windows in the room at all, and pallid light from electric fixtures does not disperse the gloom that clings to the sombre wood-panelled walls. The room seems designed to function like a sensory deprivation chamber from which all external reality has been deliberately excluded. Up front, the judge's bench is raised above us. On the wall behind it hangs a large three-dimensional coat of arms showing a lion and a unicorn against a shield, and a scroll beneath the animals bearing the inscription "Dieu et mon Droit."

"I like the motto," Caitlin says, sitting next to me, "and the unicorn, but they ought to have a bear, not a lion, don't you think?"

"A roaring beast, anyway," I say. We're almost whispering; there's a stuffy solemnity about the place that suppresses conversation, seems inimical to open disclosure.

"Roaring beasts we got," Caitlin smiles, indicating Waddy with her eyes. "I think he's girding his loins for battle." Caitlin's doing her demure turn this morning: hair tied back, small silver earrings, a faint blush on her cheeks, and pale lipstick. She's wearing a silk blouse and dark suit, even nylons, like an upmarket businesswoman.

"And you?" I say to her.

"You leave my loins alone," she says and digs my ribcage with her elbow. Dear Caitlin, I think to myself, she's truly back and I'm so glad!

Mr. Goukas and Mr. Chang bustle and fuss about at a table in front of us. Mr. Goukas' billowing black gown is shiny and threadbare, and I swear there's soup stains down the front of it. The lawyer representing Peewee and Julia, Mr. Christopher, is a thirtysomething fellow who looks as though he should be in the movies. Richard Gere perhaps. A handsome profile, perfectly layered hair, a long and easy elegance in his physique. He chats offhandedly with the clerks, every corpuscle oozing charm and success. Across from the defence sits the Crown prosecutor, a narrow character with a moustache and the lean and ruthless gleam of a predator. He stares at a heap of documents on the table in front of him, as though awaiting the emergence of some small creature, a rabbit perhaps, or a dull-witted vole, that he can snatch by the throat and eviscerate.

The court recorder takes her seat. The clerks compose themselves. An expectant hush falls. A door to our right swings open noiselessly and a uniformed sheriff calls out: "Order in the Court!" We all stand up as into the hushed and tingling courtroom steps the imposing figure of Mr. Justice Smollet.

"Great entrance," Caitlin whispers.

Mr. Justice Smollet ascends to his bench, bows ever so slightly in our general direction, and seats himself. We all sit down too, like schoolkids, on our benches. The judge surveys his courtroom without expression but with the unmistakable intimation that whatever does or does not happen in this room is entirely at his discretion. His gaze—is it disdainful or merely disinterested, I wonder—lingers for a moment on us defendants. We've worn our Sunday best to try to create a favourable impression, but Sunday best on Upshot is a good long throw from haute couture, and it's doubtful Mr. Justice Smollet is favourably impressed by our appearance.

My first take on this man who will eventually pass judgement on us is not encouraging either. He's a gaunt and ascetic-looking character, and gives the impression of being utterly humourless.

"Oliver Cromwell, do you think?" Caitlin whispers to me. "Or Captain Bligh?"

I think more of Martin Luther, but I'm reluctant to talk in the courtroom, for fear of being caught and punished.

"Jesus Christ!" Waddy whispers to me urgently, "that's the same snooty bastard I had last time!"

Oh great! What a start. Knowing old Waddy, there'll be fireworks sooner or later. Nobody's said a word yet, and already our case looks hopeless.

Proceedings begin with the Crown prosecutor, Mr. Inkstrup, summarizing the allegations against us. He has a peculiar mannerism of pulling his lips back as he approaches the end of each sentence, exposing his teeth in a half-smile, half-grimace. The exposed teeth, yellow and pointed, sharpen his feral aspect. Mr. Goukas, meanwhile, gazes across at his opponent with a look of languid indifference. Alongside, Mr. Chang maniacally scribbles notes on a pad. Mr. Christopher sits with his exquisite chin poised upon the fingers of his right hand, the way upwardly mobile junior executives pose for photographs.

Next Mr. Christopher, Mr. Goukas and Mr. Chang rise, identify themselves to the court, and indicate which of us they are acting for. Mr. Christopher and Mr. Goukas carry this off well enough, but Mr. Chang reveals preliminary indications of a terrible affliction, a peculiar habit of speech that inclines him to pepper his sentences, his clauses, even the simplest of his phrases, with the word "actually." I hadn't noticed this quirk at our pretrial conference yesterday, but it blossoms instantly in court, like an evening primrose flower popping open.

"Actually, M'Lord," Mr. Chang begins, "I'm actually representing Mr. Watts, but will as well act actually on behalf of Ms. Slaney and Mrs. Stone actually as well."

"Oh, oh," Caitlin whispers to me after this actual announcement.

Mr. Justice Smollet instructs that each of us stand when our name is called. We go alphabetically, and the judge stares balefully at each of us in turn. What an odd sensation I feel standing up and being scrutinized by this stranger. Waddy's name is second-to-last on the list. Waddy stands up when Mr. Chang calls his name, then quickly sits down again. He's wearing a grey polyester suit that's several sizes too large for him, a wrinkled shirt and the same absurd tie as yesterday. It features a picture of Betty Grable in her famous gams stand.

"Mr. Watts," the judge's voice has a weird sepulchral quality, somewhere between Boris Karloff and Vincent Price, "please remain standing."

Waddy gets back on his feet with a little grunt.

"Mr. Watts," the judge asks him, "is Waddy Watts your full legal name?"

"Yep," says Waddy, ignoring Mr. Chang's repeated pretrial advice to always address the judge as "My Lord."

"You were christened by the name Waddy Watts, were you?"

"Nope."

"No? What then?" The sepulchral judge seems to circle above Waddy the way a turkey vulture spirals down over carrion.

"Never got christened," Waddy offers. "Buncha mumbo-jumbo."

"Does your birth certificate bear the name Waddy Watts?"

"Dunno. Never seen it."

"You've never seen your birth certificate?"

"Nope."

"Mr. Watts." I can see a small tic begin to twitch below the judge's left eye. For sure he must be remembering Waddy from his prior appearance. "Mr. Watts, when addressing the bench, kindly do me the courtesy of referring to me as My Lord."

"Okay." Waddy's digging in.

"What is that in your mouth, Mr. Watts?" This is going from bad to worse.

"Plug a tobacco," Waddy says, then tacks on a belated "My Lord."

"Kindly remove it."

You can see Waddy work his plug, and I hold my breath, hoping to God he isn't going to spit it onto the carpet. But Mr. Chang, bowing like crazy to the bench, scuttles over and hands Waddy a wad of Kleenex, into which Waddy deposits the offending lump.

"Thank you," says the judge. "Now would you please tell the court your correct Christian name before I lose patience with you."

"Leander," Waddy says as though he were saying something obscene to the judge. Caitlin and I titter nervously, and the judge glowers at us with a stare as cold and sharp as basalt.

"Thank you," he says to Waddy. "Now please sit down."

Waddy sits down with a scowl that hints this skirmish won't be the last.

Zyrk's name is the final one on the list. It identifies him only as Mr. Z. Zyrk. Nobody knows where he is, or if he even intends to show up. Mr. Justice Smollet says he's issuing a bench warrant for Zyrk's arrest. I picture a SWAT team in full riot gear with tracking dogs combing the countryside in pursuit of poor Zyrk.

Then Mr. Goukas rises up in his full and fecund rotundity and requests leave to present several preliminary motions.

"Very well," says the judge drily. "Proceed."

"M'Lord," Mr. Goukas begins with a great flourish of his gown, "M'Lord, I should like to move for an adjournment of these proceedings." This is not something Mr. Goukas bothered to inform us he was going to do.

"On what grounds?" asks the judge.

"On the very substantial grounds, M'Lord, that the court injunction these defendants are alleged to have violated was originally issued without jurisdiction."

"Without jurisdiction?" echoes the judge distastefully, as though his personal integrity is being called into question. "I think you'd better explain yourself, Mr. . . . ahh . . . Goukas."

"Gladly, M'Lord." Mr. Goukas seems to feel himself on solid legal ground here and my opinion of him begins to improve ever so slightly. "The issuing of this injunction amounts in effect to the making of civil law by a court. By attempting, as it does, to restrain 'persons unknown,' the injunction in effect attempts to bind the whole world which, with all due respect, M'Lord, the court has no jurisdiction to do."

Mr. Justice Smollet looks at Mr. Goukas as though he were a cockroach. He pauses for a minute or more, and then replies, "Madame Justice Bunting has already ruled on the legitimacy of the injunction"—Bunting was the initial Kumquat trial judge, now reported to be recuperating from the ordeal at an exclusive resort in Hawaii—"and I have no intention of overturning her ruling." Through the previous mass trials, we'd heard, Bunting's rulings were treated as divine revelation, to be accepted as articles of faith, notwithstanding any insult to reason they might offer. Apparently Mr. Justice Smollet is setting a similar course. "Therefore," he concludes, "your motion is denied. Do you have anything else?"

"Yes, M'Lord, indeed, thank you," Mr. Goukas seems entirely unfazed by the summary demolition of his first initiative. "I should like to make a motion that these alleged offences be tried before a jury, as a right guaranteed under Section 11-F of the Charter of Rights and Freedoms." Mr. Chang continues scribbling diligently through all this.

The look Mr. Justice Smollet gives Mr. Goukas indicates that his judicial patience is already beginning to ebb. "This is not a proceeding under the criminal code, Mr. . . . ah . . . " The judge shuffles papers looking for the name.

"Goukas, M'Lord."

"Yes, thank you, Mr. Goukas. It is a matter of contempt of court and will be dealt with by the court. Your motion is denied. Now may we get on?"

"A third motion, if I may be permitted, M'Lord." Mr. Goukas holds his ground with a certain stateliness of character, and I begin to entertain a radical revision of my initial impressions of the fellow. Our old lecher is showing that beneath his pampered fat there lurks a rawboned legal warrior in perfect fighting trim. Caitlin and I exchange small glances of surprised approval.

"Very well." This is almost a sigh from the judge, who lays his pen down in a tiny but telling indication that nothing Mr. Goukas has to offer will be worth making note of. The Crown prosecutor bares his awful teeth again in his peculiar semi-smile.

"M'Lord," Mr. Goukas sets his wattles trembling for enhanced effect, "there exists, in my opinion, no compelling reason why these proceedings should be taking place in this city. The alleged offence occurred up-island. The defendants all live up-island, and their having to journey to, and find accommodation in, this city represents an unnecessary and unwarranted hardship on them, many of whom are persons of limited means. I therefore submit that these proceedings be moved to a courthouse within easy travelling distance of my clients' homes."

This time Mr. Justice Smollet doesn't pause a heartbeat. "This court is in session in this city," he says, with thinly disguised irritation, "and I have no intention of moving it up-island or anyplace else. As for the alleged inconvenience inflicted upon the defendants, this is a matter for which I can muster very little sympathy. The court, too, has been greatly inconvenienced by their activities and the activities of their accomplices. Those who break the law," the stern judge's strength of purpose is awful to behold, "can at the very least anticipate a little inconvenience for their efforts, can they not?"

Mr. Inkstrup smiles his gruesome smile again and Mr. Chang looks worried. But Mr. Goukas is not so easily shaken. "With all due respect, M'Lord," he says, bowing slightly, "it has yet to be proven that the defendants have broken any law."

"Mr. Goukas," now we see a flash of steel in the sallow judge's glower, "I want you to get on with the case before us and stop wasting the court's time."

"Jesus," Caitlin whispers out of the side of her mouth, "I wonder if he's got the hangman waiting outside the door."

Next thing we know, the judge rises from his bench, the sheriff bellows "Order in the Court!" again, and the judge disappears through the door like Banquo's ghost. It's time for lunch.

"Told ya he was a snooty bastard," Waddy says out loud. Several sheriffs and cops are well within hearing range, and we try to hush Waddy up. There's a weird sense of paranoia floating in the courthouse air, a feeling that people are listening, that one ought to say nothing incriminating for fear it might be overheard and later used as evidence against you.

But I share Waddy's sentiments. I'm feeling irritable about sitting around in that stuffy room while these absurd legal rituals are enacted. We've squandered a whole morning to no apparent purpose and haven't even entered our pleas yet. At this rate we'll be here for months.

21

Mr. Goukas and Mr. Chang, still in full courtroom attire, stride purposively across the street and into the Sliced Pear. Peewee and
Julia and Richard Gere have disappeared. Elvira and Caitlin have
brought bag lunches and are sitting on a bench in a little outdoor court-
yard nibbling tofu and bean sprout sandwiches in a chilly spring wind.
They invite us to share their lunch with them, but Waddy isn't the tofu
and bean sprout type.

"Thanks anyway, ladies," he says to them, "but I never heard such a
load a horseshit as all that this mornin', and it's given me a real hankerin'
for a ploughman's lunch. C'mon, Joey-boy," he says to me, "I know a real
good place just around the block."

I'd prefer to spend time with Caitlin and Elvira, and after a morning
in court, lunch with Waddy seems like a sacrifice above and beyond the
call of duty, but someone has to keep an eye on the old duffer, and I
dutifully trudge off with him to the pub.

"Soon as I seen old Smollet, I knew our goose was cooked," Waddy
tells me, striding along, holding his Betty Grable tie against the wind.
"But we ain't goin' down without a fight, no sir, we'll take a coupla them
bastards down with us."

I suppose I should try to explain to Waddy that this whole non-
violence, civil-disobedience thing is predicated on not making pitched
battles out of issues. How it's supposed to be about finding a non-com-
bative way of making social change happen. What did Gandhi call
it—Satyagraha.

But it feels like wasting your breath with Waddy, an old dog who's not about to learn new tricks no matter how hard you work on him. And I guess I'm reluctant to try to press information on Waddy; it would be like telling my father what to do. Plus I'm not all that convinced that this "turn the other cheek" business is everything it's cracked up to be. There's no shortage of greedy, selfish screwballs on the planet, and I'm beginning to believe that a big stick is the best way of dealing with them. The piety I learned at my mother's knee and from the good nuns was thick with messages about suffering quietly in this life so you could be happy forever in the next. Love your enemies as yourself. But once you cease believing unconditionally in the existence of a next life, the rationale for suffering without complaint in this one begins to wear a bit thin. You want to start pushing back. It's what I'd come to feel about my father's anger, and felt again that night at the peace camp when the yahoos came storming in—that awful feeling of impotence and fear and rage against the bully. I don't want to turn the other cheek, I want to lash out and hurt them in return. Mind you, Mistral Wind routed those clowns just by keening. Truth is, I don't really know what I want or believe in, which makes Waddy's conviction, however misguided, far more powerful than mine.

Waddy and I walk into the pub. It's a dark and abysmal little dump, blue tobacco smoke writhing against yellow lights, most of the tables empty, Tina Turner wailing "What's Love Got To Do With It?"

"Now, looky here," Waddy says to me, pointing. Sitting in a booth against the wall, there's the cop who arrested us and two other cops and three company representatives we'd seen in court. "Ain't that cozy," Waddy says, "cozy as a buncha slugs chewin' on a dog turd."

The whole group of them are huddled together over their table, so they don't see Waddy and me come in. Waddy makes a secretive gesture for me to follow him, and we sidle over to an adjoining booth without them noticing us. Tina stops screaming, so the only noise is the suddenly-too-loud talking of the few patrons in the place.

". . . crazy old bastard!" we hear the cop who arrested us say, before he lowers his voice. Waddy peeks over the divider between the booths, like an infantryman in a trench, then pops down again.

"Them sons-a-bitches!" he snarls. "They got all our pictures spread out on the table, and they're helpin' each other identify who's who, and makin' dumb cracks about us."

"You're kidding!" I say. I mean, there's been some talk about complicity between the cops and company guys, but this is outrageous.

"We'll see who's kiddin'," Waddy says, getting out of the booth. He's got fire in his eye.

"Waddy!" I whisper to him urgently, "what're you gonna do?" I want to tell Waddy to leave well enough alone, to not stick his nose in and make things worse for us.

"No need to whisper," Waddy says out loud. "We'll leave that to these sneaky bastards!" And with that he goes right up to the other table.

"What the hell you sons-a-bitches think yer doin'?" Waddy gives 'em both barrels and everybody in the place turns to look. "You low-down, dirty bastards!" Waddy calls them. "You oughta have your balls cauterized crappin' all over honest workin' people for that stinkin', son-of-a-bitchin' company that does nothin' for anybody but line their own goddamn pockets!" Waddy's roaring like a bull moose in rut, the sinews in his scrawny throat stretched like ropes.

I want to get the old guy out of there, tell him to shut up. I'm convinced the cops are going to charge him, and maybe me too, with something else. Waddy swings around and announces to the whole pub crowd who these guys are—"company stooges and cops workin' together," he calls them. Waddy stands there, like an Old Testament prophet in polyester suit and Betty Grable tie, calling down the wrath of Jehovah on these infidels. After a few moments of stunned silence, Waddy's rage ignites the room. People start booing and yelling. One guy even wings a cop with a breadroll. So finally the cops and company men pick up their photographs and files and hightail it out of the pub with the indignant patrons hurling abuse after them.

Everyone gives Waddy a cheer. There's a sense in the room that we've struck an important blow against the empire. The house stands me and Waddy a round to go with our ploughman's lunches. Somebody flips on Tracy Chapman singing about revolution, and Waddy and I bask in our temporary celebrity.

We get back to the courthouse just before two, and meet up with Caitlin and Elvira in the corridor. Waddy tells them about how he routed the enemy in the pub.

"Good for you, Waddy!" Caitlin exclaims, clapping the old guy on his shoulders and laughing. "We'll fight them in the bars as well as at the bar!"

Waddy grins from ear to ear, delighted by Caitlin's attention. The old codger's really having his day in court, but I fear he's riding a bit too high for his own good. Or ours. I'm remembering that he and Mr. Justice Smollet have already banged antlers long ago and that Waddy came out the loser. I can tell by the look on her face that Elvira's upset too.

"I've always believed in the law and our system of justice," Elvira says, a little sadly, "but this is beginning to look like a sham, a terrible, disgraceful sham." Ever since I've known her, Elvira's been an upbeat, positive character, and it's disconcerting to see her these days, so gloomy over winter, and now losing faith at our trial as well.

"Well, let's wait and see what happens," I say, trying to take on her usual role of always looking on the bright side of life. "Maybe it's not as bad as it looks." Mr. Chang and Mr. Goukas had maintained from the outset that Smollet is a very broad-minded and progressive judge, and recognized as one of the brightest lights on the Supreme Court. But my words of encouragement sound hollow even to me.

"Tell ya, our goose is cooked," Waddy quotes himself again, not helping at all. "Only one battle, though, ain't the whole bloody war."

We re-enter the courtroom and the ritual recommences. First we're each called upon to stand up and enter our plea. Peewee and Julia are the first ones called. They each enter a plea of not guilty, coupled with what's called an admission of fact, meaning they don't dispute any of the evidence entered against them, but do deny that it proves them guilty of criminal contempt. They'd worked out this clever dodge with Mr. Christopher so that he can remain in court representing them while they get back home to their Jacuzzi and the lucrative bosoms of Monique Manlotte. "It's called a win-win," Peewee told me this morning. "Everyone's happy."

It's my turn next. I stand up with a dry throat and confront the judge's dismal stare. "Guilty of civil contempt," I say and sit down. That wasn't so hard. Caitlin does the same. And Elvira. Waddy's last.

"Not guilty," Waddy says with a ringing tone of defiance, and the judge looks at him narrowly. Waddy pleading not guilty means we're in for a full three-week trial with all the bells and whistles. You can see the judge isn't the least bit pleased by the prospect. Those of us pleading guilty to civil contempt aren't required to sit there through the whole trial, but we'd already decided to do so anyway, partly out of interest and partly to show solidarity with Waddy. "Solidarity forever, eh?" Waddy chortled yesterday at our blue-collar comradeship. After half a day in court, I'm beginning to regret the decision. Frankly, I'd rather be home planting.

The trial quickly degenerates to the level of farce. The Crown produces a videotape shot the morning of our arrest. It is introduced as evidence by the camera operator, a dyspeptic young man wearing an ill-fitting suit and cursed with terrible acne. The tape has been cunningly edited to show us protesters in the worst possible light. Every crazy in the crowd is featured prominently. One particularly hairy character who called himself Mad Dog and expressed his innermost feelings by frenzied barking and howling shows up repeatedly on the screen. There's the raven person. And goofy-looking Starstream. But respectable citizens, of whom there'd been plenty, are nowhere to be seen. Neither, of course, is the bear. Our magical morning in the forest looks on screen like a pathetic assemblage of burnt-out old hippies and mindless groupies. Was it really that ridiculous? Were my perceptions that far off? Beneath the judge's disapproving glower I feel humiliated, ridiculous, even a flash of the old resentment towards Caitlin and the rest of them for dragging me into this fiasco.

Unfazed by the damning evidence on tape, Mr. Goukas opens up a line of cross-examination with the apparent purpose of demonstrating that the video camera operator is not the simple working stiff he pretends, but in fact a malicious psychopath. However, the watchful Mr. Inkstrup springs to his feet with an objection, and this is sustained by the judge.

Mr. Chang wades into the fray, advancing a hypothesis that the Crown has failed to prove that the persons on the screen are, in fact, the accused. The force of this argument—which is pretty flimsy to begin with, as each of us plainly stated our names to the arresting officer while on camera—is eroded yet further by an attack of actuallys that completely overruns poor Mr. Chang's oratory. Mr. Justice Smollet's tic flutters erratically as Mr. Chang's actuallys fall from his lips multitudinous as maple leaves in a November gale.

On and on it goes. A parade of company men and cops take the stand against us. Acting on Waddy's information about the cops and company men discussing our particulars in a pub, Mr. Goukas rises with an unprecedented flapping of wattles and accuses the RCMP of "breaching its fiduciary obligations," which I think has a wonderful ring to it. Even Mr. Justice Smollet seems scandalized by this beery collusion and refuses to accept the RCMP's tainted polaroid photographs of us as evidence. Retiring with our learned counsel to the Sliced Pear, as we do after each session, we arrestees take this particular incident as overwhelming evidence that the tide has now turned in our favour and that our complete vindication is at hand.

And that's the marvellous thing about the whole process as it unfolds, day after dragging day, for weeks—this fantastic illusion that all the players help create and sustain, an illusion that any of what is happening in the stuffy confines of Courtroom Number Two will make any difference at all to the eventual outcome. We seem gripped in a conspiracy of denial, a collective longing for relevance, a hankering for the whole exercise to be something more than a set piece whose outcome is fully determined long before the actual performance begins. Poor fools that we are.

Finally, all the evidence has been heard, the relevant documents and tapes entered, the witnesses cross-examined, objections based on relevancy sustained or overruled, motions to dismiss debated, rebuttal evidence called—after all of this, the two sides sum up their cases in oral submissions to the court.

Mr. Inkstrup leads off for the Crown. He describes our behaviour at Kumquat as wanton and flagrant, characterized by a reckless disrespect for lawful authority, contemptuous, opprobrious, insubordinate, and scurrilous.

"He must've been up half the night with his thesaurus," Caitlin whispers to me as the dogged prosecutor gnaws away at the bones of our characters. Caitlin's not wearied by this numbing ordeal, these weeks of senseless nitpicking; neither is Waddy. Elvira and I have done less well. A profound sadness has enveloped Elvira. She has lost her footing somehow. I've become irritable and snappish. This thing must end soon.

Mr. Goukas rises from his chair with the ponderous solemnity of a hippopotamus rising from its mud hole. "M'Lord," Mr. Goukas rumbles, and I swear to God his wattles slap together in counterpoint as he speaks, "M'Lord, in all my years before the bar, I have never before encountered such a gimcrack, dilapidated, jerry-built excuse for a prosecution as this one. My learned friend," and here Mr. Goukas strikes a demonstrative pose to indicate it is the Crown counsel of whom he speaks, "my learned friend has laboured to cobble together a ramshackle prosecution on the very flimsiest of foundations. It is a niggling, piddling, trifling case my learned friend attempts to construct against the honest and courageous citizens I have the honour to represent."

On and on Mr. Goukas goes in this florid manner, assailing the prosecution's case at every turn, hurling himself against its evidentiary headlands like an overblown typhoon. The heater hums and the leatherette seats stick to our bums. I believe anew in the existence of Purgatory.

But then, just as we've been lulled into stupefaction by Mr. Goukas' rococo flourishes, the proceedings ignite at a flashpoint. Waddy Watts has had enough. Before Mr. Chang can rise to make his concluding submission, Waddy abruptly dismisses him from the case.

"Do I understand, Mr. Watts," the judge asks him, "that you have dismissed your counsel and will now represent yourself for the remainder of these proceedings?"

"Judge," Waddy says, his cheek bulging with a defiant chaw, his fists on his skinny hips, "you don't understand the first goddamn thing about anything."

A seismic tremor shakes the courtroom into a shocked and bewildered silence. After three weeks of what I now realize was a slow but inevitable building to this climactic moment, suddenly it's High Noon. Gunfight at the OK Corral. Waddy Watts and Mr. Justice Smollet are face to face at last. I want to jump up and grab Waddy, tell him to sit down and be quiet, to quit making everything worse for us with his confounded temper. Caitlin puts her hand softly over mine. I realize I'm trembling all over.

"Mr. Watts," the judge begins sternly, but Waddy isn't about to listen.

"I been sittin' here for three bloody weeks," Waddy cuts him off, fuming, "listenin' to all this high-priced crap, and I ain't gonna listen to no more. I didn't start out with any contempt of court, but you bastards have managed to convince me otherwise. This bloody farce ain't justice, this ain't your goddamn equality before the law . . ."

Mr. Justice Smollet recovers from his shock and begins pounding his gavel and gesturing to the sheriff by the door. The sheriff's stunned too, staring at Waddy in disbelief, not registering what the judge wants.

"All you're doin' is stampin' on the little guys so the fat cats can keep their snouts in the trough," Waddy stands there, knobbly and wizened, pointing an accusatory finger at the judge, the prophet Isaiah in a polyester suit. "You're in bed with the big shots and you're a buncha goddamn hypocrites for pretending that you ain't. When it comes to havin' contempt for the likes of you, I'm as guilty as hell!"

God, Waddy's making a mess of it. I reach up to pull on his sleeve, to make him sit down and stop this, before the whole thing blows apart on us, but Caitlin takes my hand in hers and squeezes it, and Waddy's left standing, defiant. My heart is pounding wildly.

Mr. Justice Smollet's gavel-banging and shouting succeed in rousing the stupefied sheriff. Two other sheriffs rush in. Waddy's dragged out of the courtroom by the three sheriffs, cursing as he goes. Mr. Justice Smollet's face has turned a deathly white and his tic is flickering alarmingly. He stares blankly out into an unspeakable void for several moments, then bolts from the courtroom, like a giant bat from its cave, his black robes flapping. There's no sheriff left to cry "Order in the Court!" and none of us rise at the judge's departure.

My body's still pumping adrenaline when Caitlin and I sit down for lunch at a little vegan place we'd discovered a few blocks from the courthouse. Elvira's supposed to be joining us shortly.

"Well, Waddy's made a royal botch of it at last," I say. "I knew it was a mistake including him in the first place."

"Including him?" Caitlin uses that tone of hers on me. "If memory serves, it was Waddy's idea to begin with."

"Oh, come off it!" I'm not having any of that. "We both know that you and Mistral orchestrated the whole thing from the start. Waddy was only . . ."

"Yes?"

What? Should I say it? Yes! "Only a pawn."

"A pawn? Of Mistral and me?"

"Sort of."

"And what about you?" Caitlin doesn't look angry, but intense enough to bend angle iron. "Were you a pawn too?"

Back and fill! an urgent message flickers from the back of my brain. Float like a butterfly! But, damn it all, I'm worn out and burned out and sick and tired of this whole frigging fiasco. Waddy's made a total bollocks of everything, first dragging us through this ridiculous trial and now attacking the judge. You couldn't make more of a mess of things if you tried. So I certainly don't need Caitlin Slaney lecturing me in condescending tones. I tear off my hair shirt and leap into the bear pit.

"Maybe I was!" I say, a bit too loudly for a vegan place.

Caitlin looks at me appraisingly, then delicately forks a small bit of polenta from her plate. I brace myself for a drubbing.

"You didn't want to go to Kumquat?" She frames the question with just a trace of incredulity, the slightest tinge of disillusion.

"It isn't that I didn't want to go."

"But you were a pawn, a dupe, manipulated into going, against your better judgement."

Why is she trying to corner me? Why pick a fight? Or is it me who wants to pick it?

"No, I wouldn't say manipulated exactly."

"What would you say exactly?"

Help, is what I would say, but there's no help at hand. I wish Elvira'd show up.

"More like seduced," I say, trying for a lighter spin, but missing.

"Seduced?" she cries out loud, so that two bald guys with Z Z Top bushy beards, sitting at the next table, stop eating and peer at us.

"Seduced!" Caitlin says again, for their benefit, rolling her eyes like Bette Davis. "You think I seduced you?"

She's talking far too loudly, attracting attention. I want to tell her to quieten down, but that could be suicidal. The bald guys look away, back to their table, but they're listening so hard you can hear their eardrums beating.

"Well, of all the self-indulgent little twerps!" Caitlin wades in, wielding her fork like a rapier. "You think I've got nothing better to do with myself than seduce reluctant virgins?"

The bald guys look over again, startled. One of them's got a little cascade of alfalfa sprouts down his beard. I catch his eye by accident and we both look away quickly. I sense the whole café is pondering the circumstances of my virginity.

"Let me tell you something, J.J." Caitlin says, more quietly, perhaps sensing she's gone too far, humiliating me in public this way. "You're a lovely man in many ways, but you're also a craven coward."

I won't deny this, but I don't think it's the sort of thing should be said over lunch.

"Waddy may be a little pepper pot," Caitlin carries on, "but he's nobody's fool and he's certainly nobody's pawn. What he said to old Smollet just now is the first whiff of truth we've had in that stuffy dump for three weeks. Why shouldn't he say it? Why shouldn't he cut through all the bullshit and just speak the plain honest truth? Which is what he did. And I honour him for it."

Caitlin puts her fork neatly on her plate and stands up, as though the national anthem were starting.

"And as for you," she says, standing over the table, everyone in the place straining to hear, "you can keep scratching away in the archives of ambivalence for the rest of your life if you want. But don't you go blaming Waddy, and don't you go blaming me, every time the least little draft makes your candle flame flicker. They're your choices, J.J. You make them, you live with them. You want seduction, try the phone sex lines. Personally I've got better things to do!"

She picks up her purse, throws some bills on the table, and stalks out of the café, leaving me sitting there like a bloody fool with a polenta-smeared fork through my heart.

22

"Been listenin' to the ravens?" Waddy asks us as the ferry slips out of Rumrunners Cove into open water. We're gathered in the ferry lounge, off on the latest leg of our legal marathon. A light chop shimmers across the waters of the open strait; the dark mountains of the big island loom ahead. None of us has been listening to the ravens.

"Sittin' in that big snag at my place all day long," Waddy tells us, "yappin' to beat the band. You know them bloody ravens always got somethin' to say."

"Nevermore, usually," Caitlin says, and we all laugh.

"Never mind never more." Waddy hasn't read his Poe. "Gonna be a cold late spring, you watch."

After our trial, ending in Waddy's intemperate outburst, before judgement was rendered, we were able to go back home for a bit, even Waddy. We'd straggled back from the city, relieved that the numbing boredom of the court was for the moment behind us. I felt smothered by depression after my argument with Caitlin. I don't think the others noticed the cleft that had opened up between her and me.

Still, Upshot never looked better than that bright April afternoon when we arrived home, weary and infinitely wiser than we'd left. The novelty of our noble crusade had by then worn pretty thin on-island. There'd been the normal springtime spate of relationship break-ups, wild affairs and reckless recouplings, and these, as Professor Pipes discovered long ago, have a way of capturing the popular imagination that more sombre themes do not.

We had a few blessed weeks in the sunshine and showers to get spring planting underway and catch up on our lives. I guess we each retreated to our gardens as to a sanctuary. The Japanese cherries were in blossom just then, and one afternoon I allowed myself the unaccustomed luxury of simply lying for several hours on warm grass under a large Mount Fuji cherry in full bloom, gazing up through the perfect clarity and purity of the pendulous white flowers, vivid against a deep blue sky. My jangled spirit at last began to settle.

What had become of me? I lay under the tree, a single blossom falling now and then, like one of Lucifer's angels. Where was I now? The earth was shifting under me, had been shifting and heaving ever since this Kumquat episode began, since Mistral Wind stepped ashore that evening. And what had become of her? What of Elvira? Dear Elvira in a darkness deeper than I'd seen in her before.

But, mostly, what of Caitlin—brilliant, fiery Caitlin. I hated her for what she'd done to me in that café. But loved her too, I knew it now completely. Loved and feared to touch her. Be touched by her. Had I lost her at last? Was she ever mine to lose?

Under it all, I felt my faith shaken, the old hand-me-down faith I had thought lost long ago. But it hadn't been really lost, I realized, it had just changed its colours a little. I may have quit whispering repentance for my sins to an omniscient God, but I'd still believed implicitly in an ordered universe, a reason for being, some evolutionary process that makes sense, that moves logically from this point to that. I'd still believed in a guiding purpose of some sort. All of that was shaken now, I realized, lying there on a perfect spring afternoon. Looking at what's going on all over the globe, the violence and pestilence and brutality, the only outcome I could see was a terrible darkness descending, a new Dark Ages coming. I craved the simplicity and clarity of the Holy Rule.

I took refuge in study. I knew I should address the court before sentencing, and I set about gathering some information for my statement. I read Thoreau and Gandhi, and I devoured everything I could get my hands on about coastal temperate rain forests. I was astonished by what I read, about how these ecosystems function, and how most of them have already been destroyed. I realized, I think for the first time, that what was going on at Kumquat was extraordinary. I'd undersold the importance of what we'd done there, allowed my cynicism to devalue it.

The more I learned, the more I saw us arrestees as bold crusaders for a noble cause. I felt fanaticism gaining a toehold in me.

But then I'd find myself, miles away from the books in front of me, thinking about Caitlin. I wanted to be with her. And didn't. It was up to me to initiate something. Did I want to? What if I didn't?

I was still groping in gloomy indecision when we dragged ourselves back down to the city for our verdict. In the courthouse foyer, we greeted Mr. Chang and Mr. Goukas, even blow-dried Mr. Christopher, as old comrades in arms. We made our way back into the dreary courtroom. Mr. Justice Smollet entered in due course, took his seat, and proceeded to read out his reasons for judgement. These were not distinguished by any great originality of thought. Rather, they were a catalogue of precedents previously established by Madame Justice Bunting. Not surprisingly, this scrupulous following of Bunting's script and score led to a finding that we were all guilty of criminal contempt of court. We were instructed to return in two weeks' time for sentencing, after Corrections Branch had completed an assessment.

However, there was a new quality in Smollet's sepulchral voice that morning as he read his verdict. A slight quavering, as though his assuredness were shaken. He would not look at us at all, and his tic seemed to have spread its unsettling influence over a larger area of his gaunt face. He appeared haggard and careworn.

"They better get that feller off to Hawaii for a spell too," Waddy said on the courthouse steps afterwards. But none of us were rejoicing in Smollet's discomfiture.

Today Elvira, Caitlin, Waddy, Peewee, Julia, and I are on our way to an interview at Corrections Branch. They will assess us as to our suitability for serving our expected sentences not in prison, but confined in our own homes, under an electronic monitoring program.

Zyrk is still criminally at large, though rumour has it that he's somewhere back on Upshot.

We enter the corrections office five minutes before our scheduled appointment. A receptionist who looks disconcertingly like Lucille Ball instructs us curtly to "take a seat over there," pointing to a derelict waiting area in a dark corner. Following our conviction we are now officially known as contemners, a term which seems to invite expressions of distaste from honest citizens like the receptionist who, having put us in our proper place among the dog-eared *People* magazines, turns her undivided attention back to filing her nails.

We wait. And wait. And wait some more. An hour goes by without any word of explanation. We can hear occasional bursts of laughter coming from the inner office area. Finally, Caitlin walks up to the receptionist, who has spent the last twenty minutes, upon completion of her manicure, picking invisible bits of lint off her sweater.

"Excuse me," Caitlin says to her, sweet as a Nanaimo bar, "could you please find out why our appointment has been delayed for more than an hour?"

Lucy stares for a moment at Caitlin as though she's been asked if she wants to buy cocaine. "If you'll resume your seat, I'll endeavour to find out," she says primly. Another burst of laughter from the interior.

"I'll wait right here while you're endeavouring, if you don't mind." Caitlin's smile packs enough menace that even Lucy recognizes the prudence of not minding. She swings around on her swivel chair and wobbles off down the corridor on lethally high stiletto heels, the muscles of her calves, thighs, and rump bulging from the strain.

We hear the laughter stop as she enters a room at the far end of the corridor. Then another burst of laughter. A scraping of chairs. She reappears, smiling coyly, with a tall man alongside. He's in shirtsleeves and as the two of them make their way up the corridor, talking together, he tucks his white shirt back into his trousers.

Lucy's facial gesture to him indicates who and what we are and the fellow hails us from beyond the reception desk. "Hello there!" he cries. "Won't you come in."

We all exchange glances as we proceed down the corridor behind him. He's whistling "Yesterday" between his teeth. He ushers us into an interview room where we sit around a large table. From here the laughter and chatter sound much louder.

"A party?" Caitlin asks our man.

"Just a little staff get-together," he makes a face. "Super's birthday. The big five-oh."

"I see," Caitlin smiles. "Sorry to drag you away."

"Not to worry," the fellow seems impervious to sarcasm, "this won't take a minute."

He's at least six feet four, with thinning hair, ostrich eyes, a Groucho Marx moustache, and imbecilic smile. Mr. Charles Vitale,

Corrections Officer, reads the business card he hands each of us.

"You folks can call me Chuck," he grins at us idiotically. "I know you're not common criminals."

"How d'you know that?" Waddy's sounding snappish, but Chuck seems not to mind.

"Well, Kumquat and all that. Hardly big potatoes compared to what we get in here, believe me." He winks at Caitlin.

"What do you get in here?" she asks him, all sweet innocence while her talons are emerging.

"Oh, all sorts," Chuck ignores the rest of us and focuses his charm on Caitlin, "murderers, rapists, queers, all sorts of slime."

"Slime?" Caitlin echoes, "and you're not afraid that some of it might stick to you then?"

"Nah," Chuck brushes off the notion with a chuckle, "we're a pretty professional bunch here at C.B.—oh, sorry, I mean Corrections Branch."

Waddy lets a squirt of juice go, right there on the floor. Chuck doesn't see.

"Yes, we were all just commenting on the professionalism of the place, weren't we?" Caitlin looks over at us drolly.

Peewee and Julia are taking notes. They've already exploited Mr. Goukas, using him as a template for a besotted stepfather in their latest opus, and now I can see they're sizing up Chuck for a starring role as well.

"Anyways, let's get down to business, shall we?" Chuck pulls a pile of files towards him, and begins leafing through them randomly, the way seagulls peck at beach washup on ebb tide. "Bloody paperwork," he flips the files shut in disgust. "We're drowning in it, you know?"

"Are you then?" Caitlin's terribly interested.

"It's all we do any more, work on our files," Chuck confides, sticking the little finger of his right hand into his ear and excavating a lump of wax that he studies for a moment. "There's murder and mayhem out on the streets and they've got us in here writing files." Another round of laughter erupts, and Chuck's eyes dart towards the door and back. "Anyways, I'd like to recommend to the court that you all serve your sentences under the Electronic Monitoring Program."

"You mean house arrest, don't ya?" Waddy asks him.

"Well, only in a manner of speaking. You'll each wear an anklet with a radio transmitter, and there's a box attached to your telephone. This ensures that you remain indoors throughout your sentence."

"Why indoors?" Julia asks.

"Because this is a period of incarceration. We can't have you just wandering around outside, can we?"

"What about having a Jacuzzi on the deck?" Peewee wants to know.

Chuck blinks a couple of times. "You've got a Jacuzzi? In that case, I'll have to come over and do a site evaluation. But listen, all that can wait until after sentencing."

He plainly wants to get back to the party, and we have a ferry to catch, so the interview draws to a close with Chuck telling us how much he looks forward to assisting us in paying our debt to society and in working on our rehabilitation. Then he bids us a distracted farewell, gathers up the files that are the burden of his life, and dashes back into the party.

We leave Corrections Branch with a refreshed sense of the absurd.

I walk back to the car with Caitlin, behind the others.

"How's your mum doing?" I ask her, wanting to talk about something, but not our fight.

"Oh, it's awful really," Caitlin says, I guess not wanting to either. "The nursing home's dreary and understaffed. She lies in bed most of the day, staring off at nothing. God knows what goes on in her brain. I feel so guilty that she's there and I'm so far away and can't be with her."

"Can you put her in a home out here?"

"I think she's too far gone. The trip would probably kill her. She was beautiful, you know, as a young woman, beautiful and vivacious."

"Yes, you showed me her photographs."

"That's how I remember her from when I was little, a gorgeous woman with lovely laughter. I so wanted to grow up to be just like her."

"I think you have," I say. "I'm sure it's just how Jenny sees you now."

Caitlin stops on the sidewalk and looks at me. "You're a sweet, dear man, J.J.," she says to me, just as she'd said in the café before the firefight started. "I'm sorry I called you a coward. You're not. You wouldn't be here if you were."

"I'm here because of you," I barely get the words out.

"There you go again. It's innocence you have, not cowardice at all. No matter what the judge says, I think you're completely innocent, and I love it in you."

"You do?" I can manage nothing more intelligent than this. I feel as though I'm hanging upside down, like a rabbit in a snare, all the small change of my life dropping out. How close this woman is to me, to my own feelings about myself. How this leaves me dangling, captive. She sees me vulnerable, but she is not laughing.

Caitlin's just about to say something more when we're interrupted by Waddy calling across the parking lot.

"You two aimin' to swim home after the ferry's gone, or what?" he yells. We have to break off and join the others. I'm still in mid-air, disconcerted, though feeling better, much better, than I have for a very long time.

23

We return to Courtroom Number Two for the final time, to receive our sentences. Seated in our familiar front-row bench, we rise at Mr. Justice Smollet's entrance, and I swear we all gasp to see him.

"Good God!" Caitlin whispers, "what's happened to him?"

The judge seems to have aged overnight, his hair gone grey, his shoulders stooped, his face lined and sallow. He walks with a cane. I've never seen anyone deteriorate so dramatically in just a few weeks.

He sits down with a sigh. He shuffles some papers randomly and peers out at the courtroom with such a look of horror on his gaunt face, you'd have thought the room was full of Holocaust victims. When at last he speaks, his voice sounds cracked and dry, an echo of Ezekiel in the desert.

Mr. Inkstrup, the Crown prosecutor, rises to speak first. With the withering judge now an object of pity rather than of fear, Inkstrup looks more the devious weasel than ever.

I pay no attention to what Inkstrup's saying in his bloodless monotone. I can't take my eyes off the judge. Surely our little farcical trial hasn't brought this great sorrow down upon him. It's not as though he's mistakenly sentenced some innocent wretch to death. What mysteries, I wonder, are dancing in the dark of his judicial mind.

Mr. Inkstrup concludes his remarks by suggesting that the long prison sentences handed down by Madame Justice Bunting in identical circumstances establish "a not-unreasonable precedent" for the sentences we should be given.

Mr. Christopher rises next, to speak for Peewee and Julia. He parades out a list of their Who's Who credentials and associates, their attainments and high standing in the academic community. No mention's made of Monique Manlotte, just of "numerous books published." Out of the corner of my eye I see Peewee and Julia preening like coloured cockatoos at the suave Mr. Christopher's delineation of their distinguished characters and careers. But the judge is miles away.

Waddy leans over and whispers to me, "Could use this gandydancer to help spread manure on my potato patch." And Waddy's right: Mr. Christopher's a bit too slick for his own good, polished to such an exquisite sheen on the surface, one instinctively recognizes that surface is all he's composed of. His presentation ends like a Hollywood epic, impressive but devoid of substance. Still, Peewee and Julia look pleased.

Mr. Goukas rises to present his arguments. He is in full and splendid fettle this morning. He begins slowly, almost mournfully, as though to match the judge's pitiable state. But soon Mr. Goukas is lifted and borne away on the slipstream of his own grandiloquence. On and on he goes, stacking hyperbole upon absurd hyperbole, eventually retreating to a rhetorical promontory of such outlandish bombast I think the only recourse left him is to plunge from its impossible height and be smashed against the rocks of reality far below. After more than an hour of this, Mr. Goukas collapses into his chair, wheezing, like a typhoon that has blown itself out at sea.

Mr. Chang follows up with a discourse so laced with actuallys, so riven and strewn with affirmative and declarative actuallys, it becomes first painful, then amusing, then hysterical to listen. Caitlin gets a fit of the giggles part-way through, then so do the rest of us, and we have a terrible time suppressing our chuckling so as not to provoke the judge or hurt earnest Mr. Chang's feelings.

"Actually, M'Lord, that is all I have to say, actually," Mr. Chang concludes and sits down, his dignity intact, making me feel meanspirited for snickering at his affliction.

The time has come for us contemners to speak to sentencing. The tyranny of alphabetical order dictates I have to go first. The mood in the room is intense and before I even stand up, I'm assailed by acute nervousness. Feeling queasy in my stomach, I rise and come forward to stand before the judge. I have a prepared statement printed out, containing a number of quite brilliant insights that occurred to me during my research work into civil disobedience and coastal temperate rain forests. All I'm now required to do is read the statement aloud. But after only a sentence or two, I begin feeling short of breath, like I can't keep speaking. Cold little beads of sweat start trickling from my armpits down over my ribs. Words seem to snag in my throat, and several times I have to gulp for air in mid-sentence.

By way of justifying our civil disobedience, I sketch in outline the peril facing rain forests generally, but especially coastal temperate rain forests. How there'd been fewer than forty million hectares of temperate rain forests worldwide to begin with. How most of them have been destroyed in Europe, South America, and New Zealand.

Halfway down my second page, I'm convinced I'm boring everyone to death. The dryness in my throat is doing me in. I actually begin saying "actually," and catch myself in horror. Did I hear someone snicker? Caitlin?

"Here in North America," I continue, almost asphyxiating, "the greatest coastal temperate rain forest on earth is disappearing forever. More than 60 per cent of the B.C. rain forest has already been lost to clearcutting, with less than 7 per cent protected. Three quarters of the Washington forest has suffered the same fate. A measly 4 per cent of the original Oregon coastal forest remains, with less than 2 per cent of the original in protected status. And 96 per cent of the great redwood forests have been felled."

Looking up from my notes at the ghastly spectre of the judge, I realize with perfect clarity that he represents for me all the formidable figures of authority I was trained to fear and obey—father, priest, teacher, God. Although I know our cause is just, our actions honourable, that we are, as Caitlin says, on the side of the angels, still I fear to disobey our father who art in heaven. My own father who art not. Obedience. Yes, it is for me a question of obedience. The third sacred vow. To willingly and lovingly submit in all things to the directives of the superior.

But who or what to obey or disobey? The Church? The state? Absurdly, I remember the "suscipe" of Saint Ignatius of Loyola, words by which I'd guided my life for so long: "Lord Jesus Christ, take all my freedom, my memory, my understanding and my will. All that I have and cherish you have given me. I surrender it all to be guided by your will. Your grace and your love are wealth enough for me. Give me these, Lord Jesus, and I ask for nothing more."

I've lost my place in my text. I don't know what I've said already or not. In a panic, I look up at the dreadful judge. I see the huge coat of arms hanging behind him. "Dieu et mon Droit." God and Law? Or Right? Or Duty? Yes, more like God and my Duty.

I realize that the moment has come to say exactly what I want to say, what it is my duty to say. If not now, when? How much older do I need to grow before I speak my truth without equivocation? What's the alternative—to spend the remainder of my days hiding out, as Caitlin said, in the dusty archives of ambivalence?

And it comes to me in a sudden transformative flash, right there in the courtroom, like lightning striking a tree, what Ignatius really meant about surrendering to grace and love. Letting go of all you have and cherish, all that you cling to. I thought I'd known this years ago in the seclusion of the cloister, but not really, not like now, down to the marrow of my bones. A wonderful clarity alights in my mind.

I abandon my notes completely and speak from my heart. "M'Lord," I say to the judge in a clear voice, no longer shaking, no longer afraid, "I respectfully submit that no right-thinking citizen can in good conscience sit idly by while the last fragments of these amazing ecosystems are being systematically demolished in the name of corporate profit. What I and my friends here did, I know to be right. I broke a law that I know to be wrong. Whatever punishment you assign, I readily accept. And in your own present predicament, M'Lord, I recommend less of Madame Justice Bunting and more of Saint Ignatius of Loyola. Thank you." I sit down with the silence of the courtroom ringing in my ears like the Angelus bell.

Caitlin, sitting beside me, squeezes my hand in acknowledgement.

I'm vaguely aware of Julia speaking next, but I hardly hear a word she says. Or Peewee after her. I've done it, I keep hearing my frenzied brain repeat, I've stood before the police and priests and magistrates and said my piece. I've held my ground. I've been afraid, yes, but not so afraid I could not speak, not silenced, not so afraid I need lie to myself, deny to myself what I know is right and what is wrong. There is still meaning, I realize with a sudden rush of exhilaration, a beating heart, a pulse, despite the battering accidents of life. I feel as though I've rediscovered something precious—I don't know if I'd call it faith exactly—something I'd had once upon a time and lost.

"Thank you," I hear Mr. Justice Smollet whisper into the hushed courtroom just as Peewee's finished. I am back in the courtroom, back in the world.

Caitlin stands before the court, a picture of cool, radiant composure. She begins to speak, and her words flow out as pure poetry. She talks of the great trees and plants, the creatures and waters of the rain forest, as though she's describing her lovers. Her poet's voice rises and falls, lilting and rhapsodic, as she characterizes the rainforest valleys as living, pulsing systems powered by rain—"amazing places," she calls them, "among the richest, rarest, and most complex ecosystems on earth. And we're battering them down, for what? Toilet paper? Telephone directories? Daily newspapers full of violent trash that are perused in minutes and thrown away? For this we squander one of earth's great treasures? Are we mad? Do we want to be damned for fools by our children? Are we not the guardians of the earth they'll inherit?"

No one could stand against the force of Caitlin's convictions. Her questions ring against the courtroom walls like a battering ram striking timbers. And I know, as surely as I've ever known anything, that it is she who has stirred me to life, helped me find what was lost.

"Thank you, Ms. Slaney," Mr. Justice Smollet whispers when Caitlin is finished. His face is shaking awfully.

Caitlin turns on her heel and strides back to our bench. I can feel the heat steaming from her body as she sits down beside me. She squeezes my hand again, and winks; her eyes are full of lovely mischief.

Elvira's name is called. She stands and steps forward. She's wearing a plain brown dress—Elvira's not much on fashion statements—but at her throat hangs a beautiful silver necklace. It belonged to her grandmother, a gift on her wedding day. Elvira showed it to me long ago, explained the stylized representations of eagle, frog, wolf, and bear.

She pauses before speaking, looks at the judge with what feels like immense compassion. Elvira seems to root herself in places, wherever she goes, and that's how she looks now, like a native oak rooted in the barren courtroom floor. She speaks just a few simple sentences about the plundering of the coast that has gone on since the first Europeans arrived. The devastation of the forests and rivers and native communities. She speaks without anger, but with the power born of an enormous sadness.

"No court in this country," she tells the haunted judge, "could impose a punishment that's harsher than seeing what they're doing to the forests and the creatures and the people. Even now. Even with all we know about our past mistakes. It's criminal, isn't it?" Elvira finishes with a pensive smile, fingers her magic necklace and sits down.

Again a silence, broken only by a few sniffles from the spectators' benches. We are almost done. Only Waddy Watts remains to speak.

Waddy takes his stand before Mr. Justice Smollet, but now there is none of the explosive tension that hummed between the two of them on their previous encounters. The judge is reduced to a figure of pathos, and Waddy's demeanour is more of conviction than combativeness.

"Your Honour," he begins, from watching "Perry Mason" and "LA Law," "I ain't got any facts nor figures in my head, and I don't know the finer points of law. But I worked in the woods for more than forty years and I seen what's goin' on out there, Kumquat and every place else there's still an old tree standin'. It's got nothin' to do with forestry, what's goin' on. It's greed, naked greed, pure and simple."

Waddy shifts around a bit and hums to himself for a moment before continuing. "I'm an old man," he tells the judge, "and I been around the track enough times to know which trestles need replacin'. Remember an old engineer name of Lafreniere, French feller o'course. Taught me plenty. Handle a locie like no one I ever seen, that feller could. Knew his tracks. There was one old trestle on that show'd wobble like a gimpy hip every time ya went across her. Laffy, that's what we called him, he kept tellin' the bosses, that trestle, one of these days she gonna come down like an old whore's drawers. But they didn't listen. Greedy bastards, y'know, tryin' to squeeze the last nickel outta that show before they shut her down. Well, Your Honour, old Laffy went across that trestle one too many times and down she came, just like he said she would, with him on it, and when they dug him out of the wreck, there wasn't hardly enough of him left to bury. That's what's happenin' in the woods right now. Greedy bastards wreckin' everythin' and not carin' who gets hurt or what's left for the people who come after us.

"You can call what we did over there at Kumquat criminal behaviour if you want," Waddy says to the judge, "but that don't make you right. Anyone who knows the forest knows what's right in this. And knows who the real criminals are."

Waddy finishes by saying he will not under any circumstances accept house arrest—"Nobody's gonna make me a prisoner in my own house," he says. "I'd rather go to jail. That's all I got to say, Your Honour, thank you."

Waddy sits down. Silence engulfs the courtroom, like the silence in deep caverns, resonant with depth. Mr. Justice Smollet's haunted stare seems fixed on a point above our heads, far, far away. His tic flickers erratically. His thin lips scarcely move in thanking Waddy. He plainly has no stomach for sending an eighty-one-year-old man to prison.

"Very well," the judge says at last, in a voice that might have come from the grave. "We'll break for lunch and reconvene at two o'clock." Then he stands up slowly and makes his painful way out of court.

"Attaboy, Joey," Waddy says to me on the courthouse steps. "You done us proud in there." This praise from the old guy touches me profoundly.

Over lunch at the Sliced Pear, Mr. Goukas and Mr. Chang commend us all for our presentations. Between salacious glances at the statuesque waitress, Mr. Goukas assures us that Smollet has bent before the force of argument presented by our learned counsel, and that we'll likely get off very lightly, with perhaps no more than a suspended sentence. Mr. Chang is less confident, but still his beaming and affable self, and I feel worse than ever for snickering at his actuallys.

"You were wonderful in court," I say to Caitlin as we make our way back to the courthouse. "I loved what you said."

"You were pretty good yourself, my learned friend," she says to me. "I was inspired by you. Remember I said, way back when, that we needed your soul-force on this expedition?"

"I remember. I thought it a clever ploy at the time. Like the anonymous letter."

"Maybe it was at the time, but it was also true. It's what we saw in court this morning, and it was inspiring, truly. It's what I meant by soul-force. It flows from a pure heart, and that's what *you* have, J.J., a lovely pure heart."

I suppose I should confess that I'm not at all pure, that I'm as lewd and lascivious in my own secretive way as goofy Chuck or our learned Mr. Goukas. But before I can say anything, she leans across, right there on the sidewalk, pins me against a parking meter and kisses me full on the lips.

"I'll go to the electric chair a happy man!" I cry, hugging her close, and over her shoulder I see Elvira smiling at us from the courthouse steps.

I stride back into the courtroom three feet off the floor.

The judge returns to pronounce sentence: four weeks' imprisonment for each of us, with an option to serve the sentence at home under the

Electronic Monitoring Program, and one year of probation. Waddy Watts will go to prison for a month if that's what he chooses. Again a shocked silence in the courtroom.

The judge picks up his gavel to conclude the case, but before he can bang it, Elvira stands up.

"My Lord!" she addresses the bench.

"Yes?" Mr. Justice Smollet seems overcome with a great weariness.

"My Lord," Elvira says, "if Mr. Watts is to be sent to prison for his actions, then I want to be imprisoned as well."

We're stunned by this announcement. Mr. Justice Smollet gapes.

"As you choose," he says at last in a whisper, barely audible in the numbed courtroom.

Caitlin stirs beside me, as though she's about to rise as well, and instantly I think I too shall rise and say something, that we shall not be cowed.

But before anyone can do anything, there's a commotion behind us. The judge looks up, and we turn to look too. And there in the aisle stands Zyrk. He's wearing his classic black leather, shaved head, ear studs and all, and smiling beatifically.

My instant thought is that we may have created a monster by encouraging Zyrk in these dramatic entrances.

"My Lord," Caitlin's up in a second, far faster on her feet than any of our legal team, "this is Mr. Zyrk, for whom you issued a bench warrant. I believe he's come to these proceedings of his own free will."

The judge just stares. Zyrk advances up the aisle, past our bench, past the lawyers' tables, and stands before the judge. The sheriffs aren't sure what to do. The lawyers and clerks stare, stupefied. Zyrk slowly, gracefully, lowers himself into the lotus position on the floor and takes up his mantra.

The courtroom is perfectly still, with only Zyrk's mantra humming in tune with the heating unit. I close my eyes. Rising and falling, Zyrk's magical chanting coils like a cobra through our brains, coiling back upon itself in loops and rounds of sound, back again in altered form, like clouds drifting and reforming in a summer sky. It is a hymn to the universe that absorbs us all, dissolves the walls of prosecution and defence, absolves us of whatever sins we haven't yet confessed.

Opening my eyes and glancing up, I see a marvellous thing. The grim mask of Mr. Justice Smollet's face has relaxed. His tic has ceased its awful flickering. His eyes are closed, his jaw unclenched. A faint smile drifts and lingers on his face. He seems to me at peace, at least for now. What's he thinking, I wonder, this austere judge, what fragments of his life, what dreams, is he remembering under the ensorcelling spell of Zyrk's peculiar magic?

His mantra draws to a close, and Zyrk stands up again. Then he speaks the first and only words I've ever heard pass his lips:

> Waddy Watts has taught us lots
> Of growing with forget-me-nots;
> Elvira Stone sits home alone,
> Freddie's gone with Oberon;
> For all the rest,
> Silence is best.

Zyrk bows profoundly to the judge and to each of us in turn. Then he walks back up the aisle the way he'd entered, and out of the court-room, leaving all of us sitting there in absolute amazement.

$$\text{---❊--+❧ } 24 \text{ ❧+--❊---}$$

The spell is broken. Mr. Justice Smollet exits our lives, perhaps to face his demons, perhaps to find peace. Still dazed from Zyrk's enigmatic intervention, we contemners bid our legal team farewell, and are herded into a holding room in the courthouse. Our names, addresses, and other particulars are laboriously recorded, for the umpteenth time, by a pair of muddle-headed marshalls scribbling like schoolboys with stubby pencils on smudged foolscap.

"I thought Big Brother was at least computer literate by now," Caitlin jokes them, but her meaning sails over the plodding sheriffs' heads.

They process Waddy and Elvira first. Waddy's as docile as I've ever seen him, and Elvira's sadness is like a deep pool into which dark things have been cast. Why did Zyrk single them out, I wonder. What did he mean by forget-me-nots? Or by Oberon, invisible king of the fairies?

Four big sheriffs bustle into the room officiously, talking in excessively masculine voices. One carries a large metal case which he places on a table. He snaps the case open and takes out a pair of handcuffs, then another, laying them on the table. Two big sheriffs each seize one of Waddy's arms and a third snaps the handcuffs on. Waddy doesn't say a word. Then they do the same to Elvira. I've got a knot in my stomach like I've just been punched and I see Caitlin's face flashing with anger. The sheriff takes more hardware out of the case, and as the two large men bend down in front of Waddy, I realize they're putting leg irons on him, and on Elvira too.

"Now just one bloody minute!" Caitlin explodes at the sheriffs, but they push us back, put the leg shackles on, and quickly march Elvira and Waddy out of the room.

It's no joke seeing our friends taken off in leg irons like that, hand-cuffed and shackled like vicious thugs. I remember what Caitlin said the morning of our arrest, about men with guns arriving in the dark to prey upon the innocent. I thought at the time that was just more of Caitlin's histrionics, but I don't believe so now. What else but the henchmen of evil, these bumbling fools who'll shackle women and old men for no crime other than saying government policy is wrong?

Peewee and Julia look shaken, and I see tears in Caitlin's eyes, which I don't think I've ever seen before. So strange to see her vulnerable. I take her hand in mine and hold it, though I have nothing to say. Her tears are brimming.

"What was that about Ignatius of Loyola?" she asks me, sniffling.

"All that I have and cherish you have given me," I quote the saint to her. "Your grace and your love are wealth enough for me."

Caitlin smiles and tenderly brushes my cheek with her hand.

The sheriffs return. They handcuff and shackle Peewee and me and lead us out, like a very small Georgia chain gang, to a waiting prison bus. Through the bars I see Caitlin and Julia being put in another similar vehicle. Caged like animals, we're driven several miles to a provincial jail.

We're held all afternoon in stinking little cells in the jail basement while Corrections Branch officials once again try to get our names straight and to figure out how to program our electronic monitoring devices. They have a marvellous facility for not letting their incompetence diminish their officious self-importance. Finally they herd us up to the prison reception area, where they attach electronic anklets to each of us and give each a monitoring device in a little case.

Just then, visiting hours at the prison begin, the big front doors are opened, and a stream of visitors crowd in. They line up across the foyer from us in order to pass through a security check. There's a smattering of worried-looking older people in the crowd, parents or relatives I suppose, and several young men. But mostly the group's made up of young women, some of them carrying babies. Obviously the wives and girl-friends of the inmates. They stand there quietly, not talking at all, in a sullen and defeated queue, dressed in cheap patent leather boots and fake furs, their faces masked hideously behind overdone makeup, their hollow stares a pathetic mixture of defiance and defeat.

"Oh, God," Caitlin says, "just look at them. Talk about despair. Compared to them, we're just on a lark. We're free as birds. I can't imagine what it's like to be caged the way those kids are. To have no way out, ever. They make me feel like a tourist slumming for fun."

We leave that dark place and limp home, catching the last ferry back to Upshot. The gloom of the day trails after us like wraiths of mist across a bog. We each go home to our private prison.

But for me it's a prison in paradise. The clarity of my courtroom epiphany, the tenderness of Caitlin's kiss, remain with me as vivid memories. I feel like Richard Lovelace writing "To Althea, from Prison."

We are forbidden to go outdoors other than for specific purposes. The anklet and monitoring device are in constant contact with Corrections Branch. We've been told that if we violate the terms of our confinement, we'll be sent to prison instead.

We stay in touch with one another by telephone. Corrections Officer Chuck Vitale soon becomes a favourite conversation piece. Chuck obviously knows a good thing when he sees one, and he sees two in our little Upshot contingent—the Overstalls' Jacuzzi for one, and Caitlin for the other.

"He's over for site evaluation today," Julia tells me by phone one morning. "He just left. Well, of course, Peewee and I could care less about this idiotic confinement. We're busy with the new book . . ."

"What's this one titled?" I ask.

Love Among the Antique Roses. We think it's going to be the best we've ever done, thanks largely to Goukas and this crackbrained Vitale."

"What did he say, about where you could and couldn't go?"

"Well, Peewee has to ask him whether we could go out to the Jacuzzi. Big mistake. The fool has a thing about Jacuzzis and he somehow invited himself to join us whenever we plan to use it."

Peewee calls me a few days later. "You won't believe this nut," he says to me. "He's here every day, wanting a Jacuzzi. I asked him yesterday how he had so much spare time to come all the way over here and loll around in a Jacuzzi during working hours. He told me he was monitoring our compliance. Can you believe it?"

"There's nothing I won't believe about these people any more," I say.

"Chuck's monitoring more than compliance at my place, I'll tell you that!" Caitlin's laughter spills over the phone like surf over stones.

"I'd like to see you, Caitlin," I say to her.

"And I'd like to see you, J.J., no one more. It's the worst part of this stupid confinement."

My heart soars like a nighthawk to hear her say so, but then she has to clip my wings.

"I guess I'll just have to make do with Chuck," she says, "until you're more available."

Once he's twigged there's no man on Caitlin's premises, Chuck takes to dropping in at the oddest hours. As he frequently reminds us all, the electronic monitoring regulations allow corrections officers to enter a prisoner's premises unannounced twenty-four hours a day.

"It doesn't take much to figure out what premises old Chuck really wants to enter," Caitlin says to me on the phone. "You know that great gangly fool actually showed up last night after ten o'clock. Claimed he'd missed the last ferry off, but he just happened to have a bottle of wine in his car and thought perhaps we might spend the evening discussing my rehabilitation."

"How'd you get rid of him? You did get rid of him, I hope."

"Naturally," Caitlin says. "I reminded him that we contemners are forbidden to consume any alcohol, then I showed him the door."

But Chuck, his concupiscence roused, and notwithstanding his having a wife and kids over in town, is not easily dissuaded. Caitlin has worked out an arrangement with the ferry crew that they'll call her whenever Chuck's on his way over. Forewarned, she calls around and gets somebody to come over before Chuck arrives. But two nights ago, she tells me, the system broke down and she caught Chuck hiding in the shrubbery outside her bedroom window and spying through a pair of binoculars.

"The astounding thing is," Caitlin says, "that dingbat actually believes he's contributing to our rehabilitation. It boggles the mind. Jenny's far more mature than poor Chuck, and she's only in grade one."

"Is she doing all right with you confined?"

"Oh, she's fine. People have been really helpful taking her where she needs to go. And she's so wise. She says if I've been grounded for a whole month I must've been really bad."

"Too true."

I'm allowed five minutes outside each weekday, at exactly twelve noon, so that I can walk up my driveway to the mailbox to pick up my mail.

I'm also permitted one hour a day to tend the garden and do my out-door chores. Once a week I can go to the general store for supplies. Other than that, an occasional sprint to the outhouse is as far as I can go.

The short jaunts through the garden are thrilling expeditions into the voluptuous beauties of May. Weeds everywhere, of course, and a million things to do, but intoxicating nevertheless. Draped against the kitchen wall, a purple clematis is bursting into bloom, its five-petalled flowers like the trumpets of tiny archangels, royal purple in their depths, downy soft, a striped pale purplish cream at their lips. A pair of yellow-striped garter snakes bask in the sunshine, their serpentine bodies twined together, on a block of warm sandstone. In the middle of the lawn a flowering crabapple tree is splendid with white blooms set against new coppery green leaves. A pair of sparrows alight on one of its branches, flicking tails and adjusting positions in a ritualized mating dance as peculiar as the one I've been dancing myself. All the earth seems to me throbbing and pulsing with thrilling sensuality. I suspect myself of reading too much D.H. Lawrence.

Thoughts of Caitlin greet me everywhere, like Jenny's little people down among the flowers, and always now they're thoughts of joy. No longer a prisoner of doubt and misgiving, of fearful suspicion, I come upon myself rejoicing in the knowledge of her love.

I realize I'm dawdling and hasten up to the mailbox. There's a letter from Elvira. Feeling happy to just have it in my hand, I hurry back to the house, my five minutes of freedom expired.

Sitting at my kitchen table, I tear open the envelope and take out a letter written in Elvira's large and carefully formed script.

Dear Brother Joseph,

I hope this letter finds you well and enjoying the spring weath-er even though you're under house arrest. I'm fine here, but I miss Upshot terribly. Some days I want to be home so badly I could cry. I miss my garden and even those dumb birds of mine. Have you heard from Jimmy F.? He's supposed to be looking after things at my place, and I hope he is. You know what he's like.

Jail is not so bad after all. I'm quite content here, other than wanting to be home for spring planting, and of course missing all of you. And I'm worried about Waddy. Have you heard from him? I don't think he should be in jail, a man his age. They took us off, me and Waddy together, in a paddy wagon, and drove us up to the jail. Waddy had to get out there. Just before he climbed out, he said to me, "I hope your man comes back, Elvira. If I was him I would if I could, 'cause you're one hell of a fine lady." I thought that was so sweet of him. As the wagon pulled out, I could see them leading Waddy into the prison, and I had the strangest feeling right then that I might never see Waddy again. That's why I worry about him. They flew me over to the mainland, and I had to wear leg irons and handcuffs for the whole trip, as if I was going to overpower those two giants I had with me and jump out of the plane. They've all been watching too many Hollywood cop shows, these people. Anyways, I've settled in here quite nicely and I'm getting to know some of the other prisoners. Of course there are lots of native girls here, lots from up-country, and I enjoy chatting with them about their lives on reserve and their families. Most of the women here are not real criminals, just mixed up or maybe addicts. Alcohol or drugs. It's too bad. But some of their stories, oh my! Abuse and battering all their lives, some of them. Sometimes, talking to them, I feel just awful. I share a room with a girl named Eva. She comes from a village up the coast. She's a real sweetheart and we get along great. We talk and talk and I haven't laughed so much for a long time. She's in here for drugs too.

One thing about this place is that everything's arranged for you. When you get up. When you eat. What you eat. You don't have to decide anything. Being here I realized how much I have had to decide about everything since Freddie disappeared. This feels like a vacation. You don't have to be responsible at all, just do what you're told. I have been thinking a lot about Freddie lately. It's partly why I was feeling so blue this winter. I guess what I've been doing these past few years is sort of putting my life on hold waiting for Freddie to come back so I can start really living again. I didn't know it at the time. But now I see what a mistake it was. Something Mistral Wind said to me is what opened my eyes, that night she came to the garden club meeting, the second time I mean, the night she passed out the seeds.

She said to me we must let go of the past, let go of our illu-
sions, let go of those we love even. I didn't want to believe her
at the time. I thought she just meant to forget about Freddie
and get on with my life. I couldn't do that, but it worried me.
That's why I was feeling so glum for the past while. But being
here I realize she meant much more than that. She meant stop
holding on in general. Stop holding on to the way things used
to be, or how you thought they'd always be, or want them to
be. She meant start seeing them as they are and as you are.
Start seeing the real world. Then you can move forward to
maybe help make a better world. Mistral said it but I didn't
understand it until I got here, which is a totally different world
from Upshot. And then Zyrk saying that in court about
Freddie. Can you believe it? Talking with these girls, I realized
what Mistral meant, and even Zyrk too. Everything suddenly
came clear for me. All of a sudden my heart was glad again,
which is funny for being in prison. So there's no need to worry
about me, I'm as happy as can be. I hope you are too. I guess
you haven't seen much of Caitlin, being as you're both confined. I'm writing to her too. You know my thoughts about you
and her, that I feel you belong together. Write me if you like. I
guess I'm here for another two weeks. Please let me know if you
hear about Waddy.

Your friend,
Elvira Stone

p.s. I'm planning to bring Eva home with me. She and I get out
around the same time. She's a lovely girl and I've told her she
can stay on with me for as long as she likes. You'll like her too.

I go over the letter again, feeling a great upwelling of affection for
Elvira, and then I phone Caitlin.

25

My mind will not accept what Caitlin's saying over the phone. It's like that vivid, numbing flash right after you've seen a dreadful accident, when your brain scrambles for an instant to decipher what's real and what's not.

"Are you sure?"

"Absolutely," Caitlin says. "I just got off the phone with the superintendent. Waddy's dead."

"But how? I don't understand." Caitlin's news has caught me completely off guard. I can't quite catch my breath. I think back to the time the abbot called me to his study to give me the news that my mother had died suddenly. Without my having said "goodbye" to her, or "thank you." A sudden, lurching turn in your life that you hadn't seen coming. Now Waddy the same way. I can't put a name to what I'm feeling. It's as though a violent wind has torn some part of your home loose and carried it off in the dark, though you're not sure just what. Just something missing that you can't yet see.

"They don't know for sure what happened," Caitlin says. "They found him this morning. They think his heart just stopped in his sleep last night. I guess they'll do an autopsy."

"I don't know what to say. I feel stunned."

"Me too. Apparently he passed away peaceful as can be. No signs of distress at all. In fact, they said his whole face looked absolutely tranquil when they found him, as though he was still in the middle of a lovely dream."

Tranquil? Old Waddy? "I feel I'm in a dream myself," I tell Caitlin. "I can't believe the old duffer up and died like that. He seemed so vigorous. Sometimes I'd be scared he was going to blow a gasket from getting too riled up, but I never thought of him as someone death was stalking."

"Me neither," Caitlin says, "except those final days in court, remember how docile he was? Like all the piss and vinegar had drained out of him."

"Yes, you're right." I did think it odd at the time that Waddy'd stopped kicking against the goad. Even when the sheriffs put the cuffs and leg irons on him, he was sort of passive and accepting. Not like old Waddy at all.

"It was like he'd made his peace with something," I say, "not like he was defeated or beaten. Still, I hate to think of him dying in prison like that, with none of us around."

Caitlin says, "It probably wouldn't have mattered all that much to Waddy, even if he knew he was dying. He'd hardly have wanted us all hanging around giving him maudlin appreciations."

"Do you think he knew?"

"He knew a lot, that old guy," Caitlin says, "and he was always strong on his signs and portents. My guess is he saw death coming, maybe even before he went to jail. I wouldn't put it past him that was half the reason he went to jail."

"I don't follow."

"Oh, there'll be hell to pay for this, you can count on it," Caitlin says. "An eighty-one-year-old war veteran dying in jail for civil disobedience? You think the media won't have a field day with that? I think it's Waddy's last kick at the can. The more I think about it, the more I'm sure he saw death coming down the tracks and laid his plans."

"Spat in its eye."

"Perhaps. One thing I know is I'll miss him."

Something in Caitlin's voice carries the knowledge of death to me. We both fall silent. Hesitant. Remembering.

"Me too," I say. "He was such a crusty old fart, but somehow you ended up loving him anyway." I hear my own voice choking with sudden emotion. "I loved him."

"I never realized how much he meant to me till that moment when they led him off in leg irons."

"Elvira knew. I think that's why she chose jail as well. She told me in her letter she'd been worrying about Waddy, and she'd had a premonition of not seeing him again. I think she'll be devastated when she hears."

"I don't think so," Caitlin says. "I think she knows already in her own way. And Zyrk told us as much in the courtroom. It seemed like a silly riddle at the time, about Freddie and Oberon, and Waddy growing forget-me-nots. But here it is."

"Hmm. What about a funeral or memorial service?" I ask. "Is there something we should be doing?"

"I guess not," Caitlin says. "Apparently there's a committee of the church looking after arrangements."

"The church?"

"I know, isn't it a hoot? I mean, who's ever seen Waddy go anywhere near a church? What did he say to Smollet about being christened—a bunch of mumbo-jumbo? Well, it turns out Waddy's been just about single-handedly supporting the Anglican church here for years."

"You're kidding."

"Their biggest benefactor by far."

"And it never got out? Unbelievable!"

"Best kept secret on Upshot," Caitlin says.

"The only kept secret I know about," I say. "That crafty old codger. Cursing a blue streak day and night, and all those stories about whores and booze-ups and all the rest of it, and meantime he's a secret church benefactor. That's just like him!" Waddy's posthumous trick takes some of the acrid taste out of his dying.

"I guess he had something about a proper church funeral," Caitlin says. "Apparently he left quite specific instructions with that priest who comes over. He's already been notified." There's no resident clergyman on Upshot, but one comes over from the big island once a month to conduct a communion service, and for weddings and funerals. The little church is not what you'd call a hotbed of religious fervour, but it's there when needed.

"Do you know who's on the funeral committee?" I ask Caitlin. We haven't had a funeral for several years.

"Yes. That's another one of Waddy's last laughs, I think."

"What do you mean?"

"Elsie Pitfield and Geoffrey Munz."

"No!"

"Isn't it brilliant? Fibber Miller and Gertrude and a couple of other people too. I can just hear Waddy telling it as a story. Laughing his head off, slapping his knee, repeating his punch line, same as always. It's pure Waddy having Elsie and Geoffrey bury him. Anyway, it falls to them to arrange things; there's nothing for us to do."

"When's the funeral?"

"Next Saturday."

"What about this infernal house arrest?" We still have over a week to go on our sentences.

"We'll have to get special dispensation from Chuck to attend the service."

"You think he'll give it?"

"Of course. I'll whisper salacious secrets to him on his next compliance-monitoring, and he'll do whatever he's told."

"Caitlin!" God, she can be irreverent sometimes.

"All right, all right," she laughs, "I'll whisper them to you too!"

"Oh, for God's sakes," I say, "poor Waddy's barely cold and you're making sex jokes."

"Waddy's favourite kind," Caitlin says.

Which I can't deny. It's true there's no sense getting all pious and proper on Waddy's account. It would almost be insulting to his memory.

"What about Elvira?" I ask Caitlin. "Do you think they'll let her over for the funeral?"

"I doubt it somehow. Not with all the handcuffs and armed escorts bullshit they go through. My guess is she'd have to be a blood relation for them to let her out."

"I guess Chuck doesn't have any influence over there."

"Chuck doesn't have any influence anywhere," Caitlin says.

Just then there's a screeching, scrambly noise on the phone line, a signal from Corrections Branch that their computer is trying to link up with one of our electronic monitors.

"Better go," Caitlin calls through the screeching. "I hope you're okay. I miss you. Talk to you later. Bye."

I hang up the phone. I think of Waddy lying dead in his prison cot. I feel a profound sadness about it, a loss, but it doesn't feel tragic somehow. Not one of those deaths that smacks you down, shattering everything, the way my mother's did. But not insignificant, either, not at all.

Thinking about it, I realize that Waddy's time has already passed into history, like his beloved Pacific Shay. His whole world was steam and big timber logging, rough-and-tumble camp life, and drunken blow-outs in town. That's all gone now, passed into legend and museum exhibits, swept away by bright young accountants at corporate headquarters moving capital around the globe electronically without regard for the likes of Waddy Watts. For good or bad, Waddy's time is gone.

Thinking about him, I realize how much Waddy meant to me. In a strange way, he'd become like a father, someone I looked up to for his age and experience. Already I'm feeling his death more acutely than I felt my father's. Waddy was as gruff and angry as my dad, but under his rough surface, he was solid. Someone who wouldn't mess you around. And he had such fierce determination once his mind was set on something. Like our Kumquat expedition. Once he was in, he was in with both boots. Good old Waddy. Already, I miss him.

Within days, Waddy's death provokes a firestorm of controversy in the media. The papers run pictures of him as a much younger man smiling down from the cab of his Pacific Shay. The government and court system are pilloried unmercifully for locking up an eighty-one-year-old man, whose only crime was civil disobedience. The indignity of a war vet dragged off in handcuffs and leg irons is discussed at length. As the lead editorial in one of the big dailies puts it, "Even mindless treehuggers deserve better consideration than Mr. Watts received."

But as chance would have it, a few days later a gymnast from the city thrills and stuns everyone by winning a surprise gold medal at the world gymnastic championships, only to several hours later test positive for a banned substance in her urine, and be stripped of her medal. In the ensuing media frenzy, Waddy is forgotten.

Saturday dawns clear and bright, a gorgeous May morning. Chuck has granted us two hours of freedom to attend the funeral. Elvira's been denied leave to attend. I decide to walk up to the church. I've scarcely been off my own property for three weeks, and everywhere I look I see a new and splendidly different world. May's like that anyway, but today especially so.

A good crowd has turned out for the funeral service. People are gathered in small clusters on the lawn outside the little wooden church. There's an almost festive air. I spot Caitlin over near the big dogwood tree. Amazingly, she's chatting with Mistral Wind.

I hasten over to them, and the two women smile in greeting.

"Hello, J.J.," Caitlin beams, reaching out, and we hug one another warmly, all awkwardness gone, the feel and scent of her intoxicating.

"Hello, Mistral," I say, still embracing Caitlin, only reluctantly letting go. "How are you? I'm really glad you're here. I was afraid maybe we'd lost you forever."

"Hello, Joseph," Mistral says, her husky voice as seductive as ever. "No, you won't get rid of me that easily."

"Mistral's thinking of moving to Upshot," Caitlin says, holding my hand, watching for my reaction.

"God help us all!" I say, and we laugh, perhaps a bit too gaily, for some of the mourners glance over disapprovingly.

"Actually, I'm flying to India in just a few days," Mistral says.

"Broomstick or plane?" I ask her.

"Oh, the cheek of it!" Caitlin laughs, slapping my arm.

"A pilgrimage, of course," Mistral says. "No tricks at all."

Peewee and Julia join us, and it almost feels as though our company of adventurers is restored. We laugh a bit about Chuck and the absurd anklets.

We file into the little wooden church—Elsie, Geoffrey and Rose, Fibber and Blackie and Margaret May, Jimmy Fitz, Philip, Ernie and Gertrude and several dozen more. A closed coffin rests before the altar. I sit next to Caitlin, her right hand held lightly in mine, her left in Mistral's.

The service is awful. The poor priest, who knew Waddy almost exclusively through the regular arrival of his cheques, tries to give us a vision of Waddy that includes a catalogue of virtues, most of which Waddy despised. I'm thinking we should have done the service ourselves, but Waddy specifically requested these traditional last rites, full of the resurrection and the light, and the Last Judgement, at which I hope he behaves himself better than he did at the previous one. Geoffrey Munz even has the nerve to stand up and say "a few words about the dearly departed." I'm certain Waddy would have let a squirt go at that.

We file out of the church behind the coffin, with the tower bell tolling in mournful single rings. The graveyard's on a gentle slope below the old church. It's a Garry oak meadow, with big gnarly oak trees widely spaced, the grass below them a tapestry of colour from hundreds of wild bulbs blooming yellow, blue and white. It looks to me the most beautiful place on earth. We gather around the grave. The priest consigns Waddy's remains to the earth, "ashes to ashes, dust to dust." And there's an end to it.

The crowd drifts off, but I linger for a few minutes by the graveside. I picture Waddy lying in his coffin. I hope he's wearing his Romeos and his Betty Grable tie. I remember him the morning of the blockade, sitting in the bus right after I got arrested. "That's the stuff, Joey-boy," Waddy greeted me, "that'll fix the bastards!"

I can't help smiling, remembering the old guy, missing him. I pick up a handful of soil from the mound beside the grave and cast it onto the casket. "That's the stuff, Waddy," I say aloud, choking back a sob as I say it. "That'll fix the bastards."

I do not stay for the white bread tuna fish sandwiches and tea, though I do manage to swipe a pocketful of Charles' dainty pastries on the way through. Caitlin asks me to come along with her to drop Mistral off at the ferry. A lovely pensive silence holds the three of us together as we drive down to Rumrunners Cove. I'm thinking of Waddy, and remembering far too many extraordinary events to even begin discussing in this short time. I no longer feel a need to ask Mistral multiple true-or-false questions. Caitlin will know what there is to know and will tell me in due course.

The ferry is already loading. Just before Mistral takes her leave, she looks at me squarely, right into my eyes, the same way she did that first time I met her, here on the wharf, part enchantress, part pilgrim. Only now there's nothing in her gaze I do not want to see.

"I hope you share a great happiness," she says to us both. She hugs me warmly, and then Caitlin. She places Caitlin's hand in mine and kisses our joined hands, theatrical to the end.

"Farewell," she says, and turns towards the ferry.

As she walks down the ramp with that lithe, loping stride of hers, we see a figure in black leather on the deck come up to meet her. Zyrk. Of course. Standing on the open deck, laughing together as the ferry pulls out, the two of them wave goodbye to us.

We wave back, Caitlin and I, laughing like fools ourselves, at all that's gone on, and at the untold possibilities of things yet to come.

About the Author

A former monk, teacher, and social worker, Des Kennedy has spent the last twenty years writing professionally from his hand-hewn house on Denman Island in British Columbia's Georgia Strait. An award-winning journalist and regular contributor to *The Globe and Mail*, he has written many articles on gardening, environmental issues, and rural living for a variety of magazines, including *Harrowsmith*, *Canadian Geographic*, *Nature Canada*, *Gardens West*, *Country Life*, and *Fine Gardening*. His books include *Living Things We Love to Hate* and *Crazy About Gardening*, which was short listed for the Stephen Leacock Medal for Humour. Des has long been active in environmental issues, especially in forestry. He sits on the board of a community land trust and has participated in civil disobedience campaigns to preserve several wilderness areas. In his spare time, Des can be found writing and performing satirical material on the environment and other issues, appearing as a regular guest on radio and television, or enjoying the gardens he and his partner have created on their island acreage.